The Spooky Isles Book of Horror, Vol. 1
edited by
Andrew Garvey & David Saunderson

Copyright © 2018 by David Saunderon
All rights reserved to David Saunderson of The Spooky Isles and to the individual authors of these stories. This book or any portion thereof may not be reproduced or used in any manner whatsoever without the express written permission of the publisher except for fair use by the authors (including excerpts for promotion and inclusion in portfolio) and the use of brief quotations in a book review.

Printed in the United Kingdom

First Printing, 2018

ISBN 978-1-9164227-0-4

Dark Sheep Books
Flat 24
316 Green Lanes
Manor House
London, N4 1BX

For more offerings from the night side of the fold, see www.darksheepbooks.co.uk

CONTENTS

INTRODUCTION BY ANDREW GARVEY 1
INTRODUCTION BY DAVID SAUNDERSON 2
SPARKS 4
THE BLACK DOG 18
LETTERS FROM A TOXIC HEART 31
LAMBS TO THE SLAUGHTER 55
HAVERGILL'S FETCH 72
HUNGER 87
JACKFEST 103
DUST TO DUST 115
AM FEAR LIATH, THE GREY MAN OF BEN MACDUI 128
THE HANDFAST WIFE 138
RING AROUND THE ROSIE 154
CHURCHGOING 167
THE EAR 182
CREATURES OF RATH AND BONE 192
THE FINAL ANSWER 209
CAMP 46 225
STRANGER THAN BEFORE 238
THE PIED PIPER OF ESSEX 253
SPOOR 263
COME AWAY 277
ABOUT THE AUTHORS 291

INTRODUCTION
BY
ANDREW GARVEY

Some editors like to bang on endlessly in their introductions. To me, that seems like a bit of a waste of your time, and mine. So I'll be brief. You're about to read a collection of fiction and non-fiction, culled from the strangely twisted imaginations of eighteen authors from three different continents. It's only truly unifying theme - that all the stories are, in some way inspired by British and Irish folklore. From spontaneous human combustion to Ireland's Faerie folk to Jack the Ripper to vampires to ghostly churches and undead Nazis, it's a wide ranging witch's brew of malice, creeping dread, death and bloodshed.

Stylistically, there's epistolary historical fiction, there's slasher movie brutalism, there's something unmistakably M.R. James-ian, there's rural horror and there's the quietly unsettling. Each story is accompanied by a short essay detailing the myth or legend that inspired it. As varied as the tales themselves, these include examinations of the authors' chosen myth, personal reflections and insights into their storytelling techniques.

This first volume of the Spooky Isles Book of Horror has been a pleasure to work on and, I hope, a pleasure to read.

INTRODUCTION
BY
DAVID SAUNDERSON

Congratulations to the writers who have submitted their fiction and true-life inspiration tales to The Spooky Isles Book of Horror Vol. 1.

Over the years, www.spookyisles.com has published thousands of articles relating to the horror, paranormal and supernatural goings-on throughout Great Britain and Ireland.

We know that our lands are drenched in the blood of those who have come before us, not only through the history books but the knocks and cries out in the night we hear unexpectedly.

The British and Irish are some of the most superstitious people in the world. That is why we have produced the very best writers specialising in horror and the supernatural, like M.R. James, Bram Stoker, W.B.Yeats, Robert Louis Stevenson and indeed, William Shakespeare included ghosties in his writing.

This volume was produced due to the dedication of Andrew Garvey, who has been long committed to the success of the Spooky Isles website, joining shortly after its inception in 2011.

I'd like to particularly thank him for his patience, and working with the talented writers in this tome, to produce new, scary works that will all keep us up at night.

David Saunderson

Spooky Isles founder and managing editor

June 2018

SPARKS
BY
MICHAEL CONNON

The last of the 19th-century tiling slipped into shadow behind an insulting slice of MDF and I began painting. It seemed a shame; an original Edwardian fireplace would be a bonus for most homebuyers, but not us.

We'd both fallen in love with the house as soon as we set eyes on it. 'Inglenook' was perfect in both size and location yet still, she-who-must-be-obeyed had pretty much made it a deal-breaker that I fill in this particular feature if we were to buy the place. I didn't know why it was so important to her, just assumed she didn't want to risk an open fire with Caitlin around, even though our daughter was now coming out of her mad phase and settling down into a nice, mercifully sensible six-year-old.

A weekend of final modifications was progressing well, ready for us all to move in properly next week. Moira hailed from these parts – across the glen in Crianlarich – and was keen to make the move back. Currently visiting family in England, she would join us on Monday and I wanted it all to be perfect for her arrival, before the bulk of our belongings arrived on Wednesday. A burst of giggling and a flurry of feet brought me round. Caitlin, excited about her new room, passed through busily engaged in arranging accommodation for her dolls and stuffed animals. We'd given her the room at the front of the house overlooking the garden and the long gravel driveway which led into the pine forest beyond.

Leaving the paint to dry, I took a look around at my handiwork. That should meet with Her Majesty's approval, I thought. A few final odds and ends to do tomorrow, then I could enjoy the rest of the weekend with Caitlin before rustling up something special for a nice family meal together on Monday evening.

That night, all of the excitement and exploration seemed to have taken their toll on Caitlin and I was able to leave her halfway through a story, sleeping soundly as I gently flicked off the light.

It was a freezing night and snow fell throughout. The view from the back bedroom was spectacular as I dreamily watched the flakes gently dusting the moonlit fields behind the house, convinced that we could be nothing but happy here.

I was just drifting off when I heard the sound of feet in the corridor, a wail of crying, and Caitlin burst in, bounding up onto the bed next to me.

"Hey, honey, what's up?"

"Daddy, I'm scared of the man!" she sobbed.

I must admit that for the briefest moment I did wonder. Given the isolated location, a house empty until this week could easily have attracted unwanted attention. Then I reminded myself of the power of a six-year-old's imagination, especially in strange, new surroundings and encouraged her under the duvet where she hugged me tight. I could feel her little heart racing but didn't pay too much heed. Dog tired, I wasn't even really listening to her any longer.

The man at the window had wanted a cuddle, she said. Just a child's dream, I thought.

* * *

We rose late and I made us both a nice lunch, after which Caitlin took up the challenge of the snow as I worked on. When I'd finished up the last of my jobs I thought I'd indulge in a few snowballs with her. The snow lay deep everywhere except the drive and immediately before the house, owing to being in the lee of last night's fall, I guessed. Intending to surprise her with an unexpected volley from the flank, I began quietly gathering snow from the roof of the car.

Immediately, even through my thick gloves, something felt wrong. Brushing off the snow revealed beneath it the paintwork, raised and blistered. To say I wasn't pleased would have been an understatement. Like many of us, I'd sacrificed my little two-litre pride-and-joy for a people carrier in the name of fatherhood but all the same, it was mine and I was furious.

Running my hand over the swollen bodywork, the red paint giving way to angry black and oily blue eruptions, I could only wonder what kind of searing heat must have been applied to cause this. And there was more, all along the passenger door.

When the hell had this happened? Instinctively I looked around for an explanation, even for overhead cables despite knowing already there were none even close.

"Did he do that?" Caitlin appeared at my side.

"Who?" I asked irritably.

"I told you he was a bad man."

"Who?" I persisted.

"Sparks!" she stated indignantly. "You never listen, do you? I told you he was here last night. At the window."

And with that she ran back inside.

That was when I saw the rest. Wiping the snow from the double-glazed window of Caitlin's room, just feet from the car, it was obvious that the same terrific heat source had been responsible. The plastic sill was bevelled inwards, bubbled black at the edges and the seal holding the glass had gone, or at least been driven away from the centre, forming into rivulets of black rubber over the sill and onto the brickwork. I pulled at it uselessly, not sure what to think. There'd been a fire of some intensity out here, inexplicably, and the thought of someone messing about like this was something I could really do without.

Despite feeling faintly ridiculous about it, I decided Caitlin was probably my best source of information and followed her uncertainly into the house.

Before I could track her down, the phone rang in the hall. Moira. It was wonderful just to hear her voice and for an instant I forgot the aggravation outside, which was fortunate as I knew better than to ever sound at all ruffled to my wife the inveterate worrier.

"Yeah, I'm fine, but missing you. Can't wait to see you," I said, genuinely longing for the company of another adult, even the flappable, excitable Moira.

She asked about Caitlin.

"Absolutely fine... enjoying the house, the garden... loving the snow..." I waffled on convincingly and, after years of experience, might have even got away with it if only our daughter hadn't chosen that moment to reappear.

"Is that Mummy? Tell her about what Sparks did last night," she said brightly and went back outside again. Thanks a lot, I thought.

"What?" I heard Moira stiffen over the line.

"Don't worry, sweetheart, it's just some bad dream she's had." I glanced at the car through the open door.

"What did she say? Michael, what did she just say?" Moira implored, agitation rising in her voice.

"Calm down, love, you know what kids are like."

"No!" She was hysterical now, yelling at me. "Get out! Get her out of there now! Michael, promise me you'll leave that place right now! I'm coming up there. So help me, if you two don't get out of that house now... I'm on my way!"

I could hear her begin to hyperventilate.

"Moira, don't be ridiculous! Stay where you are. Look, we'll go up to Kenmore Lodge for the night, OK? How's that?"

I had no intention of it.

"We'll stay over there tonight and I'll see you tomorrow. We can talk about it then. Please don't worry. Promise me you'll try and relax?"

She began on her deep-breathing exercises and I hung up.

She'd always been a bit odd. Strange, often obsessive childhood fears still haunted her but she was never willing to talk about them. I'd learned to live with it over the years but the last thing I wanted was Moira's hang-ups infecting Caitlin.

Still, I thought, it wouldn't do any harm to bring her in for the night and keep an eye on her.

Deciding to forego any questions about the incident, I bombarded Caitlin with hot chocolate and cartoons for the rest of the evening and made an early supper. That night I kept her in my room, snuggling her close, and a few stories later she was sleeping soundly and I followed soon after.

* * *

Around 2.00am I had to answer the inevitable call of nature and got out of bed as quietly as I could. The nearest loo was just off the front hall and as I headed for it, bleary-eyed, I slowly became aware that something wasn't right.

Washing across the walls and floor, a pale, blue, shimmering light filled the hallway. With a flicker like that of a welding torch and completely silent, the effect was almost beautiful in the pitch-black tranquillity of the early hours.

Convinced I was onto the idiot responsible for the damage to the car – but not quite reckless enough to charge straight outside – I slipped into Caitlin's empty room for a better look.

Directly outside her window, standing in the drive and looking straight at me – if something without a face can look – it stood.

Not a man, but human in outline. And of fire; fire of the most brilliant intensity, sparkling blue.

A hulk of violent, roaring flame, its interior fizzed in unrelenting, fiery motion while from every inch of its surface, sparks spat ferociously. With the light of a thousand gas jets, whatever it was cast everything as far as the eye could see in an eerie, shimmering glow.

All about it, the snow retreated hurriedly as though in dread and I was suddenly put in mind of that morning's shallower drifts at the front of the house.

At first I thought someone must have lit an effigy in the garden, some kind of twisted greeting from the locals, perhaps. But no, this was alive, at least in some sense of the word. And aware – certainly aware of me – I was in no doubt.

Despite its lack of features, somehow among the morass of roaring flame where its face should be, I discerned an intelligence – and a purpose – and immediately wished I hadn't.

Its intent was one of pure and unrelenting hatred; within the intensity of that firestorm burned its absolute detestation of all things living.

And yet still I watched, entranced by the unearthly luminosity, even as I knew that its very essence boiled with unspeakable, raging fury.

"Is he back?" Caitlin's voice came from behind me.

The spell broken, I turned instinctively, protectively, gathering her up tight in my arms. When I looked back, the thing, whatever it was, had gone.

Gathering a few scraps of the day's clothing for both of us and as much money as I could lay my hands on, I bundled Caitlin into the car and floored it until we reached the road to Kenmore.

* * *

The overnight receptionist at the Lodge Hotel was clearly perplexed but thankfully didn't press his concerns. I understood how a partially-dressed man covered in snow clutching a shivering child in the middle of the night might well have attracted the attentions of the authorities.

Muttering over and over about some inexact emergency, throwing in words such as 'flood' and 'disaster', I showered him with money for any room at whatever inflated off-season premium he cared to impose.

In the room, Caitlin lay on my chest and I quietly stroked her head and, hopefully, any fears away while wishing someone could do the same for me. I didn't want to probe too much for fear of upsetting her but I still wanted to know what she knew. So when she talked, I let her.

Oddly, she insisted on being quite matter-of-fact about it all. She kept stressing that the man had only wanted a cuddle. Even bad people wanted cuddles - didn't they? – she wanted to know.

I told her they may well do but they're no less bad people. Who did she think he was interested in? Was it her? Me?

She said she didn't know but somehow felt sure it wasn't us. Eventually she dropped off and I began my impromptu vigil.

In a tumult of emotions I think anger dominated, albeit an impotent one. I thought of the intruder in the garden – in my garden – and what I could do about it. How could we possibly still live there after this? And then there was Moira; that wasn't a conversation I was looking forward to.

And yes, I admit I was frightened too, of the figure and the hate inside it but that was quickly sublimated in my role as protector and responsible adult, allowing me to keep it together for the time being. I can remember feeling glad of that.

I still didn't have a clue what to do even as the weak morning light came over the mountains and through the curtains. In truth I just wanted to stay there in the twilit limbo of inaction and indecision. The longer I lay in denial, fending off the morning, the longer it seemed I could avoid facing up to it all.

* * *

I left Caitlin with a copious breakfast in the care of a nice girl from the hotel. After pressing more money onto the staff and promising to be back imminently while again hinting heavily at some family drama, I extricated myself and faced up to going back to the house. The plan was to quickly collect a few essentials. And to call Moira...

The first sign of trouble was the profusion of tyre tracks on the road which led only to our property.

In the drive stood a Grampian Police patrol car. Alongside it were parked a large red car and an unmarked grey van. Behind that, I could see the front of Moira's Ford Focus peeking out.

It was in a daze that I strode to the front door where a teenager in a police uniform stood uncertainly on the step. He was already on his radio as I approached.

'Mr. McKenna?' He held out his arm across the open doorway.

'That's me.' I brushed past aggressively and he renewed his pleading transmissions for back-up; Mr McKenna had arrived unexpectedly, what was he supposed to do?

Crossing the threshold I might have been traversing dimensions; in one short step I passed from a crisp, bright Highland morning into a steaming, orange hell.

Straight away I could see the interior was bathed in an unearthly glow and the air, hot and close, offended my senses with its sickly, sweet odour. From all around me the walls – each of them smeared in black soot – were radiating a tremendous heat.

Mystified, I somehow managed to move forward into the living area, just as some primal sense of dread began rising in my soul.

The two bare bulbs which hung at either end of the blackened ceiling were lit and both they and the windows were coated in a sticky, orange substance, imparting their light with an unnatural radiance.

Yet strangely in the midst of all this there seemed to be no damage; furniture, packing cases and toys all stood as they had been left and it was this very normality in the midst of the uncanny, the enforced union of certainty and dreadful unreality which made the scene so disturbing.

But the horror had only just begun.

In the centre of the living room floor lay a mass of ashes, white and delicately powdered. At its edge a pair of human feet, clad in white trainers and completely intact, protruded from the lower portions of a pair of blue jeans. From the top of the neatly scorched edges of the trousers projected short lengths of blackened leg bones, quickly merging into the shapeless heap of pale powder where the rest of the body should have been.

The final remaining feature I simply didn't recognise at first, being as far from ordinary experience as it's possible to be. At the opposite edge of the ashes lay a blackened skull, seemingly shrunken in the complete absence of flesh.

Everything between the upper and lower extremities of what was once a human being had been completely and efficiently reduced to a heap of fine, white ash in the centre of my home.

Totally benumbed, I scrutinised the scene quite calmly, looking on it all with a merciful stupefaction, insensible from all feeling which, in hindsight, would prove to be my salvation.

Because, of course, I knew by then I was looking down at the remains of my wife.

Close by lay her mobile phone, warped and buckled into an outlandish form by a terrible heat.

It was at that point I understood the significance of the room's orange cast and the bizarre glaze on the bulbs and windows.

They were stained with a deposit of vaporised human flesh.

"You weren't supposed to see this, sir. I'm sorry."

A uniformed man – senior in rank but not a police officer – stood at my side.

"What happened here?" I asked dumbly.

He didn't answer.

"Have you seen anything like this before?"

He nodded. Something in the nod told me he'd never managed to get used to it.

"I think you should leave, sir. There's nothing you can do," he said gently.

And he was right. I had to leave and never come back. There was nothing I could do or ever could have done.

Moira's obsession had pursued her across more than twenty years. That's a long time to be running from anything. How can you ever be free of something prepared to wait that long to get what it wanted?

Some things never give up. Some hatreds never grow cold.

BACKGROUND ON SPARKS
BY
MICHAEL CONNON

As a child, I remember well my schoolmates and I rushing out to buy 'The Unexplained' partwork every week in our lunch break. We bought it principally because we were into UFOs, maybe the odd ghost or two, but what we didn't expect was to be introduced to the horror of Spontaneous Human Combustion (SHC). The grim pictures of charred body parts and the notion that it could happen to anyone at any time frightened the beejeezus out of us all. I'm sure a whole generation was scarred by that magazine.

As an author, I wanted to deal with the subject and set myself the task of making something already absolutely terrifying even more so. I hope I have achieved that. It was also important for me to work into the story the notion of a childhood fear which persists into adulthood as well as including some key aspects of SHC lore.

The classic SHC case usually involves a lone victim, often elderly or disabled, who is discovered with large parts of their body burned to ash while leaving the extremities intact, sometimes still clothed. Typically, surrounding objects and furnishings are untouched and the mystery asks how can the central torso be incinerated, requiring temperatures in the region of 800 – 900 °C and yet leave surroundings unscathed?

Unsurprisingly such a subject has appeared in fiction many times over the years. Herman Melville, Mark Twain and Charles Dickens are just some of the authors who have dispatched characters by means of a mysterious, consuming fire while the movie 'Spinal Tap' and TV series 'South Park' have sought to find a funny side to the horror.

For those new to the mystery, an excellent starting point is Spontaneous Human Combustion by Jenny Randles & Peter Hough (1992). Devoid of sensationalism, the authors set out to investigate a series of alleged cases before examining the main theories put forward and I would highly recommend their work to readers.

Officially, of course, the phenomenon does not exist. Or, at least, that was the case until 2010 when an Irish coroner recorded the death of Co. Galway man Michael Faherty as SHC in his verdict. It would seem there are those in authority who are prepared to consider the possibility of SHC and Randles & Hough quote several senior fire officers who have spoken out. The idea of official interest is something I could not resist hinting at towards the end of my story.

Sceptics pour scorn on paranormal explanations, pointing to the fact that isolated and vulnerable people may well take ill or fall, not being found by family or neighbours for some time. Add to this the proximity in many purported SHC cases of sources of combustion such as fireplaces, cookers or cigarettes and surely we have an answer? A human body full of fat, it is argued, can burn like an inside-out candle, the clothing providing the wick. The so-called 'wick effect' was held up as the solution from the 1960s [1] and many perhaps breathed a sigh of relief at this down-to-earth, 'natural' explanation.

Others, however, point out that burning fat produces a great deal of water and that initial ignition is very difficult to achieve despite claims of replication of the effect under laboratory conditions.

Former Police Scenes of Crime Officer John Heymer thoroughly dismisses the wick effect in his excellent book 'The Entrancing Flame' (1992). Heymer began investigating the phenomenon after being called to the scene of a mysterious death in 1980 and posits a theory based on a chain reaction of rupturing mitochondria. He also suggests that a reluctance to admit to the reality of SHC amongst the medical establishment means that there could potentially be around 200 cases per year in the UK alone.

In a New Scientist article in 2012, Brian Ford suggested that in rare cases a process of ketosis could produce large quantities of highly flammable acetone in the body [2]. Other theories include a build-up of methane in the gut and even ball lightning. However, the reader of the literature must be left with – and disturbed by – the fact that the human body is actually a difficult thing to burn, as any crematorium operator will attest.

For lone victims lying undiscovered for many hours, the wick effect may well explain some of the deaths attributed to SHC but what about those troublesome instances where eyewitnesses were present? Jeannie Saffin began burning in front of family members in 1982 and in 1985 Frank Baker burst into flames in front of a friend - and lived to tell the tale. It is perhaps from the study of cases such as these that the mystery may eventually be solved.

The most frightening aspect of this mystery may be that the explanation, whenever we arrive at it, is something beyond our current understanding. And as readers of this volume will know, the unknown is always the most frightening.

THE BLACK DOG
BY
TRACY FAHEY

The day I pull my own hair so hard I cry, I know it can't go on. Or to be more precise, that I can't go on. Everything has become muddled and chaotic, infused with anxiety. I operate in a panicky zone of uncertainty. I can only work alone; anything involving other people is problematic. I work on evading anyone who annoys me because I might – no, I will - become unreasonably angry. I am enveloped in a suffocating, selfish fug of dread. The possibility of intimate conversation terrifies me. The simple question – how are you? – could provoke any manner of honest and terrible responses. My fear of dogs, always present, intensifies. The sight of a tense, bristling dog makes me sweat and shake.

Even my body is breaking down. My energy dips and wanes each day. I crave sugar and salt, chocolate and meat. My skin itches. My leg has developed patches of eczema, like rust on metal, lichen on stone. I scratch them mindlessly till blood leaks under my fingernails to form a perfect burgundy crescent line separating the white from the pink part of the nails. My chest beats fast, staccato one-two, one-two, like a tight red drum in my chest. I sleep with earplugs in to dim the sounds that might make me panic. I read to dull the thoughts in my head. In moments of lucidity, I am scared. I sit in traffic, thinking – Is this it? Is this ever going to end? – And, most terrifying of all – Is it still me? Because, you know, it doesn't feel like me anymore. It feels like a bad version, a blurred photocopy, a self of newsprint smudged with tears.

I'm no longer in the driving seat you see.

* * *

The Black Dog. He names it for me, the kind doctor. His eyes squint at me in sympathy. "I'm sorry," he says, gently. "It's a brute, that dog."

I've listed my ailments, those strange, pressing urges, the blank undertow of sadness that smothers me, night after night. I've told him of the fear that disrupts my rest with teeth-clenching anxiety. Of the long, heavy, blank sleeps that can overpower me, so I wake, dry-mouthed and heavy-eyed.

"Maybe it's my hormones?" I suggest. Slow, fat tears trickle down my face. I wipe them away, absently. These days I cry so much I barely notice the constant flow.

The doctor straightens up. He cocks his head to one side and says quietly, "Poor old you." It is such an un-doctorly statement, I forget to cry. "Well, I don't think this is PMS. What you describe – the listlessness, the panic, the overwhelming feeling of sadness, these all tally with the definition of depression." That's when he names it. The Black Dog. I feel a terrible sorrow mixed with a dawning relief at his diagnosis. His face is calm and kind.

"Is there a history of depression in the family?" he asks.

* * *

Is there a history of depression in the family?

Yes. Yes, there is. I can see that now. Like an ancient poison it has infected us, generation after generation. I see it now, exposed for what it is in the clinical environment of the doctor's office. I see it in my mother's despairing rages, my grandmother's glassy stare and the strange, asynchronous workings of her mouth. And now I see it in my own mirror, in the ugly lines at the corner of my mouth. I see it in my flat, panicked eyes. It's a dreadful, quiet homecoming, a recognition of what has always lain beneath. Is it still me?

It's been inside, quiet, dark, waiting. As a child, when I bit my hand in rage or pulled my dolls to pieces...was that it? Like a detective I examine myself for clues. That night I hit my head off the wall to stop thinking. That was definitely it.

Maybe in time I'll be proud of this. I'll see it as part of my family heritage, as genetically distinctive as the dimple in the cleft of my chin, my long fingers, or the slight upward tilt of my nose that I see replicated, endlessly familiar, on strange faces at family funerals. For now, the tears trace lines on my face, a map of erosion, the long, slow slide of hot salt over sore skin.

* * *

I start taking the pills. They are tiny, like little dots of white on my palm. I find it implausible that they can stem such a huge and weighty tide of emotion. But I try. I remember to breathe deeply when I can.

As the days go by, the tautness in my chest loosens, little by little. I can now drive my car without visualising all the possible accidents that will happen; the flickering images of blood and twisted metal begin to pale and recede. I sleep past the white-night hour of three in the morning. I say hello. I ask how people are. Once I catch myself laughing, unguarded. The sound shocks me.

Some things don't get better though. As the general anxiety fades my fear of dogs intensifies. There are so many dogs. They are everywhere. Little dogs bark at me from gardens, short, throaty, angry yaps. When I go by, they hurl themselves against gates, in a blurred frenzy of pink gums and sharp white teeth. It's the big ones that terrify me most. I see them throw their large bodies against their leashes, their powerful chests working with ribby muscles as they strain and pull. I stop walking around the city to avoid them. These animals are only domesticated on the outside. I can see them for what they are. In their rolling eyes, their curled snarls, I see their true nature; they are jackals, wolves, carnivores.

The heavy wall of anger and despair is lifting, slowly but surely. Now, like a recovering car-crash victim, I feel the pain in my limbs. I can't stop eating. Everything tastes pungent and delicious. I don't fall asleep anymore, I crash into sleep, and it's heavy and blank, a flat, implacable wall.

It's then that the dreams start.

The dreams are always the same. I'm walking down a road, a flat, unmemorable country road. It's summer. I can smell the dry heat, the cut, shrivelled grass. I hear the hum of insect-buzz, and feel their tiny wings bat against my face. I'm walking parallel to a deep ditch, backed by a large dark-green hedge. Suddenly I realise I'm seeing with a curious double vision, one that remains fixed on the dusty road, and the other which has risen to give me a birds-eye view of the hedge. Behind the hedge I see him.

He's a huge black dog, crouching, his hackles raised and his powerful body coiled and tense like a bowstring. I know he is waiting for me, but I can't stop my feet leading me inevitably towards the hedge he lies behind. I wake just as he is about to spring, my mouth parched and open, hot, damp patches livid on my chest and the back of my neck.

I call my mother. This is unusual. We don't phone each other a lot in my family. Years of tense silences and uneasy conversations lie behind this.

"Was I ever frightened by a dog? When I was little?"

My mother is silent for a moment. "No," she says eventually. "Not to my knowledge. You've always been afraid of dogs."

I persist. Maybe if I'm more specific.

"Is there any time you recall that I saw a dog pounce from behind a hedge?" I need to know the origin of this dream.

"No." Her voice is sharper now. I'm a little startled. In recent years, she's been so much calmer.

"Sorry," I say automatically. "Sorry for bothering you."

"It's fine," she says in a softer voice. "When are you coming to visit me and your granny? I'd love to see you."

"Me too," I say. There are tears in my eyes. I mean it.

I put down the phone. A patch of eczema flares on my ankle, pink and angry. I scratch it until the blood wells up in dark beads.

* * *

Last night, the dream changed. I was walking down the road, when I realised my viewpoint had changed. I could still see from the birds-eye view, but when I looked downwards, my old trainers had disappeared. In their place were two glossy black paws, stretched out to show long, cruel nails. The wave of horror wakes me abruptly. I'm sweating, panting, lungs bursting with effort.

Is it still me?

* * *

"So now you dream you are a dog?" The doctor is making interested notes. He shakes his head. "The good news now," he says. "I'm very happy that your symptoms have dissipated, and that your blood-pressure is down. You're feeling better in all respects but this very particular anxiety."

He puts his pad down. "I'd recommend cognitive behavioural therapy to you. It's a good way to address these kinds of fears, which seem to come from nowhere." He pauses, head cocked on one side "But I'm curious. Are you sure you've never been bitten by a dog? Scared of one as a child?"

I consider the conversation with my mother. "Almost positive that I wasn't."

He considers it. "Maybe you heard a story about one that frightened you?"

I think. Something in that last sentence sounds familiar. I close my eyes and raise a hand to stop him. There is silence. I hear the clock tick on the white-painted wall, slowly, calmly measuring the seconds, the minutes, the hours...

"Yes," I say finally. "Yes. I heard a story."

* * *

I'm five years old. My grandmother is making a new dress for me in the kitchen, her clever fingers pulling and tugging the material under the whirring needle of the sewing machine. I am tiptoe-stretched, head following the flashing movement of the needle. Quietly I reach out one chubby hand towards it – "Stop!" shouts my grandmother, suddenly, pushing my hand away. I'm opening my mouth to cry, when she pulls me onto her lap. I rest my head against her soft, warm neck. "Hush now," she says, and her voice is quiet, murmuring. "Hush or the Black Dog will hear you."

* * *

The Black Dog of Cratloe. How could I forget about him? According to my grandmother, the Black Dog ran beside the road beyond Limerick. If he ran alongside you, that was good, and you'd have a safe journey. If he jumped out at you, Fate would follow you, like the dog itself, until you met your bloody end. My grandmother claimed to know a man who had died a week after a cycle home. The dog had run at him repeatedly during the stretch of road by the estuary, he told her, run at him over and over again, so he had to keep cycling and shouting, faster and louder, until it finally vanished at the foot of the Cratloe hills. "It did him no good," my grandmother says, nipping off the thread with her sharp teeth. "Sure wasn't he dead a week later. God rest him."

* * *

I get to my feet and leave the surgery, rejecting all offers of referral. There is nothing wrong with me anymore. My fear is real. It is out there in the woods, hiding by the road, waiting for me.

* * *

That night I dream again. I'm back on the road. This time it's dark. Beyond the hedge is the silver salmon-flash of moonlight on water. The air smells different, moister, and loamier than before. I stretch myself out. Every muscle in my body lengthens and tautens as I flex slowly behind the hedge. Then I hear it, faint in the distance, the whirr of bicycle wheels. I tense. Nearly there. The whirr grows louder, and I am running quick, sure, low to the ground, the grassy earth under me damp and firm. He sees me. His mouth opens in a perfect round 0 of shock. I keep running, darting out and back from the hedge. It is intoxicating, the dew-fresh smell, the speed, the frightened, phlegmy catch of his breath as he pedals faster and faster. The chase goes on, I run in and out, just missing his front wheel, until the bike swerves, and with a ripping sound of rubber on tarmac, it stutters, and crashes to the ground. I grab his collar in my mouth and start to drag him away. He is crying now, in hot, blurting breaths, face contorted, but the faint light shows me who it is.

The doctor.

* * *

When I wake up, heart blundering in my chest, everything has changed. There's blood in my mouth, but I can't find a cut. There's blood under my nails, but there's no scratches on my legs. I feel a glass-shatter of pure, high terror in the soft pouch of my stomach.

Is it still me?

What do you do when what you fear most becomes invisible?

When it hides inside?

* * *

I sit down with my mother and my grandmother. Their eyes tell me they know what I am going to say. My grandmother is already nodding.

"I have it too," I say simply. "The Black Dog." My mother's face is gentler than I have ever seen it. She brushes a hand over my hair, with a gossamer-light touch.

"We know."

Wordlessly, I extend my hands to her and my grandmother.

Is it still me?

Their eyes are warm, reassuring. We grip each other, palms warm, fingers taut. Together, our weakness is our strength. I feel the power coursing between us, from generation to generation, from Black Dog to Black Dog.

BACKGROUND ON THE BLACK DOG
BY
TRACY FAHEY

'The Black Dog' is a story that weaves together strands of a local legend, that of 'the Black Dog of Cratloe' with the wider apparition of the Black Dog in folklore. It also intermingles these legends with shades of pathography, genetic illness and lycanthropy.

The Black Dog is a popular trope in global folklore. Its most popular manifestation is probably in English folklore, with variants of the Black Dog legend in most counties in England. The Black Dog may be a direct descendant of Cerberus in Greek mythology; most stories tell of it as a pre-shadowing of death. It also makes several appearances in Irish folklore. T.J. Westropp, in his 'A Folklore Survey of County Clare' documents the story which directly inspired this one, that of the 'Black Dog of Cratloe'. He writes:

> *Many believed that they had seen the apparition, which used often to accompany the D'Esterre's coach and the mail car...I was present at its first telling, before they heard*

> *from our old servant, Mrs. Julia MacHugh, of the local belief... A large, dark, shadowy dog seemed to run upon the moonlit water, first to one side and then to the other of the carriage, and was more than once lashed at by the driver. It disappeared near where the road ascends from the low marshy 'corcasses' along the foot of the Cratloe hills. Julia MacHugh, a woman of wide local knowledge, at once 'explained' the apparition and said that the omen was good if the dog ran alongside, but bad if he leaped at the carriage or horses.*

Westropp's account is one of several recorded in the south-west – another, more local one heard anecdotally is that of the Black Dog of Thomondgate, in Limerick city, where I live. All of these accounts have several features in common; the Black Dog is larger than life, with glowing eyes, and his presence is a malignant one, often a portent or a warning.

When I write, I'm particularly attracted to ambiguous images that call to mind a range of meanings. In 'the Black Dog', I wanted to pay tribute to the folkloric story, but I was also interested in the wider meaning of the black dog in contemporary culture, as a euphemism for depression. Diarist Samuel Johnson first used the term in the 1780s as a metaphor to describe his own struggles with a depressive disorder, and Winston Churchill popularised the term to describe his own encounters with the illness. This image is a striking one; the idea of a dog who follows, who won't go away. Writing about a mental disorder also introduces the idea of the unreliable narrator – to my mind, a story always works particularly well if there are several different explanations for how the narrative unfolds.

Illness, and the feeling of dislocation is brings, is a theme that runs through several of my short stories. Illness itself is a liminal space where the sufferer is plunged into the intensely introspective terrain of one's own body and mind. However, it's also a space of 'Unheimlich' alienation from the self; a stark realisation of the divorce that has happened between the 'normal' terrain of wellness, and the uncertain, grey world of illness.

However, there's another strand to this story that borrows from folklore, that of lycanthropy. We're familiar with the legends associated with the werewolf, rising to prominence in Germany in the 1591 with the trial and execution of Peter Stubbe, a serial killer who believed that he became a wolf and committed his crimes while in this state of physical and mental transformation. This notion of lycanthropy as a mental disease is one that has survived until the present day. Today it is recognized as 'clinical lycanthropy', a rare syndrome whereby the sufferer is convinced that he or she can transform into an animal. This belief in transformation of self is connected both with body-image ideas and as an add-on expression of a psychotic episode caused by another mental health condition such as schizophrenia.

Lycanthropy is most commonly associated with men and male werewolves, which is strange, as in most fairy tales and legends, the wolf is a complex character; not only a vicious male predator, seeking out young girls to seduce and eat, but also as female, operating on a lunar cycle, ruled by blood and the moon, prey to monthly shifts in mood and hormonal changes. Many horror movies such as the Canadian 'Ginger Snaps', which align women with wolves, can also be read as a metaphor for the darker side of the transformation from childhood to womanhood; lycanthropy is used as a signifier of mental illness.

In 'the Black Dog', I was interested in drawing these different strands together – from global trope to local legend, from illness to werewolf stories. It was important that the narrator's illness could be read in a variety of ways, from depression to menstrual psychosis to lycanthropy.

Which is the true reading? I'll let you decide.

LETTERS FROM A TOXIC HEART
BY
ED BURKLEY

The following articles were discovered hidden in the inner lining of a portmanteau that had been procured from an estate auction. Engraved on the trunk's handle were the faint remains of a name: CREAM. The collection of enclosed papers was found bound in twine. Atop the collection sat a photo of two young boys sitting together, on the reverse it read, "Daniel and Thomas." Underneath the photo, the first slip of paper had written on it but a single line, an address: 103 Lambeth Palace Road, Lambeth, Central London.

* * *

From The Chicago Daily Tribune (Chicago), Saturday September 24, 1881:

DR. DEATH RECEIVES LIFE

The jury took only three hours to deliberate, returning with a verdict of guilty. Sentencing is to be life imprisonment. Dr. Thomas Neill Cream, who received his degree studying the effects of chloroform from McGill Medical College in Montreal, will be taken to Illinois State Penitentiary at Joliet to be incarcerated and serve out the remainder of his life. The victim's wife, Mrs. Julia Stott, turned state's evidence and will be set free.

The trial of who murdered Mr. Daniel Stott was overseen by trial Judge Kellum and was fueled by much fanfare. The prosecution, led by state's attorney R. W. Coon and Senator C. E. Fuller, claimed that Mrs. Stott, 27, was unknowingly lured into a most insidious poison plot perpetrated by Dr. Cream, 31, to swindle money from Chicago druggist Buck and Rayner. Mrs. Stott, the prosecution claimed, was intent on purchasing harmless medication for her husband's epilepsy. It was Dr. Cream who tampered with the medicine, switching it with a poison before handing it over to the naive Mrs. Stott.

The defense, led by Hon. Col. D. W. Munn, relied on a different allegation. Mr. Stott, who was 77, was originally assumed to have died of natural causes. But upon hearing of his death, Dr. Cream reportedly sent a telegram to R. W. Coon suggesting that Mr. Stott's death was not natural, rather he suspected it was the result of Strychnine poisoning. Three other letters from Dr. Cream were to follow, one went to the district attorney, and two others went to the coroner demanding an autopsy. Despite the allegations, none of the officials were willing to exhume Mr. Stott's body, so money was raised to properly investigate Dr. Cream's claims. The findings from the laboratory assessment confirmed Dr. Cream's hypothesis of death by poisoning. Based on this, the defense argued why would a guilty man send letters to public officials demanding that Mr. Stott's death was something other than natural causes, more to point a murder by poisoning. Surely, if no one were aware that a crime had originally been committed, a guilty man would not openly proclaim as such. As of recent, sympathizers have already begun rallying for Dr. Cream's release.

* * *

Illinois State Penitentiary, March 3, 1887

Miss Clover,

My heart soars with more affection than I can possibly find words to express. You do me a great honor and I warmly welcome both your sympathy and your upcoming visit. Nothing would bring me greater joy than support from someone so sensible as you.

Until we meet, your humble servant,

Thomas Cream

* * *

March 20, 1887

Dr. Cream, Thomas,

I find such reassurance in finally meeting with you. All my hopes regarding your character were assuaged after hearing your account of your present predicament. You had only the most sincere intentions for your patient Mr. Stott. A man so true as yourself should never find himself attached to the likes of such a charlatan as Mrs. Stott. She has tarnished your name kind sir and I fully concur with your sentiment regarding reparations against her being taken. Gain peace of mind knowing that others such as myself feel that a great injustice has occurred. I do not wish that this letter or our meeting be remembered with such lamentable circumstances. Let us, however, dwell on what I most assuredly gained from our encounter, that you are a kind, honest and giving man. Allow me to be so forward as to say that I, too, felt something between us. Please do not hesitate to call upon me again. I will do all that is within my power to assist you and aid you further in any manner necessary.

    Yours truly,

    Miss Matilda Clover

* * *

Illinois State Penitentiary, April 1, 1887

Dear Matilda,

Never kinder sentiments were spoken. I cherish the light you bring in such a dark place as I currently find myself. If you but find it in your heart to continue meeting with me, I would very much enjoy both your company and an opportunity to discuss how I might rely upon your assistance in righting the wrong done to me by Mrs. Stott. Please do visit again soon.

    Yours,

    Thomas

* * *

April 20, 1887

My Dear Thomas,

These past meetings and letters have overwhelmingly confirmed my initial feelings for you. I, with bated breath, hope you feel as I do. I have developed more than mere fond feelings for you. For someone so dear to me I would be willing to do just about anything to prove my unwavering affection for you. As discussed, in an attempt to ascertain the location of that vile creature Mrs. Stott, I have sequestered the resources of the Pinkerton Detective Agency. I assure you I will find her for you. I will so you know how deep my affection for you runs. She gave you a life sentence, so I will take hers. Then we will finally be able to put this awful blemish beyond us and be together completely unburdened.

    With sincere affection,

    Matilda

* * *

Illinois State Penitentiary, April 22, 1887

My sweet Matilda,

My affection for you is unbound. Handling Mrs. Stott would be more than enough of a display of your affections for me. As always, I look forward to our upcoming visit. However, in the event that you are unable to meet with me, I find my love for you too great to delay in expressing it. As such, I am sending this letter promptly. Find Mrs. Stott, deal with her, and it would bring me no greater pleasure than to have you as my wife.

Fondly,

Thomas

* * *

April 30, 1887

Dear brother,

I was fortunate enough this time during my visit with you to finally confront the women you have been meeting and corresponding with. I concur with you that she is quite mad. She most assuredly believes you to be in love and going so far as to speak of a betrothal. I gather you have commandeered her service to track down Mrs. Stott. Again, I implore you to let the matter lie. I understand you must fill your time in some fashion, however, stay clear of her. In other matters, support for you has drifted from the public's attention since the trial and I find the burden of your release falls squarely on my shoulders. I am attempting to make the appropriate connection and funds to result in your liberation. I have heard speak of corruption and that bribery may be a solution to your incarceration. I will do what I can.

With much affection,

Daniel

* * *

May 13, 1887

My love,

I believe I have found her! She appears to be hiding in Whitechapel, London. It is rumored that out of financial desperation she has turned to prostitution under a false name. I want nothing more than to prove my love to you; however, at present I am unable to afford the voyage. Please advise me on what we should do now.

Your betrothed,

Matilda

* * *

May 14, 1887

Dear Dr. Thomas Neill Cream,

It pains me to inform you that your father has passed away. He has bequeathed sixteen thousand dollars to you. In addition, I have looked over your case and with family and friends have petitioned Governor Joseph W. Fifer for your release. I am confident that your freedom is in the making.

Your friend,

Thomas Davidson of John Ross Co., Quebec.

* * *

Illinois State Penitentiary, June 25, 1887

Matilda my love,

I have news that brings me both great joy and great sadness. My father has passed away. However, he has left me quite a sum of money. With this I will send you to England to finish what we had planned.

Safe voyage my darling,

Thomas

* * *

July 15, 1887

Thomas,

I leave straight away, bound for Whitechapel, London. The most fortunate of circumstances has occurred, a murder just this April. I will use this as a ruse to cover what I intend to do to Mrs. Stott or whomever she now pretends to be. Wish me luck.

Your future,

Matilda

* * *

Packet of letters from Matilda Clover sent together on Oct 20, 1888, Whitechapel, London, England:

August 8, 1888

I have done it! I have found and removed that which ails you most. I approached her from behind. I had to move slowly as to not arouse my presence. I waited until we were in a sufficiently darkened area, a landing directly above a flight of stairs; there I made my move. She was completely unaware. I took my knife, cut her lying throat so she could not scream, and then plunged my tool deeply into her more times than I can count. I finished with one final wound to her licentious heart. I hope you approve of me, my love.

September 1, 1888

Alas, the last person was not she, but I have since corrected that mistake. I believe to have found her and have now removed her from existence. On Buck's Row I approached her and like the other, I sliced her deceitful throat, silencing her lies for all time. My rage was not sufficiently quenched, and as I looked her over I found myself cutting the place she gave life. I removed her womb and stood proud over my accomplishment. I pray you are proud of me too my dear Thomas.

September 10, 1888

Oh, my darling. Again, I find myself flummoxed. I felt assured I had her, yet she slips through my fingers. So I made further inquiry and pursued whom I believe to be the obstruction to our being wed. That simply will not stand. Like the others, I followed her and, after her meeting with a tall man wearing a deerstalker hat and overcoat, took her as she made her way into an unlit backyard. First, I gave her a most suitable crimson necklace across her throat, never to espouse falsehoods again, and then I procured her womb. She was wearing some beautifully fashionable rings so I took those too! I dare say that I very much enjoyed disposing of Mrs. Stott!

Oct 1, 1888

I feel my heart grow weary, as does my mind. I was wrong again. There are so many licentious women in this town with false names, finding the right one is a difficult task. But I think I have finally done it, only not without casualties. Last night, while I pursed the real Mrs. Stott, another interfered and I was forced to silence her, cutting her throat. I felt sorry for this poor girl, as she had not intended to disrupt me, but I could not let her live for fear of what she might say about my description to the authorities. In the tussle, I lost sight of my true pursuit. But fear not. An hour later I found Mrs. Stott again, in Mitre Square, and did as I must. First her throat and face, then when I finished I decided to take from her a souvenir from within. I believe it is finally done, but I have been wrong before. I do hope I have faithfully shown you my love. If I am wrong and have to find another, I will not abandon our plan, but I must be careful. All my pursuits have garnered quite an audience. I was amused recently when the papers reported a letter had supposedly been sent by me to the police and was signed most whimsically, Jack the Ripper. Such a silly name!

Oct 18, 1888

My love, I am ashamed to say that I must cease with my pursuit for now. More false letters, by this Jack the Ripper, surrounding my actions are being printed in the papers. Too much attention is being focused on Whitechapel. However, the good news is I believe I have found her this time. I am sure of it. I will not hurriedly undertake my course of action this time; rather I shall plan this one out. No surprise on the streets. This one I will bring back to a room and show her what it means to take the life away from the one I love. I will take her life away and be done with this for good.

* * *

Illinois State Penitentiary, Oct 31 1888

My dear,

You are doing such excellent work. Keep it going and you will find her, I am sure of it. When you are done, we will again be reunited and I will marry you once and for all, having proved your love to me and done away with Mrs. Stott.

Yours forever,

Thomas

* * *

Nov 10, 1888

My dear Thomas,

Your most recent letter fueled my action and I hope finality has come at long last. I believe I have done it, done away with that most loathsome Mrs. Stott once and for all. It took more time than expected, to have both time and place converge upon opportunity, but as all good things come to those whom display patience, I too have claimed my prize. As I last wrote, I performed her final rite in a secluded room. This allowed me ample time to show the world what type of creature Mrs. Stott truly was. I took all manner of her flesh that indicated womanhood. The spectacle was quite the depiction of horror. However, I must confirm that Mrs. Stott has truly left this mortal coil. I have been wrong so many times before and have begun doubting myself.

Matilda

* * *

Dec 25, 1888

Dear Thomas,

I lose hope of ever being with you. The last one was neither she nor the one after. I have doubt I will ever find her. I must see you in person, must feel your gaze upon mine, if I am to continue. As of now, I return to you a complete failure.

Happy Christmas,

Matilda

* * *

July 20, 1889

My love,

Our recent visit has filled me with a renewed sense of purpose. I have arrived back in Whitechapel and have begun planning my pursuit. I will not fail you.

Matilda

* * *

Sept 15, 1889

My darling Thomas,

Other murders are occurring here, making my mission most difficult. The other day under the Pinchin Street railway arch was found the remains of some poor soul, or rather merely a torso. The city is filled with all manner of twisted depravities. I long to feel your embrace amidst all this degeneracies. I must be careful. I have found someone, one final person. It is she, most certainly. This will be the one.

* * *

Feb 25, 1891

I found her Thomas! In Shallow Gardens. The act was perhaps rather mundane after all this time. I simply went up behind her, threw her to the ground, and slit her lying throat. Now you can wed me. I am not wrong this time. I have been diligent and am most certain that a one Frances Coles was a moniker for Mrs. Stott. I have proven my affections for you, now nothing stands before us. She has served her penitence for what she has done to you. Oh my sweet darling, I envy this letter, to be present when reading these words of atonement. I wait for your reply.

Matilda

* * *

March 15, 1891

Dear brother,

It seems our work has paid off. Bribery was the final key to your liberation. I have it on good authority that the person I meet tonight should put things into motion for your release. Take heart brother, soon you will be free.

Daniel

* * *

Illinois State Penitentiary, March 17, 1891

Dearest Matilda,

Great news! My brother has found a way for my release. However, you must stay in England. Once I am free I will come to you and we will marry. There will be much suspicion attached to me if you return here and it may hinder my release. Please wait patiently and I will contact you once I am released.

Your future husband,

Thomas

* * *

June 1, 1891

Thomas,

I have not heard from you in some time. I wallow in this cesspool of human depravities and salacious deaths. How much longer must I endure? Please keep me abreast; I cannot wait to be with you.

Matilda

* * *

July 20, 1891

My love,

Do not fret, any day I will be freed. And what are mere months in exchange for a lifetime together?

Your soon to be husband,

Thomas

***

July 25, 1891

Dear brother, Freedom at last! The Governor has commuted your sentence and with ten years already served you are to be released.

Ever faithful,

Daniel

***

Aug 8, 1891

Brother,

I cannot condone you leaving for London; I know it is to reunite with this lunatic woman. I have given tirelessly in shielding you from all manner of slander, yet you seemingly seek it out. Leaving for London will result in your downfall dear brother and I will be no part of it.

Daniel

***

Letter: Sept 1, 1891

My beloved Matilda,

I am on my way. Do not correspond so as to keep our meeting a clandestine one. Upon my release, I believe others may be following me, perhaps relatives of our Mrs. Stott learning of her demise, investigating possible connections to my involvement. I will contact you as soon as I make the appropriate arrangements and am sure no suspicion follows me.

Thomas

***

Pages torn from a personal diary:

Oct 1, 1891

I have landed in Liverpool from voyage aboard the S. S. Teutonic. I will make my way to London and end all connections with the madwoman Matilda Clover.

Oct 6, 1891

I have taken a 2nd floor room in London across from St. Thomas' Hospital, 103 Lambeth Palace Road. For a doctor with my particular tastes, my room is at the most serendipitous placement, for I am at the intersection of both patient and prostitute. I look forward to indulging in both!

Oct 12, 1891

I met the most delightful young lady, an Ellen Donworth. I may find something to give her, a gift of sorts, to ease her ailments. I hope she enjoys taking her medicine!

Oct 19, 1891

I meet with Matilda tomorrow. I will not be proposing an indefinite union between us, but rather an indefinite parting. My consolation prize to her will be the most unpleasant Nux Vomica.

Oct 20, 1891

It is done! I am free of all connection with the demise of Mrs. Stott. Matilda and I met over drinks and I offered her a small pill, a token of my appreciation, something I brought back from America. I told her it would take away all the turmoil she endured while waiting for me. I may now live the life I desire in this city of untold vices. It is not lost on me that now I alone know the secret of whom Jack, or should I say, Jill the Ripper was! Life is most certainly full of surprises.

Jan 7, 1892

Booked passage back to Canada on the S. S. Sarnia. Suspicion has begun to build around the poisoned women in Lambeth. I, however, will be in Quebec.

Feb 28, 1892

While staying at the Blanchard's Hotel in Quebec I met a fine fellow, a Mr. Wilson McCulloch. Over far too many drinks and much hooliganism, I fear I may have become loose-lipped. Many things discussed between us are but hazy recollections. I really should limit my Morphia pills for only my restless nights. I find perhaps some reassurance that he was not from London and knew very little of the "Lambeth mystery" as the papers have so sensationally begun calling it.

March 23, 1892

The itch has become too great and I must find an avenue to alleviate its incessant clamor. So I have booked passage aboard S. S. Britannic. Headed back to the "city of the world," London. In no other city can a person indulge in all manner of debauchery and the authorities be none the wiser. I had done so here in Canada once before and had a life sentence put upon me as a result. Only in London will I be truly free to whet my appetites. I have stayed away for far too long.

April 2, 1892

Met a young woman while buying tickets at the Alhambra Theatre. I convened with her later at the Northumberland public-house and offered her a remedy for blemishes to her complexion. Miss Lou Harvey—if I recall correctly, such a peculiar name—took my cure, two white pills, and swallowed them down. I told her I would meet her later at the Oxford Music Hall, however, I quite doubt she will make her appointment.

April 12, 1892

Last night I met two lovely girls. One Alice and the other Emma, both ladies of the evening, loitering in St. George's Square. I offered them drinks and we proceeded to their abode. To cover my identity I told them my name was Fred and after a night with them I offered them both two small pills, a cure for many of the aliments garnered from their profession. Like our lovely Jill the Ripper, I had myself a double event.

May 16, 1892

I have befriended an American by the name of John Haynes. An exceptional man, he probes me for tales of murder and mayhem from the streets of London. Last evening over drinks at the Café Paris in Ludgate Hill he was so enamored by my knowledge of the people and places of the crimes that had occurred. I spoke of Ellen Donworth and our dear Miss Matilda Clover, of the one with the strange name, Miss Lou Harvey, and the two young girls Alice Marsh and Emma Shrivell. I dazzled him with details of the crimes and showed him the locations where killings occurred. I took the man to many a darkened place within London's heart. To see his astonishment by the knowledge I possessed, I think he presumed me a brilliant detective. I do so enjoy his company.

* * *

Unsent Letter:

June 15, 1892

Dear brother,

I have now heard word of your arrest. I pleaded with you to not return to London. Your fate now hangs in the hands of God.

Daniel

* * *

From Illustrated Police News, (London), Saturday, July 30, 1892:

THE LAMBETH POISONING MYSTERY

[On the cover is a drawing of a large spider with the face of Dr. Thomas Cream at the center of a web. Across the body of the spider reads: Strychnine. Down each of the spider's legs reads: pills. Surrounding the arachnid are five women trapped in its web. One of the victims is unknown, the remaining four display the names of Ellen Donworth, Matilda Clover, Alice Marsh, and Emma Shrivell. Just beneath the spider a caption reads 'The poison spider and the poor trusting flies, his victims!']

* * *

From The Daily Telegraph and Courier (London), Friday, October 21, 1892:

TRIAL OF DR. THOMAS NEILL CREAM

Three minutes was all it took to return with a guilty verdict and a sentence of death. Dr. Thomas Neil Cream will be taken to Newgate Prison to serve out his sentence by hanging. At the Old Bailey, Justice Hawkins oversaw the case of the murder of several young women by Dr. Cream. The defense was led by a Mr. Geoghegan and the prosecution by Hon. Bernard Coleridge. According to Sargent McIntyre of Scotland Yard, numerous women of ill repute were interviewed and linked the culprit to the victims, seeing him each with Ellen Donworth, Matilda Clover, Alice Marsh, and Emma Shrivell.

Next, Coroner Braxton Hicks testified that upon further investigation of the women that all were found to have died of Nux Vomica or Strychnine poisoning. The defense testified that this type of drug is not uncommon in the tools of a doctor so it was not unusual that Dr. Cream was found to possess such a substance.

Next to give testimony was John Haynes, an ex-detective from America. During one night, Dr. Cream took Mr. Haynes to many of the locations of the Lambeth poisonings, reciting the victims' names and addresses, displaying knowledge no mere admirer could possibly gain from the newspapers. After their encounter, Mr. Haynes promptly contacted Sargent McIntyre about his suspicions.

A Mr. John Wilson McCulloch from Canada was next. Mr. McCulloch stated that he had met the culprit while staying at the Blanchard's Hotel in Ontario. After many drinks, Dr. Cream returned to his room, which was adjacent to Mr. McCulloch's, and began a conversation. Dr. Cream showed him a small box of white pills and told him that it was poison and that he used the pills to dispose of women after his liaisons. He said there was a delightful irony in the women thinking he was offering them a cure to their aliments, when only agony and death were to follow.

However, the most damning testimony came next from Miss Louisa Harris. It seems that Louisa, out of concern for her welfare related to her profession, went by the name Lou Harvey. Dr. Cream's complexion turned alabaster when Miss Harris took the stand and her gaze met with his own. She testified that she had initially met Dr. Cream outside the Alhambra Theatre. Later that evening, she met Dr. Cream at Charing Cross Underground Station. There they walked to Northumberland pub for drinks. Afterward, along the Embankment he offered her two white capsules. She didn't care for the look of them so she pretended to put them in her mouth and while he wasn't looking, threw them in the Thames. He promised to meet her later but never showed. Upon re-cross examination, Mr. Haynes mentioned that it was odd he was able to find information on all the poisoned victims Dr. Cream had mentioned except for Miss Harvey. Quite undeterred he resolved to track her down. However, whereas Dr. Cream had been so eerily correct in relaying the names of the other victims to him during their discussion, Lou Harvey was not dead. Quite the contrary, she was very much alive and had but narrowly escaped the Lambeth poisoner.

In the end, Dr. Cream was convicted of the murder of Ellen Donworth, Matilda Clover, Alice Marsh, and Emma Shrivell, as well as the attempted murder of Louisa Harris. His execution by hanging is scheduled for November 15. The press is not permitted access.

* * *

The final article of paper is a folded note:

November 30, 1892

    I have collected numerous articles, all of which pertain to your life. I was there at your trial and rather close to you during your execution, closer than most perhaps. The bells could be heard ringing in the distance as the executioner made for the final pull of the gallows, and I heard you say for but a brief moment "I know whom Jack the Ri—" then the rope cut off both your proclamation and your life for all time. Outside, the crowd cheered seeing the raising of the black flag, knowing your fate had finally been sealed. Your soul, having ample stain attached to it to fuel the fires of hell for a hundred lifetimes, may never be clean. However, I simply cannot allow it, the horror of it all. There will be no more death attached to your name. Your secret is safe with me, hidden within these letters. I have bound them and placed them where no one will scarcely think to look. Your heart may have been as toxic as the poison you used to kill your victims, but as I have been fond of doing, I find myself gazing at the photograph. Two young boys sitting together, you and me. From that memory of us as children, you will be missed dear brother. For what you have become, may God save your soul.

Daniel Cream

BACKGROUND ON LETTERS FROM A TOXIC HEART
BY
ED BURKLEY

A sound piece of advice for any serial killer is to make sure the dead stay dead. A pesky victim coming back from the grave to identify you as her killer is most unwelcome news indeed. In 1892, Dr. Thomas Neill Cream learned this lesson the hard way.

Dr. Cream had been showing an American friend, who unbeknownst to him was a retired detective, around London to all the key spots where a serial killer, the nefarious Lambeth Poisoner, had killed five women with strychnine. Dr. Cream was kind enough to even give strikingly good details regarding each of the murder scenes. Providing the former detective with such details was Cream's first mistake, but including the exact number and names of the victims in his descriptions turned out to be his most fatal.

The detective, as any good investigator would, looked into each of the victims mentioned and discovered one surprising fact: one of the victims Dr. Cream had mentioned was very much alive. Although the good doctor had given her strychnine pills, the clever woman faked swallowing them and once they'd parted ways, threw the pills into the Thames.

This discovery by the former detective led to Dr. Cream's arrest. The resulting trial that played out seemed like something ripped straight from the script of a sensational Hollywood movie. During the proceedings, Cream was quite shocked when one of his victims, who he thought to be very much dead, testified against him. It was a twist ending he never saw coming, all thanks to this not-so-dead victim, and it would bring to an end his killing and his life. That may be how Cream's story and his killings ended, but the deaths linked to Dr. Cream all started much, much earlier.

Thomas Neill Cream was born 1850 in Glasgow, Scotland and shortly after moved to Quebec City, Canada. He received his medical degree in 1876 exploring the effects of chloroform. The first peculiar death to occur within his vicinity was that of Kate Gardener in 1879. She was found dead behind his place of work in an alleyway. Her cause of death (surprise, surprise) was chloroform poisoning. It was shortly after that he fled to Chicago where several more women died under similar circumstances. But Cream was crafty and no evidence ever conclusively tied him to their deaths.

Then in 1881, Daniel Stott, a patient of Dr. Cream's, died of strychnine poisoning. Cream had taken the man's wife, Julie Stott, as his mistress and the two of them intended on eliminating the third wheel. However, things did not go as planned. In a strange turn of events, Cream attempted extortion and blamed the pharmacist for Mr. Stott's death. This ploy ultimately backfired and he was arrested. Worse still, Mrs. Stott then turned states evidence on him and he was sentenced to life in prison.

But that would not be the end of the doctor. His brother, likely through bribery, convinced Governor Fifer to commute Cream's sentence and secured his release in 1891. Once out of prison, Cream fled to a place where his name was not linked to his previous crimes, a place he could be lost in and in turn lose himself in his killings.

Later that year, Dr. Cream took residency at 103 Lambeth Palace Road in London. Days after, a young 19-year-old named Ellen Donworth died of strychnine poisoning. She would be the first in a series of victims whom the papers dubbed "The Lambeth Poisoner." Next to fall prey was Matilda Clover, a 27-year-old prostitute who also died of strychnine poisoning. After a brief vacation in Canada, Cream returned to London in 1892 and met Louise Harris, who went by the name Lou Harvey. Like his victims before, he offered her pills for her ailment and left her for dead. But Harvey was one step ahead of Cream's trickery. She palmed the pills and later tossed them into the river. Shortly after, Cream meet 18- and 21-year-olds Emma Shrivell and Alice March. They too were found dead from poisoning.

So confident was he in his ability to elude capture, that Cream often delighted in showing his acquaintances the Lambeth Poisoner's murder scenes. One such acquaintance was John Haynes, an ex-detective from America. It was his testimony, along with that of survivor Lou Harvey, that finally led to Cream's downfall. On November 15, 1892, Dr. Thomas Neill Cream's death sentence was carried out and he was hanged at Newgate Prison.

Cream's story has garnered so much attention that there is speculation he may have been Jack the Ripper. Such a supposition was fueled in part by Cream's knowledge of anatomy, but even more so because reportedly his final words as he dropped from the gallows was that he knew the identity of the Ripper.

However, there is good reason to dismiss Cream as the Ripper. Most problematic is that Cream was in a Canadian prison for the poisoning of Mr. Stott at the time of the Ripper killings. To work around this issue, some say he was smuggled out of prison, committed his killings, and then returned. Given the time a transatlantic crossing took in the 1880s - as much as a week - he'd have been missing for some three months, or have to be repeatedly smuggled in and out of jail and make several journeys. Others suggest he worked with someone on the outside. It was this latter speculation, along with Cream's life and fascinating trial, that inspired 'Letters from a Toxic Heart'. My story revolves around Cream's attempted revenge on Mrs. Stott, who actually went into hiding after his trial, by manipulating an admirer of his to get his revenge and in doing so leading to his knowledge of the identity of Jack the Ripper.

LAMBS TO THE SLAUGHTER
BY
CHRIS RUSH

Torrential rain cascaded down the winding, muddy, overgrown path, through the woods to the road below. Two hikers quickly made their way back to their car through the enveloping darkness.

"Jesus, come on, I'm getting drenched here," Brenda said to her husband.

"Two seconds." He replied.

He desperately flicked the button on the key set until the car's central locking finally clicked open. Lunging into the vehicle, the windows instantly fogged up, as they both quickly slammed the doors behind them.

"That came out of nowhere." Derek panted, turning on the ignition.

The pair placed both hands in front of the heater, hoping it would soon bring comfort to their quivering, numb hands.

"What a way to begin the trip, eh?" Brenda said, cranking up the heating further.

Why do people always do that when the engine is obviously cold? He grinned to himself.

"Yeah it was meant to be cool but they didn't forecast this."

The newlyweds were taking two weeks off for their honeymoon and travelling around Ireland, taking in some of the sights. Staying in a nearby hotel they only had a fifteen-minute car journey ahead of them.

"You know what's up there right?" Derek nodded to the darkness in front of the car, as he used his sleeve to wipe the misty windscreen.

"What, in the woods?" she replied, the only working streetlight in the carpark, shielding the car in a yellow cone.

"Just through those woods, sitting on top of the hill, the Hellfire Club."

His wife didn't share the same interest for the weird and wonderful that ran through him.

"The Hellfire Club?" Turning to him with scrunched eyes, lips parted.

"Yeah, I had planned on bringing you up this evening to see it. They say that Satanic rituals, murders occurred and even the Devil himself paid a visit up there." He replied, the rain outside beating even harder against the glass.

"Come on, you hardly believe all that crap?!" was the dismissive response, as warmth finally began to float from the heaters through the car.

"Well we're going up to see it tomorrow evening. I can't come to Dublin and miss this opportunity." Derek was adamant. Pushing the gearstick into first, they began moving from the security of the illuminated parking space.

Brenda didn't even bother arguing, she knew it would be pointless and he would go either way; plus once it was out of the way, she still had nine more days to enjoy.

The following evening came cold and frosty, but dry. The sunlight was making its final sweep across Dublin city as Derek reversed the car into the same position he had parked it in the previous night.

Cold mist surrounded them with each exhale as they reached into boot of the car, and collected a torch and a warm winter jacket each. Looking around the parking area, again Derek noticed that theirs was the only vehicle using the facility. Locking the car, they set off on their steep, uphill journey.

The natural and artificial lighting quickly lost their battle with the darkness a few brief steps into the wooden terrain.

"Why couldn't we do this during the day?" Brenda stuttered, stumbling over a falling branch.

Catching her, Derek laughed.

"It wouldn't have been as much fun and plus you spent so long shopping earlier, this was the soonest we could get here. So it's kind of your fault too." He grinned, continuing. "Seriously though, take your time okay? You wouldn't want to break a leg up here."

They slowly ventured further up the incline, brushing past some undergrowth in the process. Reaching an opening, the sunlight had finally submitted below the skyline and the only light present were the narrow beams being emitted from their torches.

"I don't believe it, there's a path over there you idiot!" Brenda panted, swinging the torch around to highlight the manmade access to their left.

"We don't want it to be too easy do we, where is your sense of adventure?" He laughed. "Come on let's keep going." Derek said shining the light up the, now dry, clay covered path.

Following another five-minute ascent, the profile of a large stone roof revealed itself against the dimming evening sky.

Derek's eyes widened with excitement taking in the haunting building, peering over the surrounding countryside. The sound of cracking grass quickly filled his ears as Brenda caught up behind him and paused also to view the ominous structure.

"That's some climb." Brenda panted, placing both hands on her hips.

"A little different than what we're used to alright." The excited man acknowledged.

Stepping closer, the long, large, arched middle window became noticeable.

"What if someone is in there?"

"Don't worry we'll be fine." Derek confirmed, turning to the worried silhouette in front of the shimmering city lighting.

Continuing towards their destination, both shone their torches against the old stone work walls and through the lower square windows. No sign of life within, not one single sound.

"Hello?" He roared.

"Jesus Christ, Derek!" She said, with her heart in her mouth.

"See no one else is up here."

The words brought no comfort to her as the cold air kissed her cheeks, looking at the large derelict hunting lodge.

"Let's have a look inside." Derek instructed, eyeing the curved, low, side entrance within the protruding, central part of the structure.

Taking small steps, the couple stooped carefully inside. The smell of soot smothered their nostrils and the taste worked its way down the back of their dry throats. Making their way further, they noticed a room to the left and right, some old stairs with a dark steel handrail lay in front of them and another chamber lurking behind it.

Turning left they ventured into the first room they had seen. Sweeping his torch through the blackness, Derek noticed the interior walls were damp, moss creeping its way through the stonework. The excited newlywed reached into his pocket and plucked out his phone.

"I still can't believe we're here." He said snapping pictures with giddy hands. Brenda stood back, not sharing the same enthusiasm.

Moving across to the next chamber, it resembled the last, cold, damp with an uncomfortable smell swaying through the air - except this one had what looked like a large fire place built within it. Taking another few photos, the pair stepped into the area located behind the stairs.

This room was slightly different. Unlike the others it had a very low ceiling. It contained numerous discarded beer cans and other general debris.

"You know when the Hellfire Club were here, they use to toast the Devil." Derek said, snapping a couple of shots once again.

"You don't believe in all that do you?" Her breath catching the light.

"Oh someone's scared." He said playfully nudging her.

"No just cold!" She replied.

Ignoring her comment, he continued looking around the small space. An ear-piercing scream suddenly bounced off the walls.

"You ok?" Derek asked, instantly turning the torch to her.

"I'm fine, it's just water." Pointing to the droplets abseiling down the wall and occasionally falling to where she was standing. "Can we go now?" She continued.

"Just a quick look around upstairs and we'll go then." Derek laughed at his skittish wife.

Brenda didn't bother arguing because after all it was his thing and he often accompanied her to local plays back home, which she knew he couldn't stand. This was the least she could do for him.

Reaching the top of the stairs, the cool country air smacked their faces, through the large main window opening. Turning right they ventured into the first dark and damp chamber, no more inviting the others.

"What the fuck?!" Derek screamed as a sudden shuffle within the blackness caused him to leap back from the old opening.

Moments later the fluttering of wings echoed through the cold, dark atmosphere. Brenda giggled as the pigeons inside the chamber made their escape.

"What's wrong, did you get a fright?" She asked, trying her utmost to contain her amusement.

"Yeah, yeah. Laugh it up." He said recomposing himself and stepping inside.

At that stage Brenda had lost all interest in examining the Club any further, and confident that no one else was anywhere near the area she decided to have a look at the city lights through the main central window as numerous camera flashes ricocheting off the walls behind her.

Happy, Derek then headed for the opposite room.

"Derek who is that?" She whispered, gripping his left arm tightly, as he joined her.

Peeking out into the dusk, Derek eyed three dark, figures slowly approaching the building in the distance.

"Turn off your light." He instructed, while placing his torch and phone on the small ancient ledge of the large window in front of him.

As the phantoms drew closer, Derek couldn't tell what the two individuals on the outside were swinging, assuming it was smoke weaving its way around their bodies and floating up into the night air behind them. The person in the middle was holding something above their head, which occasionally glinted against the city lighting in the background.

"Come on let's get out of here." The words of urgency barely made it out of Brenda's trembling mouth.

"Wait a minute, we don't know who they are or what they are doing, and we can't just run out there, they'll see us. Don't worry I won't let anything happen to you."

The pair continued to stare at the group approaching their position. Brenda tightened her grip on Derek as low chanting fell upon their ears. The terrified couples' breathing deepened, as although they were unable to identify exactly what was being repeated just feet from the entrance they themselves had used, they instinctively knew it wasn't good.

A brief sigh of relief came as the mysterious group turned and began to circle around the building.

"Now's our chance." Derek said, grabbing his wife and quickly leading her downstairs, from the structure. "Shit!" He spluttered, smacking his head off the low entrance they had used earlier.

Once in the open, the pair sped towards the steep decline. Neither dared to look back in case they eyed three dark figures watching them make their escape. They panted their way down the hill in the direction of the carpark, not caring about how much noise the loose gravel was making.

Reaching the car safely both jumped inside and automatically locked their doors. Turning the ignition, Derek tore off into the night, putting as much ground between them and Montpelier Hill as possible.

"Shit!" Derek roared, pressing hard on the brakes, bringing the car to a screeching halt in the middle of the road.

"What's wrong?" His terrified woman responded.

"I've left my phone up there."

"You're taking the piss?"

"No I grabbed the torch, but I never thought of the phone."

"We can't go back up there now." Brenda said, rattling beside him as the shock was still flowing through her.

"I have to; it has all our information on it. If they find it, they'll know everything about us." Slowly doing a U-turn Derek made his way back.

I can't believe I left my phone up there! Terrible thoughts bombarded his mind as he made the journey back to the area where had experienced fear unlike anything he had felt before.

Swerving into the carpark once again, Derek couldn't stop his hands trembling on the steering wheel. Parking, he popped open the boot and retrieved the wheel spanner for protection. Returning to the driver's door he tried to coax out Brenda.

"Come on love, I can't leave you here on your own, you'll be safer with me."

The words didn't sit easy, but there was no chance she would be able to sit in the car alone, terrified that someone may lunge at her through the glass.

Locking the car, the pair anxiously made their way into the shadow infested woods once more.

Slowly climbing the path, they tried to remain as silent as possible. Every flutter of disturbed bird wings or twig snap in the distance added to the increasing, jolting terror running through them. Glancing out over the shimmering city lighting, Derek wished he could be anywhere down there at that very moment, rather than climbing his way towards the mysterious building they had just run from. Worse again, he didn't know what or who they would encounter when they reached the top.

Once the roof of the Hellfire Club revealed itself, Derek instructed Brenda to switch off her torch. He wanted to grab his phone without attracting any attention.

Pausing briefly, both examined the area for any sign of movement or torches. Nothing.

Nearing the front of the Hellfire Club, flickers of light could be seen dancing off the walls within the ground floor.

Derek gestured his wife to remain behind him as he slowly stepped alongside the stonework, stooped down and peeked inside the low square window.

His eyes popped and his jaw lowered upon witnessing the scene unfolding inside.

The room was decorated with the light of various candles. Four more people had joined the three cloaked ones and he assumed they were the leaders of the ritual taking place inside. The cloaks were black and the hoods concealed the wearers' identities. He quickly realised the objects emitting the smoke he had seen earlier were incense burners, which had been set down on either side of a dark, old, table. Shifting slightly to get a better view, he could see there was an old plate containing what looked like soil in it, a bowl of water and lastly, a fat red candle burned proudly on the right hand side of the table like some sort of altar. The person in the middle of the trio behind the table picked up a dark cloth with a pentagram stitched into it, placing it flat onto the surface in front of them. Reaching down once more the individual retrieved a huge knife and sat it on top of the cloth. Meanwhile the others inside where humming a low chant.

What the fuck is going on here? He thought to himself, praying he was dreaming.

"What's happening?" Brenda whispered.

"We need to get out of here fast." Was the nervous response.

Thinking for a moment, he decided that he would be quicker to go in on his own and Brenda would be safer waiting outside.

"Stay here okay, I'll be back in two seconds. If anything happens just shout." he instructed. Peering into the room once more, he saw that everyone within it had their heads bowed, taking part in some kind of ritualistic mantra.

Brenda didn't argue and remained where she was.

Although the majority of the lower chambers contained windows in the back, they were a lot smaller than the ones at the front of the building. Derek gave her a quick kiss to reassure her and then walked around the rear of the lodge, in an effort to prevent himself being detected. Rounding the other side, he eyed Brenda and gave her a nervous thumbs up. Heart pounding, he quickly stepped into the low entrance once again. Standing in the inner doorway, building up the courage to continue, all Derek could picture was someone grabbing him from the darkness.

Taking a deep breath, the terrified man quickly glanced inside the room to his left. No one looking. He quickly made a move for the stairs and began his ascent.

Brenda continued to rattle with fear outside. Looking around the countryside, she pondered what kind of weirdos were just a few feet away from her.

Reaching the top of the stairs, Derek leaned forward and looked left and right, then he eyed his phone still sitting where he had left it.

Outside, Brenda decided to kneel down and take a quick peek inside. She instantly regretted it. A chalice was being filled with a red substance at the table, meanwhile one of the cloaked individuals took a live chicken from one of the other participants. Holding the bird firmly, the four newcomers knelt down in front of the table. The cloaked spectre picked up the blade, turning away from them and the people on the floor began to mutter unrecognisable words.

The animal's neck was placed over the pentagram on the altar and with one sharp, downward crunch its head was removed. The bird's wings flapped wildly as the butcher turned towards the people kneeling on the floor. Arching their heads towards the ancient ceiling the gushing, warm blood was poured over their faces and the drained carcass was placed onto the table. Picking up the chalice, each cloaked figure took a sip of the still warm liquid. Brenda fought to keep the lumps of sick from passing her lips.

Upstairs, Derek quickly snatched the phone. Turning, he was struck over the head with a blunt object from the darkness.

Sensing he was taking a little too long to come back to her, Brenda stood to her feet. She managed one step before being grabbed from behind and dragged screaming into the Hellfire Club.

As she was dragged kicking and screaming into the chamber she eyed Derek slumped on the floor, gagged and tied, blood trickling down his forehead.

Her struggling was no match for her captor. She was easily restrained and thrown mercilessly to the ground, then gagged and tied.

From behind the bloodied gang of participants and two previously unseen enforcers, stepped one of mysterious, hooded individuals. As Brenda began mumbling in fear beside her unconscious husband, the person approached them.

Lifting their gloved hands and pulling back the hood, Brenda took a sharp intake of breath, seeing a man who was at least eighty years old.

"Welcome." He said in a raspy, low tone, reaching for the chalice on the table.

Brenda squirmed with shock, while he placed the cup beneath Derek's chin. Catching a few droplets, he placed it back onto the table.

"You have both made tonight so much more significant." The elderly man stated, signaling to the others in the chamber to pick Derek up from the floor.

They dragged the man over to the unsightly table and held him above the pentagram. Muttered screams fell from Brenda's as the old monster picked up the large blade.

"So much more significant."

Without hesitation the knife was pushed between Derek's shoulder blades and ran down his back, instantly bringing him to. Crying in agony, the blade was swiped across his back in a vicious flurry. Then the fiend turned his attention to Derek's legs and sliced both hamstrings in half, causing him to kneel in front of the table.

Turning to Brenda, smiling, he placed the blade against Derek's throat. He slid it from left to right. His skin tore open like wet tissue paper and the blood splashed onto the altar and the floor beneath him. The other participants placed a hand each beneath the sliced body and rubbed his blood across their forehead, as the chalice was passed among the leaders of this evil act.

Tears of pain and screams of disbelief and despair erupted from Brenda, as she watched the group discard her beloved's corpse to the ground.

"He'll be with us soon!" The old man continued, while the two behind him remained shrouded in shadow.

Panic, pain and terror flowed through everyone inch of Brenda's body as she quickly realised her horrific ordeal was far from over. It was then the ringing in her ears began.

Looking around the room everything seemed to be moving at a snail's pace. The ringing intensified, causing her to close her eyes in pain. Whispers of an unknown language then broke through the drumming in her head. Then silence. Everything stopped. Prying her eyes open, Brenda saw that everyone was kneeling down, faces to the floor. She turned to the door and witnessed a huge, foreboding, hooded figure, wearing tattered clothes staring at her. Advancing, it was then she heard the clop of hoofs against the floor of the old building.

Picking up the blade from the sacrificial table, the heinous monstrosity began to approach the hysterical, helpless woman.

"Believe...in...me" it slowly hissed from beneath the torn robe, as the knife plunged deep into Brenda's heart.

BACKGROUND ON LAMBS TO THE SLAUGHTER
BY
CHRIS RUSH

Sitting on the Massey estate on top of Montpelier Hill in County Dublin, lurk the remains of an old stone hunting lodge shrouded in a deeply sinister history.

Shortly after being built in 1725 by the Irish House of Commons speaker William Connolly, the roof was ravaged and ripped to pieces by a storm. Many claim it was revenge for destroying and using some remaining stones of an old burial monument in order complete construction of the ominous building. The roof was repaired into an arch design, assumed to be an effort to deflect future high winds. Connolly himself died just four years after building the lodge.

It wasn't until the late 1730s when the 1st Earl of Rosse Richard Parsons, and portrait artist James Worsdale formed the Dublin sector of this club which was best known for alcoholism, orgies and occult practices. The Hellfire Club had various divisions throughout Ireland and Britain and the activities carried out on top of Montpelier hill were identical to the others. The club had a black cat as a mascot and the members would regularly praise and drink to Satan using a concoction called *scaltheen*, a mix of whiskey and hot butter. An empty seat would also be left at the table for the Devil himself to join them.

One of the most famous stories to emerge from this haunting building is that the Devil himself did join the Hellfire Club on the top of Montpelier Hill. A stranger visited the club one dark, stormy night. Inviting him in, they decide to partake in a game of cards. One of the cards fell to the floor and during its retrieval a club member glanced across and beneath the table and was shocked to find two cloven hooves. Once noticed, the stranger burst into a ball of flames and disappeared.

Further haunting stories that shroud this building include murders, animal sacrifices and other horrendous activities such as shoving a woman into a barrel, setting it ablaze and kicking it down the long, steep hill while she screamed and cooked inside.

Alcohol and fire seemed to be common elements within the club as another story goes that a club member lost his temper, drenched another man with brandy and then burned him alive. Further claims include a black cat linked to the Hellfire Club becoming possessed by some unworldly force. An exorcism was carried out on the beast and after its completion a demon is said to have fled from within the animal.

The building was reportedly ravaged by fire and to this day many claim you can still hear the screams of a woman plummeting down the hill in a barrel to her death, with further activity such as invisible hands pulling at people's throats being reported within the building.

Sitting at the bottom of Montpelier hill is the Steward's House or Kilakee House. This building, built in 1765, became the new meeting location for the Hellfire Club following the fire that destroyed the lodge, until the death of Hellfire member Thomas "Buck" Whaley.

Renovations began on the house in the 1960s and workers stated they saw many apparitions, one which included a man dressed in black, which is thought to have been the priest who performed the exorcism on the cat on top of Montpelier Hill.

In 1971 a shocking discovery was made in the Steward's House while more works where being carried out. A grave was unearthed which contained the remains of a child or small human, believed to have been sacrificed during one of the Hellfire Club's rituals.

Further activity over the years include sightings of nuns, who it is thought took part in black masses at the Hellfire Club and a large black cat with glowing red eyes. So if you are planning to visit The Hellfire Club, be sure to bring someone with you and be careful because you never know who you may bump into up there.

HAVERGILL'S FETCH
BY
CATHERINE SHINGLER

Now that the ladies have retired, pass the brandy and I'll tell you about young John Havergill. My father was parson at Havergill church. There were not many boys of good family in that part of Lincolnshire, and as lads John Havergill and I were close friends. We went to school together, and during the holidays we were inseparable. However, as we reached manhood, the necessity of earning my living drew me away to study medicine. Havergill was under no such obligation. Our lives became very different, and our letters less frequent. With one thing and another I had not seen him for several years when I returned home in April 189-.

I walked up to the Hall to see him. My father had warned me he was drinking too much and keeping bad company, and it was beginning to show, though he shook my hand enthusiastically.

"My dear fellow!"

"Hello, Havergill. What are you up to these days?"

"Pa wants me to marry one of the Bruton girls, but I keep telling him there's no rush."

He ushered me into the library.

"Do you know Harry Callaghan?"

Callaghan was lounging against the chimneypiece, smoking an evil-smelling cheroot. I knew him only by reputation. My father had spoken of him as a dissolute youth given to strong drink and foolish pranks. Havergill was generous with his father's cellar, and we were soon all chatting like old friends. I mentioned that I had left my father working on his sermon for the next day, which was April 25th.

"St Mark's Eve," said Callaghan. "What luck."

"Why?" I said.

"They say in the Havergill Arms that if you wait in the churchyard at midnight on St Mark's Eve, the spirits of all the parishioners who will die in the next year pass before you."

"So I've heard," said Havergill. "My nursemaid used to tell such tales."

I laughed, with the derision of a man of science. "You don't believe in such rubbish, do you?"

"Let's go down there tonight." Callaghan's eyes were shining, whether from drink or excitement I could not tell.

"Let's not," I said. "There'll be nothing to see."

"Then there's nothing to be afraid of," said Havergill. "What's the time?"

Callaghan pulled out a dented watch. "Five and twenty to midnight. We've got time for another drink before we go."

Havergill poured everyone a brandy. I had had more than enough, and so had the others, but we drank it and then put on our coats. There was a full moon, barely obscured by wisps of cloud. Spring was late that year, and the wind was thin and cold.

As we approached the church, the clock tolled the first stroke of midnight. Despite myself, I looked about for any signs of supernatural activity.

"This is ridiculous," I said as the twelfth stroke died away. "I'm off ho-"

There was a low moan from Callaghan, and Havergill grabbed my arm. Across the churchyard a glimmer of pale light appeared between the dark yews. A line of shimmering figures was stumbling towards us, picking their way among the gravestones. I rubbed my sleeve across my eyes and tried to think of a rational explanation.

"Marsh gas," I heard myself say.

"It's never marsh gas," croaked Callaghan.

The wind had dropped, and there was not a sound as the ghostly procession made its way towards us. No owl hooted, no fox yelped. They walked hesitantly as if unsure of their footing. Each figure was surrounded by a faint, cold glow which threw the gravestones into dark relief. As they drew near we could see that there were eight of them. In the lead walked Mrs Alldred, carrying a baby. Behind her came an old woman I did not know. Then there was Mr Hardy from the Red House, leaning on his stick; then a little boy, then Stephens, the ostler at the Havergill Arms. Second to last came Miss Palmer, the village school mistress. The final figure trailed a little behind the others. My heart lurched. That unmistakeable lock of dark hair across the brow: it was Havergill. As it came to us it raised its head and stared intently at the living Havergill.

Havergill's fingers dug into my arm. Callaghan whimpered and fell to the ground. "A fetch, a fetch," he moaned.

My heart hung between beats as those two white faces, more alike than twins, gazed into each other's eyes.

The phantom was first to look away. It turned to stumble after its fellows. Havergal and I watched them disappear into the church porch, their light fading as they went. I did not know what to say. Havergill did not speak either, although he was breathing fast. At last I said: "Come away."

We stepped over Callaghan's weeping form and I led Havergill to the parsonage. Everyone had gone to bed, but there was a light left in the parlour, and the dying fire. I sat Havergill down and poured him a brandy. He was shaking too violently to take it, so I held the glass to his lips and he gulped it down.

"Dear God," he whispered. "What have we seen?"

"It can't be - what we thought it was. Callaghan was talking rubbish."

Havergill raised his head. His eyes looked enormous. "Do you really think that?"

"I honestly don't know what to think."

We did not sleep, but sat up all night in our clothes. He was so silent that I thought he had dozed off, but a glance showed me that he was still gazing into the fire.

In the morning the maid came to clear the fireplace. When she saw us she yelped and dropped her bucket. "We were talking so late it didn't seem worth going to bed," I said.

The maid was not looking at me. "What's the matter with Mr Havergill?"

I forced a laugh.

"Too much brandy. Do you think you'll manage church this morning, old man?"

Havergill turned his white face towards me. "I'll manage church."

He had to take my arm for support as we approached the church door. There were several moments during the service when I thought he might faint. Callaghan was nowhere to be seen.

Afterwards I walked with Havergill to his home. I chattered all the way about anything that came into my head – anything except the night before. When we reached the house he turned to me and seized my hand.

"You're a good friend, Philip. I should have listened to you last night.

"I should have told that ass Callaghan to clear off. I wish you wouldn't see so much of him. My father thinks he's a thoroughly bad hat."

Havergill managed a wan smile. "He's probably right. Very well, I shan't be at home to him if he calls again."

But Callaghan did not call again. After a few days during which he drank all the brandy the Havergill Arms could supply, while raving about fetches to anyone who would listen and many who would not, his parents called the doctor, who sent for the men from the County Lunatic Asylum. You could hear his screams all the way to the Lincoln road.

I returned to work in London. I tried to put the events of that night out of my head: events which, as a doctor, I could not possibly explain. Then I received two letters. One was from Havergill, informing me of his forthcoming wedding to the elder Bruton girl and asking me to be his best man. He was in London, staying at the Havergills' town house, and invited me to dine with him at his club. The other letter was from my father. After the usual family business, he wrote that Havergill was at last settling down and would be married in the spring. His postscript caught my attention: "By the way, you will be sorry to hear of the death of Mrs Alldred in childbed last week. She will be much missed in the village."

The vision of poor Mrs Alldred leading the silent procession of doomed souls across the churchyard, her tiny child in her arms, surged to the forefront of my mind.

On the Friday, I again met Havergill at his club. He was pale but composed, and I noticed that he drank only water.

"Your father prevailed upon you to marry the Bruton girl, then."

"She's not so bad when you get to know her," said Havergill. "I can see myself becoming quite fond of her."

"What made you change your mind?"

Havergill put down his fork and looked about him. "I fear I am not long for this world, and it will please the old man if I marry."

"You're as sound as a bell. You don't carry as much weight as last time I saw you, and..."

"That's true, but you know as well as I do that I shall be dead before the end of April."

"You mean, because of what we saw? There's bound to be some scientific explanation. We were drunk, we let Callaghan fill our minds with silly stories..."

Havergill leaned towards me. "I have seen it since."

"What?"

"Several times. The first time must have been in May. It was twilight, though not late, and I was riding back from the village. As I rode past the church the horse shied. I tried to settle him, and then I saw a figure out of the corner of my eye, standing among the headstones, watching. It was myself!"

"Are you certain?"

"I know what I look like; I have looking glasses and photographs. Then at the end of June we were coming back from church in the carriage, and we passed him – it – walking along the road. He raised his head as we drew level."

"Did anyone else see it?"

"Not for what it was. Then last month I had gone on to the terrace to watch the sunset – and there It was, watching me from the other side of the lake. It's getting closer, Philip. It's coming for me. That's why I've come up to London. Maybe it won't find me here."

He spoke like a rational man and I did not doubt that he believed every word he said.

"I can prescribe you a tonic if you think it might help."

"It won't."

At Christmas Miss Bruton's father was taken ill, and the wedding was postponed. Havergill was very downcast, and had convinced himself that he would die before the wedding could be rearranged.

"Mrs Alldred was the first," he said. "Then the blacksmith's mother. Mr Hardy died at midsummer."

"He'd been ill for years."

"The Collier boy got diptheria. Stevens was kicked in the head by a horse on Boxing Day and died a fortnight later."

It had indeed been a busy year for my father.

"And now my mother writes that Miss Palmer is unwell."

"I'm sorry to hear that."

"The – the thing that was me followed the thing that was Miss Palmer. If Miss Palmer dies, then I shall be next."

"Have you told Miss Bruton about all this?"

He snorted. "I don't want to join Callaghan in the asylum."

By the beginning of April, Miss Bruton's father had recovered to some degree, and talk of the wedding resumed. Havergill horrified Miss Bruton's family by suggesting they marry quietly and quickly by special licence.

"I don't give a fig myself," said Miss Bruton, "but Mamma is set on a grand wedding."

We were lunching at the Havergills' London house. It was the first time I had met Miss Bruton. She was handsome rather than beautiful, with a square, sensible face and a good deal of dark hair. Her manner was forthright, and when she spoke she looked straight in one's eye. I thought she might be good for Havergill.

"Let's elope. Think how much money your father will save," said Havergill.

Miss Bruton laughed. "He'd rather have the wedding than the money," she said. "It's what he recovered for."

When it was time for me to go she walked with me to the door.

"You've known John a long time, Dr Cobb."

"Since we were boys."

"He seems so restless lately. I wish I knew what was troubling him. Is he ill?"

"Not in the way you think." I hesitated to betray Havergill's confidence, but I could not let this young woman walk blindfold into a marriage with a man who might not be in his right mind.

I told her everything. "I believe it was a mass delusion."

"Poor John," she said. "He must be very afraid."

"Will you still marry him?"

"Of course. Once April passes, and he is still with us, he will have nothing to fear. And you say this schoolmistress is still alive?"

"At the moment." I had asked my father to keep me informed of Miss Palmer's condition.

"Then we will both do our best to raise his spirits."

I went home thinking that Havergill had done rather well for himself. A couple of days later, on my way back from visiting a patient, I saw Havergill striding along the pavement. Although it was a cool evening he was in his shirt sleeves and wore no hat. I stopped the cab and called after him but he took no notice. His white shirt seemed to glow under the streetlamps. I asked the cabman to follow him. "Sorry, guvnor, I've lost him. Must have nipped down an alley or something."

When I reached home I found a telegram from my father telling me that Miss Palmer had died in her sleep the night before. It was April 23rd.

I scarcely slept that night and, immediately after breakfast, I set off for Havergill's house. He seemed feverish, and had not been to bed.

"Good morning, Philip. You've come to keep me company for my last day on earth?"

"My dear fellow, it won't come to that."

"Well, I have sent for my parents to bid them farewell, and we'll ask them how Miss Palmer is."

I took a deep breath. "According to my father, she is much better. You look a little flushed. How do you feel?"

"Not bad for a man at death's door." But his eyes glittered and his hands were shaking. When I felt his wrist his pulse was racing. "I wish you would get some sleep. You'll feel better for it. I'll wake you when your parents arrive."

"Will you stay?"

"Of course."

I gave him a sleeping draught and took him up to his bedroom. All the looking-glasses were shrouded with towels. I helped him undress and put him to bed; his skin was clammy to the touch.

As soon as he was asleep I took his watch and moved the hands two hours forward. I did the same with all the clocks I could find. As I went downstairs to alter the hall clock, I met Miss Bruton. She understood instantly what I was about, and went to warn the servants.

Havergill's parents arrived at about six o'clock. I explained that their son was suffering from morbid thoughts and that I advised complete rest. On no account were they to tell him of Miss Palmer's passing. Miss Bruton and I managed to persuade them to follow our subterfuge with the clocks and watches. They were concerned, but I allayed their fears by assuring them that John would make a full recovery once the night was over.

At about eleven, Havergill awoke.

"What's the time?"

"See for yourself." I showed him his watch.

"One o'clock! Have I really slept so long?"

"Don't you feel the benefit?"

"Indeed. By Jove, I do feel much better." He laughed and sat up. His cheeks were no longer flushed, and his pulse and temperature were normal. "I'll get up."

I pushed him back on to the pillows. "No, old man, you must rest."

"At least let me have something to eat. I could murder some anchovy toast."

"I'll go and find Mrs Howe," said Miss Bruton from the doorway.

"I've been such a fool," said Havergill. "All year I've been like a frightened child, afraid of my own shadow. I should have listened to you, Philip, you're always the voice of reason."

I did not feel as relieved as I had hoped.

"And poor Elizabeth," he continued, "what sort of a fiancé have I been? From now on I shall be the most attentive lover any woman could want."

There was a knock on the door and Mrs Howe the housekeeper came in bearing a tray.

"Here you are, Mr John. Glad you saw sense and went back to bed. You'll catch your death wandering about the house in your shirt."

"I've been in bed for hours. It's done me the world of good."

She set the tray down on the bed. "You fibber. I saw you in the hall not ten minutes ago. Now eat this up like a good boy."

Havergill stared at the housekeeper's retreating back. His face was whiter than the napkin that covered the anchovy toast.

"It's all up with me," he said. "It's come for me."

His parents looked at each other in dismay.

"Eat your toast, John," said Mrs Havergill.

"It couldn't find you in time," I said. "It will have to go away without you."

"That's right, of course," said Havergill. "It's the 25th now, isn't it? You've missed your chance." His voice rose. "Get away! You cannot take me now!" He stretched out a trembling finger, pointing at a glowing image of himself that stood at the end of the bed, a wild, livid simulacrum reaching out to touch his hand. Havergill uttered a dreadful shriek and fell back on the pillow – stark dead. The thing dissipated like a cloud before our eyes.

I don't know what to make of it; I am a man of science. I wrote "heart failure" on the death certificate. Sometimes my wife Elizabeth and I talk about it; but when she insists that Havergill was pursued by a spectre that took his soul I laugh heartily and tell her not to be a silly girl.

BACKGROUND ON HAVERGILL'S FETCH BY CATHERINE SHINGLER

This story first came to me in a dream, about twenty years ago.

Fetches, also known as co-walkers, doubles or doppelgangers, are ghosts of the living, identical to them in every way. Their appearance often, though not inevitably, portends death for the person whom the fetch resembles, particularly for those who see their own fetch. The word appears as an English North Country term defined as "an apparition of a person living" in Grose's Provincial Glossary of 1787. In the sixteenth century a spirit sent to fetch the souls of the dying is called a "fetch-life".

Fetches were not always harbingers of doom. In Irish folklore to see a fetch in the morning was a sign of good luck to come. Only afternoon and evening visions foretold death.

Although the fetch is often thought of an Irish superstition, which is why I have given Callaghan an Irish name, fetches abound in British ghost stories, often associated with well-known people or families. Percy Bysshe Shelley's wife met his ghost while he was still living, although she did not consider it a bad omen at the time, and John Donne is supposed to have encountered his wife's phantom abroad at the same time she gave birth to a stillborn baby back in England.

Unlike most phantoms, fetches are not usually frightening in appearance. According to most eyewitness accounts, they were easily mistaken for the person they resembled and often not recognised as supernatural phenomena until later.

For this story, I have made Havergill's fetch a little more malignant than is traditional and endowed it with volition to pursue him across the country. I've also combined the myth of the fetch with the widespread belief that, on certain dates, the phantoms of all those parishioners who will die that year can be seen entering the church at midnight. The custom was known as porch watching. Dates and methods vary with locations: St Mark's Eve (April 24th) was the preferred date in the north and the Midlands, although in other areas porch watching took place at Halloween. In Yorkshire the watcher had to keep vigil for three consecutive nights. Welsh watchers had to peer through the church keyhole. Sometimes the dead were accompanied by the phantoms of those who would be married that year – the couples would be seen leaving the church, but the apparitions of those who would die did not re-emerge.

In some villages the same person acted as porch watcher every year, and reported their visions back to the villagers. As Robert Chambers remarks in his 'Book of Days' (1869):

"It may readily be presumed that this would prove a very pernicious superstition, as a malignant person, bearing an ill-will to any neighbour, had only to say or insinuate that he had seen him forming part of the visionary procession of St. Mark's Eve, in order to visit him with a serious affliction, if not with mortal disease."

The regular porch watcher ran the unsettling risk of seeing his own fetch. Porch watching was not something to be undertaken for a lark.

In telling this story I have tried to convey something of the sort of atmosphere found in the writing of M. R. James and other Edwardian masters of the genre: an anecdotal, gentlemen's club sort of style, where the narrator cannot quite bring himself to believe his own experiences.

HUNGER
BY
ANN O'REGAN

The wind howled like a demon in his ears and the driving rain whipped at his raw and ruddy face. Liam tried to pull his cap further down over his eyes to protect them from the raging storm. The young man held the lapels of his coat together as he battled against the unseen force trying to knock him down. Liam questioned his sanity for coming out on this desperate night, but he needed a pint and some light-hearted conversation.

Things hadn't been easy since his father had passed away, he thought. Watching his father go mad, screaming at nothing and wasting away was too much to bear. His mother seemed to go through the motions and spent most nights staring into the fire until the embers died, much like her will to live. It had been three months and it seemed this was how things were going to be.

Liam snapped out of his maudlin state of mind, as a sharp gust of wind sent him spiralling into the ditch. His foot was firmly embedded in the mud and he began to pull at the top of his boot.

"For the love of..." Liam stopped as he caught sight of a tall, angular figure out of the corner of his eye standing a few feet to his side.

"Could you give us a hand?" Liam shouted over the elements without glancing up from his current predicament.

Nothing.

"COULD YOU GI..." The young man stopped and looked up to see nothing but the spindly branches of a craggy tree lurching towards him. Laughing at his own stupidity, Liam tugged harder and finally both boot and wearer were free. The thought of a creamy-headed pint of porter spurred him on and his somewhat soggier step hastened.

As he approached the Creamery, Liam could see the welcoming lights of O'Connor's pub right ahead. Of course, it served the dual purpose of being an undertaker so there were many who wouldn't find the lights so welcoming. The appearance of Ger O'Connor from the side door in his sombre dress coat and hat showed this was one such night.

"Evening Ger, busy day of it?"

"Three today Liam, two from the same family, you know yourself."

He did. The slight man before him had buried his two sisters, one brother and more recently, his father. Wallowing in his own self-pity, Liam was unable to extend any sympathy for the deceased or the weary undertaker. Still, he wasn't heartless.

"Come on Ger, I'll buy you a pint."

Liam pushed open the door of the bar. After the solitude and darkness of his journey he found his senses overwhelmed. A wave of light and the sounds of singing, conversation and clinking glasses washed over him. For the first time that day, the young man gave a genuine smile.

Of course the topic of conversation was death. 'Sure, when wasn't it these days?' the young man thought as he supped his third pint. Although the Famine was long over, it seemed his community was still cursed by it. The number of deaths attributed to madness or starvation was on the rise, yet everyone was too afraid to say why.

Ger had left for the warmth of his wife and a bowl of stew. Sitting alone, Liam leant on the elbow worn patina of the counter and listened to Billy and Micheál Corcoran arguing over the latest local tragedies.

"I'm telling you Billy, it's happening again! It's the Fear Gorta!"

"Enough Micheál!"

"I'm telling you Billy! There's folks starving to death yet not going hungry, wasting away for no reason! You remember what mam told us about the famine, YOU REMEMBER?!" The wild eyed man clutched at his brother's waistcoat.

"Would you give over Micheál, tis an ol' wives tale and you know it. They were starvin' nothing more. Whist your nonsense now before someone hears you and has you taken to Saint Kevin's." Billy roughly pushed his brother away.

Liam shuddered. He'd heard many horrific tales about the asylum in Cork city, a few miles away. As it was, several of his community were now resident as a result of similar ramblings.

"Argh!" Micheál spluttered. He kicked his stool to the floor and stormed out into the night, his temper a match for the ongoing squall.

As the latch on the pub door clicked behind them, Billy and Liam began their long walk home. The pounding rain and icy wind had subsided and their way home was lit by a watery half-moon in the Cork sky.

Reaching a fork in the road, Billy turned to Liam and placed an imploring arm on the young man's shoulder.

"If he carries on this way they'll take him in for sure. Liam…"

"I'll be saying nothing to no one Billy, yer grand."

With a sad smile, Billy turned and carried on up the lane towards the ramshackle cottage he shared with his brother.

As Liam glanced after the long suffering man, he felt an unnatural stillness in the air. The stench of decay filled his nostrils and his eyes began to water. An icy breath touched the back of his neck and every hair on his body stood up. Paralysed with fear, Liam's eyes widened as he realised he was not alone.

He cast his eyes downwards and gasped as a withered hand reached around his waist and bony fingers dug deep into his stomach. Breaths were fast and shallow as the putrid smell grew stronger. Closing his eyes, Liam began to mutter. "Our Father who art in…" The breath was now in his ear and the stench was overwhelming. Liam felt a warm liquid run down the inside of his leg and a solitary tear travelled slowly down his frozen cheek. A gravelly voice whispered: "Hunger."

* * *

Liam shot up out of the bed, blinked and rubbed his eyes. Blaming the several pints of black nectar he had consumed, he decided to put the events of the previous night down to drunken hallucination. He wearily stripped off his nightshirt and splashed cold water over his face at the basin. As he looked into the mirror he gasped. There on his stomach was the blackened outline of four long and slender fingers.

With a sore head and heavy heart, Liam went about the farm as he did every day, like a penance. Walking the boundaries, he checked fencing and hedging were secure so the few cattle they had could not escape. His mind would not rest. Stopping at a rain-filled trough, he bent over to see his shimmering reflection and gradually pulled up his shirt. Nothing. Clutching at his stomach he moved closer to the water. No mark, just the redness from his own hand. He laughed. Maybe these late night sessions weren't such a good idea!

As he reached the top field, he glanced over the hedgerow and his body gave an involuntary shiver. It separated himself and the Corcoran family. It was used during the Great Famine as a mass burial ground and contained the husks of the poor emaciated souls who had succumbed to the horror.

Nothing but the sparsest blades of grass would grow in that field anymore and no one dared to cross it. As children they were warned never to step on the Fear Gortach. They did not, more out of fear of the corpses beneath the withered ground rather than the wrath of angry parents. As a child, Liam used to think he could hear cries and screams of pain on the wind. When he mentioned it to his father, he was given the strap and told never to speak of it again.

In as much of a hurry to get away from the field as to race towards the pint he was longing for, Liam paused only to tie his unruly boot lace. As he straightened, the hairs on the back of his neck stood up and he became very aware he was being watched. Turning slowly, the young man found himself staring straight into the terrified eyes of Billy Corcoran.

"Help...me" mouthed his ashen-faced friend.

Seeing that Billy was in no state to help himself, Liam started to climb. He froze. Where Billy stood, all the grass beneath his feet was black and decayed.

"So…hungry…so …hungry!" Billy wailed.

Liam shook himself as he realised that no matter how scared he was, he could not leave the broken man before him. In that moment any doubt he had about the curse of the Hungry Grass and the Fear Gorta was gone, replaced with certainty and dread.

Reaching over the hedgerow, he grabbed Billy by his wrists. Heaving with all his strength, Liam began to pull Billy out through the foliage. Billy's shirt caught on the sharp twigs and Liam gulped. There imprinted firmly across Billy's stomach was the unmistakable black mark of a skeletal hand. An icy chill swept over his entire body and his heart began to pound. He looked up and there, on the opposite side of the field, staring back at him was the emaciated spectre from the previous day. With a rictus grin spread wide across its gaunt, empty face, it raised one gangly arm, stretched out one single bony finger and pointed straight at the terrified young man.

Liam desperately tugged harder and both he and Billy tumbled to the ground. Scrambling to his feet, he grabbed Billy again by the wrists and began to drag him away, panting and sweating as much with terror as the effort of having to haul a dead weight. Every inch of his body told him not to look but he jerked his head up nonetheless. The gaunt nightmare loomed out over the fence, still pointing a solitary skeletal finger, and Liam cried out.

The screams brought his mother running, faster than he had ever seen her. As he looked back once more, the source of his fear had vanished.

Falling to her knees, Liam's mother placed one hand on Billy's forehead. "Run and fetch the doctor, the priest and Micheál", she snapped.

"What's happen…"

"NOW!" Her eyes flashed with both anger and fear. Liam sprinted to the Corcoran house and crashed through the kitchen door. A bewildered Micheál glanced up from his cup of tea.

"Quick, it's Billy!"

The middle-aged man dropped his cup to the floor where it shattered into a hundred pieces. Without stopping, Micheál was out the door, pulling on his jacket and hat as he went. Not a word passed between them in the minutes it took to reach the crossroads. Liam continued his run towards the village, stopping only to catch his breath and look around for the horror that was hounding him.

Liam met Father Walsh on the steps of the church. He muttered that Billy needed help after being found near the Fear Gortach. The priest did not need to hear another word and he started to run towards the unfolding drama. Liam stared after him. As he reached the Doctor's House, Liam began to panic about what others might say and decided there and then not to tell a soul what he had witnessed. He told Doctor Culhane nothing other than that he had found Billy on the edge of his property and that he needed medical attention. As the medical man commandeered a passing pony and trap, Liam headed for the door of the pub.

Terrified and confused, Liam wiped away a tear with his dirty sleeve. Hands shaking, he raised the glass of whiskey to his mouth and drank deeply. After four more he felt he could face returning home.

As he reached the gate, Liam saw a large crowd gathered around… wait - it wasn't Billy. He was gone, along with the doctor and the pony and trap. Instead he faced a mad-eyed, purple-faced Micheál, raging about the Fear Gorta while under the restraint of three burly locals. He contorted his head and turned to a bewildered Liam.

"Tell them!! Tell them Liam!!! Micheál shrieked. "Tell them what did this!!!" Liam glanced around at the waiting crowd and said nothing

"Tell them, for Billy!" the restrained man roared.

"I, I don't know, I found Billy in the field." Liam cast his eyes to his boots, pulling his cap down to hide his guilt-ridden face.

"TELL THEM PLEASE!!!" Micheál began to weep.

Feeling eyes boring into him, Liam turned to see his own mother staring with contempt before she turned away and walked back to the cottage. As he opened his mouth to speak, the sound of a wagon on the dirt road caught everyone's attention. On the side it said 'Our Lady's Hospital and St Kevin's Asylum'.

Micheál was roughly tied into a strait jacket and gagged. Liam saw there was no fight left in the man, his brother's demise and Liam's betrayal too much for him to bear.

* * *

Days passed. Liam's mother refused to speak to him and the traumatised young man found himself spiralling into a dark abyss of despair and misery. Finally, he plucked up the courage to go and visit Billy. The misfortune was lying at home, wasting away to nothing with no discernible cause.

Liam gasped. Billy had aged by fifty years, his once sturdy and strong frame shrivelled to a living skeleton. Razor sharp cheek bones jutted out from his tight and sallow skin, his eyes deep in their sockets. The only sign of life were the flashes of utter terror that they sparked.

It was all too much.

"Come on Liam, time for home." Ger shook the inebriated man into a waking state. Shaking his head, the barman guided Liam out and bolted the door behind him. A chilling gust of wind whirled around the drunkard, bringing him round to a suitable level of sobriety to manage the short walk home.

Feeling whiskey-brave as he approached the crossroads, Liam began to shout out.

"Show yourself! I'm not afraid of you! Come on!" Liam staggered around the road, fists up, looking for his spectral opponent. Nothing. "Baaaah! You're not real!" he slurred as he reached the cottage door. He turned the handle, blissfully unaware of the menacing stare boring into his back and the outstretched bony hand beckoning him to the field.

Opening his bleary, bloodshot eyes, Liam jumped to see the wrinkled, angry face of his mother staring down at him.

"Billy and Micheál Corcoran are dead," she snapped.

"What?" Liam sat bolt upright.

"While you drank yourself stupid and slept it off, Billy died alone in the night. The Doctor never saw such fear on a man's face when he found him this morning on his rounds. Word came through from Saint Kevin's that Micheál was hanging by his strait jacket this morning. Those boys are eternally damned and it's because of YOU!"

Without warning, Liam's mother began frantically hitting and clawing at her son as he tried to push her away. Losing her strength, she slumped to the ground and began to sob uncontrollably.

Time passed as Liam found himself the victim of a living nightmare. He felt his sanity begin to slip away from him. Every step he took, every glance, there was that heinous, skeletal figure out of the corner of his eye, grinning, pointing, waiting. He stopped eating, stopped sleeping. If he wasn't standing at the hedgerow, staring into the Fear Gortach, he was sat on the stool in O'Connor's drinking neat whiskey and muttering to himself.

The pub was particularly rowdy as an American wake was in full swing. Liam was in his usual spot, elbow propped up on the bar and hand resting under his chin. He swayed on his stool, drowsily watching the jigs and reels before him. Liam's eyes widened in horror. He was there. Behind the dancers and fiddle player he towered over the room and he was grinning at Liam. And pointing.

The crazed and terrified man began to scream and push over stools as every sound and movement in the pub came to a complete standstill. Liam started to grab those nearest to him and shake them by the shoulders. "Can you see him? SEE? HE'S HERE!"

As hushed whispers rose to a cacophony of panic, Liam felt strong arms and hands pin him down. He looked again and saw nothing other than the shocked faces of the dancers and drinkers. Laughing hysterically, he tried to pull away, writhing and twisting, biting and snarling. Liam felt a fist connect with the side of his head and darkness enveloped him.

He blinked. The room was dingy and unfamiliar, a rotten stench filled his nostrils. The young man tried to sit up but found himself restrained. Struggling to piece his fragmented thoughts together, his efforts were thwarted by the distant sound of cries and maniacal laughter.

Liam went cold and in a brief moment of sanity his heart sank. His worst fears had been realised and he was in the one place he dreaded more than the creature haunting his every living moment. The door opened and a nurse entered with a tall, gangly doctor in a white coat. There was something familiar about the man before him. Sunken cheekbones, deep set eyes of black, matted white hair, what was it…?

"How do you feel, I asked you?" The nurse glared at her unwilling patient.

"Um…I…"

"Well the doctor will be along to discuss your treatment shortly, drink this to calm yourself." Liam tried to protest, but the sturdy matron was more than a match and he felt a warm, sticky liquid coat the inside of his mouth and drip down his throat.

"But…doctor… here." Liam garbled as he tried weakly to raise a finger and point at the white coated man behind the door.

"Yes, yes" the nurse uttered as she swept out of the room, firmly closing the door behind her.

Liam turned his head to face the man in the white coat and his eyes widened in horror. The coat turned to rags and that familiar evil rictus stretched across the skeletal face of the wraith before him. The drugs poured into Liam began to take hold and he couldn't move a muscle. Beads of sweat began to form on his forehead and drip down onto the bug-infested mattress. The creature stretched out his scrawny arm and unfurled his withered hand. He reached out to Liam whose eyes were screaming in terror, his voice held hostage by dread.

The Fear Gorta took one decaying, bony finger, the nail pointed and blackened, and slowly and deliberately parted Liam's dry and cracked lips. With a look of pure satisfaction, the vile being forced his finger into the horrified young man's mouth.

"Yes doctor he's restrained and medicated, he'll be no trouble." The nurse struggled to keep up with the fast-paced man beside her as they headed for Liam's cell.

"Good. I've been wanting to try a new..." The doctor stopped dead in his tracks as a bloodcurdling scream resonated from the very cell he was about to enter. A wailing voice full of terror and despair like no other he had heard echoed around the corridor.

"Hungry... SO HUNGRY!"

BACKGROUND ON HUNGER BY ANN O'REGAN

If you have ever found yourself in an Irish country pub and listened in on a conversation or two, you may have heard mention of both the Fear Gorta (*Far Gur-tuh*) or Hungry Man and the Fear Gortach (*Far Gur-toc*) or the Hungry Grass. Fear Gortach is a folklore tale of a cursed patch of land where if you tread, you are doomed to die of starvation, no matter how much you eat. The Hungry Grass has two origins, but the horrific outcome of crossing over it is much the same.

In the late 1840s the Irish Famine took hold of what was a green and fertile land. Man, woman and child were left to starve to death as a direct result of the Potato Blight and a misuse of resources under British rule. Over a million people died in poverty, starvation and agony. The numbers of the dead were so many in such a short space of time, that the fear of widespread disease meant bodies needed to be disposed of quickly. These victims of Famine were thrown into mass graves, usually empty fields, unblessed, their souls condemned to Purgatory.

All over Ireland there were hundreds of mass graves, or Famine Graveyards as they became known. All were originally unconsecrated, although in later years many became memorialised and recognised as consecrated ground. Some however, remained buried in cold, unhallowed ground, forgotten souls crying out for their purgatory to end. Over the top of these burial sites the grass grew sparsely. It was cursed. It was hungry.

With the extent and horror of the Great Famine it is no surprise to hear such a tale was born from it. But tales of the Hungry Grass and the emaciated figure of the Hungry Man go back much further in time and have far more supernatural origins.

The most common lore behind the Fear Gortach is that it occurs as a result of fairy magic. Found in fields, it is cursed by the fairies of the Unseelie Court, the 'unhappy, misfortunate' ones who use dark magic. Whether the result of Famine or fairy, to stand on the Hungry Grass means death. Slowly you begin to starve and descend into madness. You eat and you eat but no amount of food will ever fill the void in your stomach. The mind snaps, convincing the poor, cursed individual they are starving to death. Ultimately mind takes over matter and the victim just withers away and dies.

The Fear Gorta, or Hungry Man is not a man at all, but an ethereal being or fairy. He is associated with Famine for two reasons. The first is his dreadful appearance. Skeletal in physique, his face is gaunt and haggard. Hollow cheeks and angular bones are covered by thinly stretched, sallow skin. His emaciated figure a horrific image to behold, his clothing is nothing but tatters and rags and to all intents and purposes he has the look of the walking dead.

The second is that he is known to appear during times of hardship and Famine. The Fear Gorta can be malevolent or benevolent, depending on his mood and the welcome he receives. He is known to go begging, house to house and if he is treated kindly he has the ability to bestow good blessings and wealth on those he deems worthy. Of course those who are unkind will feel his wrath and suffer abject poverty, starvation and ultimately... death.

There are no sure-fire ways to defend yourself against either the Fear Gorta or Fear Gortach, but there are certain protections you can try. Carrying a crust of bread in your pocket may protect you from the starvation effects of stepping on the Hungry Grass. It is also believed that crumbs of bread spread over the affected area will somehow reverse the curse over those recently afflicted. Ultimately the salting and burning of the field is believed to bring closure to the curse.

So is the Fear Gortach an act of malicious fairy magic and why would they see fit to curse the land? There are accounts of fairy magic being used to keep humans away from sites of importance to the fairy realm. Fairy forts and patches of the Fear Gortach are believed to be traps that activate in the event of tampering, whether deliberate destruction or the accidental crossing of either supernatural creation.

If the curse of the Hungry Grass relates to those who died and were unceremoniously buried, then that can mean only one thing: the victims of the Famine have become predatory, seeking to drag the living into their Hell alongside them.

The Fear Gorta is a different story. He is fairy, he is solitary and he has no master. There is no protection from his power, only your behaviour and his mood decide your fate.

So when you find yourself in rural Ireland, perhaps taking a shortcut across a local field, ask yourself 'Is the brush of grass around your ankles just that or the ravenous seeking company as misery requires? Is the hunger upon you a result of your pleasant country stroll or the curse of the fairy folk?' And if you answer your door to a skeletal, withered figure asking for alms, think twice before you send him on his way.

JACKFEST
BY
PHIL DAVIES

"Are those fingers..?"

"Yeah! Neat isn't it?"

"Wait? They're real fingers?"

"What? No! No of course not! They're only pretend. Joke ones. I got them from that place over there." Brigette pointed over at a small street-side market stall about 100 yards away. I could see more examples of the necklace she wore hanging from the awning alongside similarly ghoulish tourist souvenirs.

"Lovely! It looks very... appropriate."

Shrewsbury's annual Bloudie Jack Festival, or JackFEST as it was now more commonly known, had grown into quite the event, attracting people not just from all over the country, but even the world. And where there are tourists there are those looking to make quick cash selling them cheap souvenirs. Brigette loved it all, but then she always had been interested in the strange and macabre.

The way Shrewsbury had incorporated one of the monthly population culls into this annual festival was, it had to be said, inspired. So inspired, in fact, that many villages, towns and cities in England now used their own serial killers and bogeymen in similar ways. Shrewsbury though, had been the first. They were the ones who had had started it all and so theirs became THE event to go to, even if those who came to these things never really knew whether it would be them who would become one of the state-endorsed victims.

"Jack be nimble! Jack be quick! Jack had his head stuck up on a stick!" A laughing group of costumed children ran past singing the infamous chant.

"Isn't it just fantastic, Jack!" Brigette said as she took my hand and pulled me forward. I noticed a few glances my way after she had said my name.

"Don't worry." I said to no one in particular "I'm not one of the Jacks. Jack is my given name, not one I've adopted for this... weekend."

"Oh shut up Jack!" Brigette mocked, then shouting over her shoulder: "Ooooh JACK! Look out everyone here comes JACK! JACK is coming to kill me!"

Some of the crowd started looking over. There were a couple of whoops and cheers.

"Get 'er Jack!"

"Yeah! Get 'er Jack! Kill the bitch!" Brigette pulled me onward, laughing.

* * *

We were now sat in a Shrewsbury kaffeehous. Brigette was still smiling at my earlier discomfort. "Oh don't be such a victim!"she scolded. "Loosen up, it was a joke! Nobody really thinks you're a Jack." Even this kaffeehaus had given itself over to the legend of Bloudie Jack. Garish red ribbons, echoing his bloody end hung around the place. Fake fingers and toes had been placed amongst the various cakes and pastries and even our cups of kaffee came with these same body parts on the saucer in place of the customary biscuit.

Brigette winked at me as she nibbled on a toe. "What's it like, do you think?" She asked 'The killing I mean?"

"I haven't given it much thought really."

"That moment when the light goes out from behind their eyes. That feeling of taking someone else's life, stealing all their hopes and dreams. Everything they could be, everything they are. I bet it feels like power. Like real power."

"Well, as I said, I haven't really thought about it." I laughed, feeling uncomfortable and brought the conversation to a close. We sat in silence for a minute or two, sipping the hot kaffee.

"Where shall we go next then?" Brigette broke the quiet hanging between us.

"Can't we just stay here?" The conversation had unsettled me and I wasn't in the mood for large crowds any more. "We can see the parade as it passes. We've got a good view from here."

I knew Brigette could tell I wanted to avoid the parade. It was an opportunity for both locals and outsiders to dress up and 'perform'. If there were to be deaths today (and there would be), the parade was a good time to kill as attention would focused there and not elsewhere. Not every Jack wants to be caught and then, as happens with all of the Jacks that are captured or surrender that day: ritually hung, drawn and quartered by the memorial. Some Jacks want to get away with it; they don't want their own deaths to be added to the monthly register. Some Jacks return and come back year after year, or travel the country visiting the other festivals that take place and become a Peter, a Harold or a Fred.

Although Brigette had unsettled me with her talk of killing, the main reason I was concerned was that she was very much the Mary-Anne archetype. Mary-Anne had been the last of Bloudie Jack's victims, the original Bloudie Jack that is. Mary-Anne was the one that had lead to his capture and execution and so the name had stood as a name for all girls that were culled over a festival weekend. A Jack that was able to collect a Mary-Anne like Brigette, well, it all added to the kudos of the kill, not that I agreed with it, the cull was supposed to be about necessity, not style.

I knew the argument well. I'd even repeated it myself a few times. The cull wasn't supposed to be about purging or catharsis. It wasn't about clearing out negative, animal emotions. The cull was necessary. The cull was vital. With the world's population stretched to breaking point, something had to be done. Compulsory euthanasia for those over 65 had only got us so far; we were still too many. Still putting too much of a strain on what little we were still able to produce. We were hungry. Not just for food, but for resources, living space, breathable air and so the Government had taken drastic, necessary steps. Someone in office had clearly watched one too many dystopian science-fiction films from the 1970s and so what had once seemed far-fetched and outrageous became... normal, part of the monthly routine. But these events, festivals such as the one we were at now, once a year turned the monthly cull into something else. It had become a show, a spectacle, twisted from a necessary duty into a twisted celebration; a celebration of the depraved that this country had created.

"Well, I'm going. On my own, if necessary." Whilst I'd been lost in thought I hadn't noticed that Brigette had finished her kaffee. She put on her coat and headed back out. I hurriedly thanked the *kellnerin* and dashed out after her.

Brigette was stood watching the parade. No, not just watching, more than that, she seemed enraptured. I held onto her hand and squeezed it. Brigette, so swept up in it all, didn't squeeze back. At the head of the procession were the Jacks that had been caught or surrendered that day and each played his part, pantomime villains hissing with play-hatred toward the gathered crowd. Some wore clothing still stained with blood from whichever poor Mary-Anne had been culled. Some even wore the digits they had collected around their necks as trophies. Lost in it all, Brigette fingered her own necklace as they passed by. The crowd surged forward, looking to grab a passing Jack and carry out some form of mob justice. I felt Brigette's hand slip away from mine, and just like that, she was gone.

* * *

My earlier panic at losing Brigette had subsided and had now been replaced with the dull thud of continual worry. The police officer I was talking was a relic, still using a notepad and pen where data-pad and stylus had replaced them long ago. This, alongside an apparent lack of concern or urgency about what had happened, was doing nothing to ease my worry.

"The best you can hope for sir, is that your..."

"Friend"

"That your 'friend' finds sanctuary somewhere. This is JackFE- The Bloudie Jack Festival after all, and your friend is very much the type that attracts attention."

"You're telling me that you won't be looking for her?" The dull thud threatened to turn to panic again.

"No sir. That is not what I am saying. All I am asking is for you to be realistic. Your friend..." The officer checked hand written notes.

"Brigette."

"Thank you. Let's be realistic here, your friend, Brigette, has the misfortune to be lost amongst a gathering of semi-legalized serial killers all of whom are looking to re-enact centuries-old crimes. I'm not saying that our annual festival is right, but it is necessary. What wasn't necessary was you bringing her here in the first place!"

I was just about to reply when the officer held up a hand, touched a finger to an ear. "Go ahead control." A pause. "Okay. Send over the details. Over and out." There was a faint ping and the officer pulled out a previously unused data-pad from a pocket. I caught a quick look at the top of the screen. One single word. Homicide.

This time the worry did turn to panic. My mind raced. Homicide? I didn't think homicide was even possible at these events? I'd heard that the state offered clemency to the Jacks, Harolds, Dennis' or whichever killer it was being memorialised? Not that it was ever offered in Shrewsbury, any Jack caught was culled at the end of the daily parade even though they were, after all, only doing what the state would have done anyway.

The officer stood to leave, "A colleague will be in touch if we hear anything about your friend. Good day sir." Hat in place, the officer left.

My mind was racing. How can there be a homicide? Was it Brigette? Had they found a body? But that didn't make sense. Any Jack who collected Brigette would surely be crowing about it, they wouldn't want another Jack claiming a Mary-Anne that fitted the legend so closely, pride was at stake here! If the police were so unwilling to help, I would have to do something about it myself. I would have to find Brigette before someone else did. Find her before 'Jack' did. One thing I could be sure of was that I was safe from any Jack out there. All of Bloudie Jack's victims had been female and so men were strictly off the register when it came to potential Mary-Annes. Killing a male of any age during the festival was a strict no-no and...

That was it. It must have been a male Mary-Anne. No, not Mary-Anne: victim. It was a male victim and that is why the officer left. That was the reason for homicide, this was no Mary-Anne, no government sanctioned cull victim. This was actual murder. Homicide.

The festival may have given a purpose to the cull in Shrewsbury for one month of the year, but there were still rules. The population had to follow the rules otherwise all you are left with is anarchy and Europe had bailed us out of that mess once already. The cull was clinical, not malicious. If you were selected, you were to give yourself over willingly, it was duty. The festivals allowed a little flexibility in this. Rather than cold and precisely controlled, a festival death could be more flamboyant, more exotic. As long as the basic rules are followed, anything goes. As long as the death mirrored the original modus operandi then there were no questions asked. Bloudie Jack had killed eight women. Women, not men, and so the festival Jacks don't kill men. To kill a man over a festival weekend was homicide.

Brigette, what have you done?

* * *

I found her in one of Shrewsbury's many shuts. She had already removed the fingers from one hand of, what was in her eyes, her Mary-Anne and was working on the second hand. I called out to her and she whirled around, a wild look in her eyes.

"Oh Jack! It's even better that I imagined!" She still wore the necklace she bought from the market stall, a grim parody of the fingers she herself was removing from the victim at her feet.

"Brigette," I said again "What have you done?" I spoke softly, echoing my earlier thoughts and resigned as though I always knew that this was going to happen. That all those late night conversations about the twisted and grotesque were somehow leading here. "I always said that there should be more female serial killers, didn't I?"

She laughed as she spoke. "Brigette. There are these types of...festivals for women too. You could have been a Rosemary or a Myra. You could have told me and we could have gone to one of those. You didn't have to—"

"But what if I want to be more than just a Rosemary or a Myra? Tell me who else can I be? It's ok for you, there are festivals all over the country for men. Tell me why is that Jack? Is it because there are more of you who have done it? Or is it because you men are sloppier and men are the ones who are caught more often?"

Brigette had taken a step toward me and seeing her like that, wild eyed, covered in blood and knife in hand, I took a step back. "There!" She said triumphantly "That is why! You men are frightened of us! After all this time and after all the talk of equality, you are still frightened by powerful women. You men hate it when we try and act as equals."

I noticed the policeman standing just behind Brigette. She followed my eyes, saw the officer and laughed. "Oh, how ironic! A police *man*." She looked back just before she ran at the officer. Her last words to me: "Goodbye Jack."

* * *

It was the last day of the festival. Somehow Brigette had talked herself into being treated as a Jack and so it was with tears in my eyes that I saw her up on the platform. She had been carried through the town with the rest of them and now was going to be executed in the same manner as the others had been, as Jack himself had been. I had always tried to avoid these final tortured deaths, but it was Brigette that had insisted we came to see them, and it was her that once again brought me back today.

The black-hooded executioner cut Brigette down from the rope that had almost suffocated her and then placed her, half-conscious, onto the wooden bench. He picked up the large curved blade, and, as was the custom, showed it to the crowd. Someone started the chant, but it faltered. This wasn't Bloudie Jack, this was Brigette, someone who should have been one of Jack's victims. But this was someone who had not only stood up to Jack, but had become him. A moment passed and the chant evolved from Bloudie Jack into Bloudie Brigette. She looked over the crowd and I tried to fool myself to think it was me she was smiling at, but I know she smiled because she heard what the crowd were chanting. She nodded at her executioner and the blade came sharply down.

And then the screams. Oh the screams.

* * *

A year to the day since I lost her. A year to the day and I find myself back at JackFEST. It's different this year, no market stalls, not so many tourists. To be honest I don't know why they still bothered calling it JackFEST. There used to be rules at these things, you had to follow a particular killer, some long dead psycho, but that's all changed now. Since Brigette there have been copycats across the country and now nobody's safe. If the government want to keep the numbers down, then that's what we'll do and if you're dumb enough to come to one of these things, then more the fool you. I used to think that it wasn't about the killing, that keeping things to some clean little room somewhere was best. A blue tablet, a glass of water and then a lie down, like going to sleep they say. I know now I was wrong and Brigette was right. It's that feeling of power that comes with taking a life. In a world where even death is controlled by the state an event like JackFEST lets us take that back. I understand that now, and in understanding it I embrace it.

I become Bloudie Jack.

BACKGROUND ON JACKFEST
BY
PHIL DAVIES

As it is with all the best legends and folklore, the story of Bloody Jack (or to use the name he was given at the time, 'Bloudie Jack') has its roots in local history. However, as stories are retold and embellished over the years, it becomes increasingly difficult to tell what is real history and what isn't, but let's not let that get in the way of a good ghost story.

It was during the 12th Century that Jack Blondell rose to infamy and created a local legend. Jack was a soldier stationed at Shrewsbury Castle and while there, was given the role of caretaker or warden. Not long after Jack's arrival in Shrewsbury, local girls began to go missing. Jack was apparently quite the charmer and he would spend some time chatting up the local girls, asking each of them to keep his affections a secret.

After a little while, having gained a girl's trust and confidence, Jack would invite her back to his private quarters in the castle. Here he would rape and murder the girl and, with the foul deed done, collect ghoulish trophies from his victim. He then disposed of the remains by either feeding them to the pigs kept at the castle, or by throwing them into the nearby River Severn.

The legend holds that Jack's eighth victim was a girl called Mary-Anne and it would be his targeting of her that would lead to his discovery and subsequent execution. Unlike his other victims, Mary-Anne had, in her excitement, told her sister that she was going to marry a soldier called Jack. Suspicious, and fearing for Mary-Anne's safety, her sister headed for the castle. She arrived just in time to see Jack dragging Mary-Anne's bloody corpse across the forecourt and into the castle.

The un-named sister fled in terror from the scene, but returned a few days later to investigate further. Jack was away from his post, so she broke into his quarters and found a small wooden chest. With a little hesitation she slowly opened it. Inside, sat in neat rows, were eight sets of fingers and eight sets of toes, the trophies Jack had collected from the girls he had murdered.

Mary-Anne's sister was understandably horrified by what she had found and she hurried to the find the town militia. Jack was arrested and, upon sight of the ghoulish trophies he had collected, was immediately sentenced to be executed at the top of Pride Hill in Shrewsbury, only a short distance from the castle where he lived.

Standing on the scaffold, an unrepentant Jack hurled curses and insults at the gathered crowd, but this didn't stop his punishment being carried out. He was hung, drawn and quartered and his head skewered on a spike along nearby Wyle Cop.

It wasn't long after his execution that the spectre of 'Bloudie Jack' was seen dragging a kicking and screaming Mary-Anne across the courtyard of Shrewsbury Castle to her fate and to this day there are still stories of ghostly screams heard drifting around the area.

Although today it is almost impossible to tell what is truth and what is fiction one thing is sure, it is difficult to imagine that anyone given the nickname 'Bloudie Jack' would rest easy in their grave.

DUST TO DUST
BY
HANNAH KATE

"Okay... my turn... so you know my cousin works at the newspaper printing place?"

"Nope, you're not having that. We said no friend-of-a-friend stories."

Ash held her hands up. "Hear me out. I've seen it too, so it counts, right?"

Ty and Ash looked to Danny for a ruling. He took a swig from his can and nodded. "It counts. So long as you personally have seen it, then I'll allow it."

"Thank you," said Ash, reaching for another drink. "So he works at the printer's in Hollinwood. There used to be a factory there. Ferranti's, Ferrutti's, something like that. Anyway, everyone there says the place is haunted, but he's never seen anything himself. He was working nights, so I asked him if he'd get me in. You know? So I could take a look around myself."

"Nice one," said Ty. "Video it?"

"He said I couldn't do a video."

"Gutted," said Danny, with just a hint of sarcasm. "But you did go in? You did see something?"

"I did, yes. The story is that the place is haunted by the Black Lady. It goes back to before the factory was even there. There was a big farm on the site, and it was run by some really rich eccentric woman. Something happened, and she got scared she was going to lose all her money, so she buried it under the house or in the fields or something. And then she died before she could tell anyone where it was."

"Obviously. They always do," said Ty.

"Let her finish," Danny said. "We haven't got to the manifestation bit yet."

Ash swallowed a mouthful of vodka and flat coke then continued, "This is just the background story my cousin heard. Over the years, people have seen this Black Lady ghost – sorry, manifestation – walking around the printing press or the factory before that, trying to get her treasure back. It's the usual stuff – doors banging, glimpses of a woman in old-school black clothes. Some people have even said they saw a headless woman gliding down the corridors."

"Headless?" Danny's sarcasm was more pointed this time. He twiddled a cigarette paper between fingers tipped with chipped black polish, and looked like he might be about to call time on this particular story. "I don't get that bit. Why would she be headless?"

"How did the rich old woman die?" said Ty. "I take it she wasn't actually decapitated?"

"I don't know," said Ash. "I'm sure there was something about her death. Something not right. But I can't remember all the details. Mostly, the stories were about the buried gold."

"So what did you see?" said Danny.

"At first, nothing at all. And I didn't feel anything either. No coldness, no energy, nothing like that. It was all a bit of a bust."

"But then..."

Ash put her drink down. "It was a smell, at first. I'm not really sure why I knew it was wrong, because it's not like there weren't other weird smells in the place. But it just hit me, you know? It was a bit like turps, but mixed with herbs or something. And leathery and rotten underneath it. And then suddenly the smell was overpowering, and I couldn't breathe properly. I felt like I was going to suffocate."

"What did you see though?"

"It was too much. I closed my eyes. It was like all the air had gone from the corridor. And then I smelt dirt."

"Dirt?"

"Like soil, earth, that type of dirt. It was like I was surrounded by wet soil, but with this strong chemical smell cutting through it. It was horrible." She paused, picking at her fingernail and not looking at the others. "I knew I shouldn't have closed my eyes, so I tried to get up the courage to open them again. And then I did."

"And you saw the Black Lady swishing down the hallway?" Ty tried an awkward giggle, but Danny didn't join in.

"No. It wasn't that. It was right in front of my face. Just for a moment."

"What was?"

"I don't know. It was... like a face, I guess. But more like a mask. This horrible brown leather mask, with holes for eyes and a mouth that was just hanging open. It had a kind of bandage wrapped over its head – filthy and stained, and sort of stuck to the mask. And the smell... Jesus."

"And..."

"And then it was gone." Ash straightened her shoulders and picked up her drink. "Just like that. The smell was gone too. Everything was back to normal, and I didn't see anything else for the rest of the night."

There was a momentary silence. Then Danny said, "But no pictures? And no other witnesses?"

"Nope," said Ash. "Just my word for it."

"Ah... nice try," he said, lighting the cigarette he'd been slowly rolling. "Doesn't count though."

* * *

"Who votes for Ty's headless monk who – for reasons he can't explain – haunts a pub in Blackley?"

Ty stuck his hand in the air, and then gave an exasperated "Oh, come on!" when no one else did.

Danny nodded sagely. "And who votes for Ash's Black Lady, who may or may not be searching for gold in Hollinwood?"

At this he raised his own hand, and two other hands followed suit.

Ash gave a small fist-pump and mouthed 'Loser' at Ty. Then, adopting a more serious expression, she produced a black notebook from her backpack. "Here's the research I've done so far. It was actually surprisingly easy, because it turns out the Black Lady isn't your run-of-the-mill generic ghost. She was a real person, and she really did own the farm at Hollinwood."

"Definitely beats a headless monk then," Danny breathed.

"Definitely," said Ash. "So the woman was called Hannah Beswick. The stories about the buried gold seem to have started after her death, when people started claiming she'd hidden all her wealth to keep it safe from..." Ash consulted her notes. "... Bonnie Prince Charlie and his Highlanders, who were plundering

England in 1745. People believed the treasure had never been found, and so the Black Lady was returning to keep watch over it."

"So she died in the 1740s?" asked Danny.

"No. That was the weird thing. She died in 1758. And... get this... her doctor embalmed her after she died, and put her body on display. She wasn't actually buried until 1868."

"Put her body on display?" said Ty.

"Hannah was scared of premature burial. She put in her will that she wanted her doctor to hold off burial until he was absolutely sure she was really dead. He decided to embalm her instead. He kept her body in a box and used to show it off to visitors, then after he died it was donated to a museum."

"People did that sort of shit back then," said Danny, with a vague wave of the hand. "You had bodysnatchers and those public anatomy lectures going on, don't forget. People just weren't as squeamish about studying dead bodies as they are now."

Ash nodded. "So that's the story. Hannah's farm was called Birchin Bower, and it was on the site of the Ferranti factory – it's definitely Ferranti, by the way – which is where the newspaper is now, on the industial estate. Factory workers reported seeing a shadowy figure, or hearing the rustling of silk, that sort of thing."

"And what about the gold?" said Ty. "Anyone looked for that?"

"That's what's weird," said Ash. "It looks like the gold is long gone. A man called..." She flicked through a couple of pages of her notebook. "... Joe the Tamer – he had a house on the old farmland – dug it up and sold it, years before the factory was even built."

"So our question is, why does the Black Lady keep coming back? What is she looking for?" said Danny.

"I don't know." Ash put her notebook down. "There are plenty of stories, most of them about the gold but some of them just say she wanted to keep an eye on her home."

"Maybe she doesn't like the fact that her farm got knocked down to make room for a factory," said Ty.

"We can't change that now though," Ash said. "So how do we help her spirit move on and find peace?"

"Well," said Danny. "That's what we're going to find out. Alicia..."

The fourth person sitting on the beat-up sofas in Danny's front room hadn't yet spoken. Of all of them, she was the most committed to being in touch with the dark side, and so frequently sat in silence, eyes coloured by tinted contacts and fixed on something the rest of them couldn't see. She was often absent from their little get-togethers, with no explanation as to where she'd been or who she'd been with. Ash believed Alicia was part of a coven or a cult; Ty was pretty sure he'd seen her working in Wilko's.

Alicia knelt on the floor in front of Danny's coffee table, and laid out a couple of candles and crystals. "We'll begin with the Ouija, I think. If we don't get our answers that way, we can try a full séance."

The four of them sat around the table, watching Alicia lighting candles and preparing the board. Well-versed in how this sort of thing went, they each laid a finger of their left hand on the planchette. Alicia took a series of deep breaths, and then began to intone.

"Welcome us, spirit world. We are seeking one of your number."

They'd been through this ritual many times, so Ty no longer had to fight the urge to laugh at this opener.

"We wish to communicate with Hannah Beswick. Is Hannah with us? May we speak with her?"

The planchette jiggled under their fingers. Slowly, haltingly, it scraped a path to the top right-hand corner: NO.

"Is there anybody there who will speak with us?"

Top left-hand corner: YES.

"Who is it that would speak with us?"

Under the light touch of their fingers, the planchette traced a route between the letters. W-H-I-T-E.

"White? Is that your name? Miss White?"

NO.

"Mr White? Are you Mr White?"

NO. D-O-C-T-O-R

"Dr White. Do you have a message for us? We are listening to you, Dr White."

H-A-N-N-A-H

"Hannah? Hannah Beswick? Do you have a message from Hannah Beswick?"

"The Black Lady," whispered Ash, but she was shushed by the others.

F-E-A-R

"Is she scared, Dr White? Is Hannah Beswick afraid of something?"

NO

I-A-M-A-F-R-A-I-D

"What are you afraid of Dr..." Alicia's voice wobbled slightly on the word, and she broke off to cough discreetly. "... White. Is there something you wish to tell us?"

S-O-S-O-R-R-Y

"What are you sorry for, Dr White?" Alicia coughed again.

M-Y-F-A-U-L-T

Alicia was having trouble clearing her throat, so Danny took up the questioning. "Tell us what you are afraid of, Dr White. Is it something to do with the gold?"

A-F-R-A-I-D-F-O-R-Y-O-U

Alicia's coughing was louder now, and she struggled to keep her hand on the plastic token. Danny raised his voice over the sound, a note of irritation creeping in. "Why are you afraid, Dr White?"

S-H-E-S-N-O-T-D-E-A-D-Y-E-T

Alicia pulled her finger away from the planchette, breaking up the group. She put her hand to her throat, heaving and trying to suck in gulps of air.

"Get some water!" shouted Danny, thumping Alicia on the back several times. "She's choking on something."

"What's that smell?" said Ty.

"Get some water!"

"Smells like... chemicals or something..."

Ash remained kneeling by the coffee table, her eyes locked on Alicia. "Look," she said, voice weak and thin. "Behind them. The face. It's the face."

Alicia's coughing had turned to retching. Danny had an arm around her shoulder and was ignoring the others. Ty appeared with a glass of water, but couldn't get it to her mouth.

"Can no one else smell that?" Ty's voice was at a higher pitch now, but it still didn't get a response. "It's like paint thinner or something. God, it's so strong. It's suffocating."

Danny looked at Ty as Alicia slumped across his lap. "She isn't breathing. Jesus, she isn't breathing." Ty dropped the water onto the floor.

Ash stared into the space where Alicia had been, unable to take her eyes off whatever it was she could see.

"We've got to try something. CPR. We have to do CPR," Danny shouted. And he rolled Alicia onto her back. "I don't know what to do! Who knows how to do this?" He put his hand to her mouth, and then pulled it straight back. "Jesus Christ, there's something in her mouth. There's..." he ran his fingers between Alicia's lips and then stared at them. "... dirt. Her mouth's full of dirt and..."

A worm wriggled between Alicia's lips and onto her chin.

Ty vomited onto the carpet. "That smell," he said, between retches. "I can't breathe."

Across the living room, Ash began to laugh.

"Ring an ambulance! Ring an ambulance!" Danny let go of Alicia's head and tried to fumble in his trouser pocket.

Ash's laugh grew louder.

"Ash?" Danny's voice was cracked, as though there was something stuck in his throat. "What's happening?"

Ash's eyes, hollow and dark, were still fixed on the space next to him. The laughter subsided, and her mouth drew back into an empty hanging grin. "Dr White was right. This is all his fault."

"What are you talking about?" Danny spluttered the words out around coughs.

"He shouldn't have treated me like that."

Danny choked on whatever reply he wanted to make. Beside him, Ty started to hyperventilate.

"It wasn't right what that man did. Filling me with poisons and keeping me in a box."

Ash got to her feet, rictus grin still fixed. "Thought he could do what he liked. Thought I was dead and gone. But I taught him a lesson. Gave him a taste of his own medicine. Didn't like that."

Ty collapsed on the floor, eyes rolled back and lips tinged blue.

"Ash...?"

The girl's head moved in slow jerks and her blank eyes landed on the figures doubled-over on the floor. "Hannah," she said.

She stepped over Alicia's prone form and walked to the living room door.

"And I'm not dead yet."

BACKGROUND ON DUST TO DUST
BY
HANNAH KATE

Hannah Beswick was born in 1688, the daughter of John Beswick of Failsworth, a wealthy merchant. During her lifetime, Hannah lived at Birchin Bower in Hollinwood, and she inherited part of her father's wealth on his death in 1706. Few details of Hannah's life have survived, as it was only in death that she found a degree of fame.

There are several stories that have been told about Birchin Bower and Hannah's supposed haunting of her old home. One common tale is that, in 1745, Hannah became so worried by the approach of Bonnie Prince Charlie's army marching down from Scotland that she converted all her wealth to gold bars and buried them around Birchin Bower. This led to various sightings of Hannah's ghost – reported as wearing a black silk dress and lace cap, though also sometimes inexplicably reported as headless – which was said to return to the site of her buried gold every seven years.[b]When Ferranti, the electrical engineering company, opened a works on the site of Birchin Bower in the 1950s, sightings continued, with workers reporting seeing the 'Black Lady' at the factory site.

The tale of Hannah Beswick's buried gold is local folklore, and there is no evidence that the woman really did hide her wealth from advancing Scots soldiers.

However, claims have been made that, not only was the gold buried, it was in fact recovered in the nineteenth century by a weaver who lived in the workers' tenements built on Birchin Bower. Nevertheless, the story of Hannah's ghost continued to be told and embellished until the closure of the Ferranti works. The site is now home to MEN (Manchester Evening News) Media and Trinity Mirror, who publish and print newspapers.

More notorious than the story of Hannah's spirit, though, is the story of what happened to her body. Hannah entrusted her remains to her family's physician, Dr Charles White. White was one of the founders of Manchester Royal Infirmary and a collector of natural history 'curiosities'. The story goes that Hannah had a pathological fear of premature burial, and so requested that White keep her body above ground until he was absolutely sure she was dead. Some versions of the story add that Hannah left a large sum of money to Dr White, to ensure that her last request was carefully followed.

In truth, there is little evidence of any formal arrangement between the two. Hannah's will, dated 1757, left the sum of £100 to White and £400 for funeral expenses. However, whether he was acting on his own desires or those of his patient, White had Hannah's body embalmed on her death in 1758. White was a follower of anatomist William Hunter, so it is believed he may have used Hunter's techniques to preserve Hannah's body. This would have involved draining the blood, injecting the body with a mixture of vermillion, turpentine and oils of lavender and rosemary, removing the internal organs, and filling the cavities with plaster of paris.

White displayed Hannah's body in a clock case at his home in Sale, where she was viewed by (amongst others) a young Thomas De Quincey. The influential, controversial essayist's description of Hannah's body, set bolt upright in a grandfather clock case that was only opened once a year for curious visitors, is the source of much of the legend of Hannah's afterlife, as it was De Quincey who first claimed (probably falsely) that White was paid £25000 to ensure Hannah was kept above ground due to her fear of being buried alive. Over time, this story merged with the tale of Hannah's buried gold, with some versions stating that White had been instructed to transport the embalmed body to Birchin Bower on the anniversary of her death, in order to ensure her wealth was still safe.

Hannah's body remained in White's collection until his death in 1813, when his collection passed by bequest to his friend and colleague Charles Ollier. In 1828, Ollier donated White's collection to the Museum of the Manchester Natural History Society on Peter Street, and Hannah's body was put on display in the museum's entrance hall. Known as the 'Manchester Mummy' or the 'Mummy of Birchin Bower', Hannah was displayed next to a Peruvian mummy and an Egyptian mummy.

In 1867, the Manchester Natural History Society's collection passed to Owens College (later to become the University of Manchester), eventually to be housed in the Manchester Museum (opened to the public in 1888). Both the college and the new museum made deliberate efforts to distance themselves from the 'less reputable' Peter Street establishment, and it was decided that Hannah's mummified remains were no longer appropriate for public display.

Hannah's body was buried in Harpurhey Cemetery in July 1868, 110 years after her death. Her grave is unmarked.

AM FEAR LIATH, THE GREY MAN OF BEN MACDUI
BY
KEVIN WILLIAMS

They say in these parts that if you don't like the weather simply wait two minutes. I certainly learned that lesson very quickly. When I first arrived, the weather was spectacular; early April sun bathed the entire valley, glinting off the wide meandering river and warming the air enough to allow me to strip down to t-shirt and lightweight trousers. The picturesque scene was completed by the snow topped peaks beyond the foothills. The going was good and on my first day of hiking I climbed two of the smaller hills. I even chanced a short-lived swim in the loch where I made the first night's camp. Quickly realising that a few days of spring warmth could not cancel out the effects of an entire highland winter, I dragged my blue and shivering self from the water and was dried, dressed and huddled next to a freshly assembled campfire in double quick time.

The night passed chilly but bearable and I got a reasonable sleep. The morning of my second day promised weather much the same as the first. After a hearty breakfast, chased down by a mug of black tea, I set off once again in t-shirt and lightweights, intending to conquer my third summit. The weather wasn't about to go along with my plans.

Shortly before midday, ominous dark clouds gathered above. Roughly thirty seconds later, I felt the first rain drops. Chancing my luck that it was just a passing shower I pressed on and, within minutes, found myself drenched by the torrential downpour. A storm had moved into the valley and I was soon running for a small building that I could just make out through the driving rain.

I had found a bothy. I read about these buildings whilst researching my trip; basically, four walls, a fireplace and very little else. As I hadn't planned to use any of these shelters, I had not determined any locations; this one was fortuitous, to say the least. After a quick change of clothes and a check to ensure the rest of my kit remained dry, I peered out through the one, tiny window; I was going to be here for a while. The weather had worsened, to the extent that it looked like night outside. The wind had built to a steady howl and the rain lashed against the building. The window clattered and rattled, causing me to wonder whether the glass would survive. Then the thunder and the lightning began. My nerves rattled nearly as much as the little window, as each bang reverberated down the valley; a sound felt as much as heard. The lightning made sinister shadows jump and dance around the building, both inside and out. The old wooden door banged in its frame; *thud-thud-thud...thud-thud-thud*. I busied myself, by way of distraction, in preparing a fire to dry out my clothes. It was as I searched the tiny room for paper to use as kindling that I chanced across a small book. It looked cheap; a thin hardback with no cover picture or author credit, just a title in simple black letters, 'Death on the Mountain'. Who brings a book like that on a climbing trip? The owner had probably had the same thought and abandoned it here for some other poor fool to scare themselves. Well, I wasn't going anywhere for a while, I may as well be that poor fool!

The book described the mysterious fate of a climbing expedition on some unnamed mountain. Each member of the group was found dead and somewhat mutilated, in mysterious circumstances. It told how the bodies were found at various distances from their shared tent and in various stages of undress. Apparently, they had cut their way out of the tent in a panic and fled. Some of the injuries were consistent with massive force and some of the bodies were missing various parts or organs. The mechanisms of these injuries were unknown. The story was fascinating but ultimately frustrating; it offered no explanation, conjecture or conclusions. I closed the book reflecting on what may have compelled these poor unfortunates to run, terrified and half-dressed, out into the snow; and what inhuman power could cause the terrible injuries described. I was also left thinking that there was something strange about this little book, something I couldn't quite put my finger on.

In hindsight, I probably shouldn't have read it.

I'd been so engrossed in scaring myself with the book that I hadn't even noticed the passing of the storm. The weather had calmed and the window and door had ceased their rattling. I ventured a look outside. It was calm, a mist had followed the storm and now clung to the mountainside, cutting visibility drastically. I knew I would encounter snow very soon so I dressed appropriately, packed the rest of my gear and prepared to set off. I left the book where I had found it.

It didn't take long for me to get back into my stride. My little stay in the bothy had cost me a bit of time, I would probably only manage this one peak today, assuming the weather held out. I didn't mind though, I was in no rush, I intended to take my time and enjoy myself. The mist shrouded the mountain, enveloping both me and the ground around me. It had a peculiar muffling effect; any sounds I made felt especially close and intimate. It wasn't long before I reached the start of the snow, at this point just a light covering. It wasn't enough to warrant crampons, but I made sure I had my climbing poles to hand, especially as the wind had started to pick up. The wind brought with it ice and snow flurries and the constant buffeting made walking slower than would have been ideal, but I was still full of energy and was making good progress, given the conditions. It was cold, wet and windy, but my gear was more than up to the job and I was confident in my abilities, I was already planning the meal I would prepare for myself once I reached the valley on the other side.

That was when I first encountered the figure.

I struggled to see through the mist and the snow but this person just seemed to be standing still. Possibly a photographer, I thought, but it seemed madness to stop and take photos in these conditions. Could they be in trouble? I changed course slightly and made my way up the slope towards where they stood. I was now heading directly into the wind, and I was almost bent double trying to make progress. I called out now and then, but it was pointless, the wind took my words before they were out of my mouth. I drove my poles into the ground and concentrated on putting one foot before the other. The snow was getting deeper as I climbed and the going was getting harder by the minute. As I focused on my feet, so as not to slip or stumble, I lost my bearings in relation to the figure. I looked up to check my heading. The figure had gone.

I stopped dead in my tracks. How? I doubled my efforts to get up the hill to where I thought I had seen the figure last. In my haste, I lost my footing once or twice, slipping back down a few metres each time. Not much in the grand scheme of things, but it cost me precious minutes in finding out what had happened to this person.

I pushed on, poles driving through icy snow, boots scrabbling over loose stones. All the time practically blinded by the wind driven snow. The ground levelled, I moved faster, almost at a jog. I headed for what looked like a break in the mist, hopefully a chance to see a little further and literally shed some light on the fate of the person I had seen.

There was a voice at my shoulder; indistinct, short and sharp. I froze and spun on the spot; nobody there. I looked around, still no one. I chanced a few steps, I heard the voice again, this time whispering directly behind my head. I spun, I stumbled; falling, landing on my back. The ground gave way. Somebody yelled; maybe me, I couldn't be sure. I tumbled and rolled with the sliding snow. All I could see was white. Down I slid, building momentum; faster and faster. I saw a gap between two rocky outcrops and, desperately, frantically, I jammed one of my walking poles into it, holding on with all the strength I had. The snow continued to slide over me, rocks and ice, bouncing, battering my body. I clung on.

Eventually the onslaught stopped. I realised I had been holding my breath and that my eyes were shut tight. I rolled onto my back and filled my lungs; a long, deep gasp. Opening my eyes, I surveyed my surroundings. My feet were sticking over the edge of a rock, I sat up to see what was beyond, my stomach dropped; there was nothing. The 'rock' was the edge of a crag; the top of a sheer cliff face. The snow that had cascaded over me lay on the stony ground far below.

Shit – the other person; where were they? Had they gone over? Had they got clear? I called out; heard nothing back but echoes. I sat and considered my situation; should I head back down or continue on up? My thoughts returned to the book I had read in the bothy, the chaos, fear and panic that can occur on the mountain, the changing conditions and the tricks that the mind can play. Was that it? Had I nearly died because my senses were fooled? The figure; could that have been nothing more than a rocky outcrop, or pile of stones, since swept over the edge? The voices; simply the sound of the wind in my ears or my backpack rubbing against my waterproofs? I stood, so I could regain my bearings.

It was back.

This time closer, this time larger; a lot larger. The figure stood motionless beside a tall rock formation. I could not make out any features and its outline was somewhat blurry through the mist, but this person must have been at least eight feet tall; impossible, surely. A trick of the light, I told myself, false perspective. So why did I feel those icy fingers of fear creeping up my spine?

I called out again and waved my arm, taking a cautious step, away from the precipice that so nearly claimed my life. The figure disappeared behind the rocks. Again, and without even thinking, I found myself pursuing. This time there was less wind and I was able to keep my focus and head directly for the rocks. The voice started again. It was a low murmur, I could make out no words but again, it felt like a whisper straight into my ear. I tore off my headgear, the voice was still there. I threw off my pack. Still, the voice continued. I ripped off my waterproof jacket and tore off the over-trousers; surely the source of the whispering. But, no! On it went, now growing louder, now more insistent; now more guttural.

I ran.

The rocks... the figure... protection... 'Help!'

My legs burned as my skin chilled, my feet, growing numb, pounded up the hill. I made my way towards the formation. The voice rose as I fled. The rock loomed over me, I jumped behind it; I had to escape the voice, it was practically screaming. My head felt like it might split open. My eyes streamed and my lungs felt like I was breathing fire. I hit the ground and rolled onto my back, chest heaving. I regained control of my breath and listened for the voice; silence, at last. I stood up...

It was right there!

Horror and dread rooted me to the spot. Up close, it was even bigger than I had thought. It towered over me, a menacing, formless black mass, standing in stark contrast to the white of the snow and mist beyond. I could see no face, only shadow. It barred the way back to my equipment. I tried to move, it moved with me. I sidestepped, it moved to block my path. I stepped backwards. It lunged. I fled. It roared; a sound like no other I had heard. It was deafening. It was terrifying. I stumbled and lost my footing, went over on my ankle. I was tumbling, bouncing. Earth, sky, earth, sky... crack; a sharp, agonising pain up my leg. I tumbled and slid, a chaos of snow, rocks and pain. Another sickening crack, a thud, then darkness.

Somehow, I woke up back in the bothy, in which I write this. I have no memory of making my way back here, but I have been drifting in and out for the last few days. I can't remember much since I fell. I'm in a pretty bad state. Both of my legs are broken, probably in more than one place judging by the shape of them. The pain in my head is, at times, unbearable and I think I must have lost a lot of blood. I am very weak. I'm hoping somebody comes by soon, I have no way of communicating, my gear was all in my backpack. I need my things, but I can't go back out there... can I?

P.S. I found that little book again. I've realised what's so strange about it. It's not a proper book, it's a notebook; the story is handwritten, just like mine.

BACKGROUND ON AM FEAR LIATH, THE GREY MAN OF BEN MACDUI
BY
KEVIN WILLIAMS

I remember a book from my childhood, the title of which, unfortunately, escapes me. It was a book about the supernatural. The illustrations were amazing and incredibly spooky, and the stories were fascinating. I spent many a night after reading this book waiting for sleep, jumping at shadows, bedcovers pulled right up to my chin. One of the stories that has stuck with me to this day, was that of 'The Great Grey Man of Ben MacDhui'.

It told of a massive, dark figure that haunted the summit and the passes of Ben MacDhui (often now spelled Macdui), part of the Cairngorm mountain range and the second highest mountain in Scotland. Walkers and climbers tell of being overcome by a sense of foreboding, terror, depression or dread; with some even describing having to resist a compulsion to approach, or even throw themselves from, dangerously high, rocky crags.

One of the most famous accounts of this legend, that of J. Norman Collie, speaking in 1925, is recounted on the website *Undiscovered Scotland:*

> *"I was returning from the cairn on the summit in a mist when I began to think I heard something else than merely the noise of my own footsteps. For every few steps I took I heard a crunch, and then another crunch as if someone was walking after me but taking steps three or four times the length of my own. I said to myself, "This is all nonsense". I listened and heard it again, but could see nothing in the mist. As I walked on and the eerie crunch, crunch, sounded behind me, I was seized with terror and took to my heels, staggering blindly among the boulders for four or five miles nearly down to Rothiemurchus Forest. Whatever you make of it, I do not know, but there is something very queer about the top of Ben MacDhui and I will not go back there again by myself I know."*

There have been many theories put forward to explain the various occurrences on the mountain. It has been said that the mysterious footsteps, heard by so many, may simply be the noise of rocks and stones fracturing, caused by the freezing expansion of water trapped within. One posited explanation for the sightings of the grey man is a phenomenon known as the *Brocken Spectre.* This effect can be seen, given the right conditions, when the shadow of a climber is cast against cloud or snow. This shadow is quite often magnified or distorted, giving the effect of a large, dark figure lurking within the mist.

I enjoy playing with the psychological aspects of horror in my stories; the tricks the mind can play. Having lived in northern Scotland and spent time in the hills and mountains, I can vouch for the feeling of the uncanny one can experience when alone in such a vast and remote area. I was particularly struck by how Collie, a scientist as well as an experienced mountaineer, told himself that 'This is all nonsense,' yet was to be found, moments later, fleeing in terror across five miles of highland terrain. I have tried to imbue in my hero a sense of scepticism and considered rationality, a view which he will see challenged, and maybe even eroded, as his story unfolds.

Readers may notice that I have borrowed elements from an episode of Siberian history, known as the Dyatlov Pass Incident. I hope I do not offend by transposing the event to the Scottish Highlands. Ultimately, though, who is to say that the phenomena behind this incident in Siberia and those on Ben Macdui are entirely unrelated?

We all tell ourselves stories, it is those which we choose to believe which, ultimately, define how we view the world.

THE HANDFAST WIFE
BY
ÁINE KING

Long Andrew brought the news, raw-faced from riding into the harsh February wind. He braced himself in the doorway, red hands on bony knees, and coughed out the words we had been dreading for a week and more.

"'Tis truth. John's taken. Piracy". And then to me, " And murder, Helen. I'm sorry, lass."

My father folded like a sail, a strawback chair creaking beneath him, his eyes and mouth wide and round, like a fish in air.

"The ship's been seized," Andrew was regaining breath. "She's the Caroline, not the George. John took her, and shot his captain. They are mutineers, all of them."

"Pirates." My mother, beside me, tightened herself like a fiddle string.

"John will hang, surely, for he took the ship, and shot the captain. And stabbed him. And drowned him. They are all captured and shackled and sent south for trial. John was shackled twice, and he'll hang for sure."

"Pirates!" My mother's slap came too fast for me to duck and I staggered backwards against the wall, cheek burning and eyes streaming. I blinked and swallowed, hating her, and determined not to weep.

"Your sweetheart!" she spat. "Your swaggering sea captain, John Smith. So fine in his green velvet coat! So grand! Master o' a great vessel, and so young! A pirate! And a murderer! And you-"

"Mary -" My father pleaded in vain.

"A – whore!"

"John Gow is my husband!" It was the first time I ever spoke it. The wind had been roaring in the chimney all day, but dropped just then, and it seemed I was shouting.

"Liar!" My mother was louder, pale and shaking with rage.

"I am not! We are handfasted. At the Odin-Stone." With trembling fingers I drew John's token, on its narrow ribbon, from inside my bodice. The slender slice of stone spun slowly; dark as the night we had joined our hands through the hollow heart of the great monolith, and sworn. Odin's Tears, some call them, these little wedges of rock. John said they were the heads of arrows, made long ago by the folk who raised the tall stones. John. He had laughed as he bound each one with ribbon, cursing the cold and his frozen fingers. He put one shard to his lips, and then pressed it into my palm. I kissed the other, and then kissed him. Our left hands met around the deadly little flints, and our right hands joined through the hollow heart of the Stone. And we Swore.

"Oh, Helen, you fool," my mother moaned, her anger waning.

"You liked him! You thought him fine!"

"I thought him not a pirate! He fooled us all." I thought she would strike again, but her rage was quenched in tears. "Who'll have you now? You've bound yourself for ever, to a dead man."

"I care not. I love John. I want no other."

"You will." The wind was rising again, winding its moan around hers.

"Andrew!" My father was pale, but on his feet in the doorway and yelling to the lad who had shuffled away a few yards, pretending not to eavesdrop on our shame. "Fetch my horse! What's bound can be unbound," he said. The Speywife can free them."

"No, Tam!" My mother was afraid, which frightened me. "Do not bring witchcraft here!"

"Do you think me a fool, woman?", he sneered. "Come, Helen." He turned to me, almost kindly. "Dress warmly." He threw his cloak around his shoulders and ducked out into the gathering storm.

* * *

The Speywife had lived above Brinkies Brae for all of my life and more, but I had never seen her. Every bairn knew she had one eye. A raven took the other. Ate it, some said. Some said she let it. She raised winds, fair and foul, and sold them to sailors. And curses, too. My brother, Tam swore he'd glimpsed her once, from a distance, among the graves at the Old Kirk. Tam was a tale-teller, and not everyone believed that he had picked up a stone to throw at her, and cast it, and seen it fly away, a small brown bird in the air. I believed him, hunched under my father's cloak, shaking with cold and fear, as every stumbling step of the horse took us nearer to the witch.

The sky had been low and leaden all day, and by the time we began to climb the track above Loch Stenness it was fully dark. The wind was raging out of the northwest, ripping the clouds to shreds and flinging them in tatters across the waning moon. For a moment I could see the tumult of the sky reflected in the loch, and I thought I saw the Odin Stone less than a mile away on the eastern shore, standing against the storm. Twice the moon had waxed and waned since John and I joined hands through the heart of the stone, and swore, and lay together inside the Trow's mound, wrapped in John's green velvet coat, and loved. My John.

The storm hit us sideways as we rounded the brow of the hill, drenching us with rain and stinging hail. Within minutes we were soaked to our skins. I took the lantern from my father's frozen hand as he swiped the rain from his eyes and wrestled with the reins. I tried to ask him where we were headed, but my words were whipped away on the wind.

A mile beyond Brae Hill we turned suddenly from the track into a steep valley, cut by a fast-flowing burn, clattering over stones into the blackness below. We had seen no light of croft or farmhouse for miles, and a growing sense of dread seemed to be crushing me. My father coaxed the sweating, skittish horse down the stony channel, under overhanging blackthorn and willow. The lantern guttered and went out, and suddenly the heady, sour-smelling reek of peat smoke looped about us in the darkness.

In the mossy bank beyond the burn a hovel had been dug into the dark earth and ancient stones. My father dismounted and helped me down into the sodden heather. I was shaking so hard my teeth were clattering. Any shelter would be welcome, but the ragged sail-cloth stretched across the entrance struggled and snapped like an animal in a trap, and the stench from within was foul as a week-dead sheep.

"Courage, lass." My father gripped my arm, raised the flapping canvas, and drew me into the Speywife's lair.

The turf-smoke choked us. Our eyes streamed, and the stench of graveyard rot was thick in our mouths. Blinking in the red gloom I saw baskets and creels stacked about us, piled with dried heather, cow parsley and broom. Sea weed and ribbons of kale hung from the low ceiling. Seal skins, otter pelts, gull wings and things I could not guess were crammed in every corner and crevice.

The shadows shifted. A bundle of rags rose up from the fireside, and spoke. "You are welcome, Tam Gordon." A soft, sly voice came from the huddled, hooded shade. "And your lass".

"Speywife". My father nodded, polite, in the stinking smoky gloom under the hill. There was a sudden clattering in the roots and rafters just above him, and a flurry of claws and wings as a great black bird beat into the air. The hooked beak gaped and a harsh, guttural craaaak filled the cave, as the raven swept past my face and landed somewhere behind me in the darkness.

I was breathing fast, hissing through clenched teeth and fighting down the rising tide of sickness in my guts. A long, pale hand emerged from the rags, the fingers thin and scaly with knuckles like knots. Yellow nails, curved like the claws of a cockerel clutched at my wrist, and pulled me down to kneel clumsily beside her in the fire-glow.

"So, Maggie Gow's boy came home a pirate," the shadow chuckled. Her breath reeked, foul and fetid into my face.

She was not old. I had imagined a crone. The long lank locks were silver-streaked, but the smooth cheek was high and round. She was no older than my mother and, not long since, had been far more beautiful.

Her dry lips twisted in a smile, as if she guessed my thought. And then she faced me fully, and I was looking into the wreckage of her empty eye. Twisted scars snaked from brow and cheek, pulling inwards to the livid pit of crimson and black. It glistened, as if freshly ripped, seeming to pulse and shift under my terrified gaze.

"Odin took my eye, and gave me Sight." The one eye watching me was grey and green, and treacherous as the sea. Her long hands moved on the ash-floor between us, making a circle as a boat makes a wake. A circle of talisman cards, grey as dry earth, face-downwards to Hell, some torn and stitched, some stained with streaks and spots of unguessed filth. "Ask." One hand poised above the circle, quivering; a hawk before the drop.

"I —" My mouth was dust-dry. "What will become of John?"

Out of the darkness a harsh voice rasped, "Choose." The raven spoke.

The cards seemed to shift, as if turning slowly like a wheel. I jabbed at the card nearest me, and with one yellow claw she flipped it over. Crude but clear brown ink lines formed tree, rope and hanging man, with bulging eyes and lolling tongue. There were rune-letters, too, that I could not read. "Foolish question." She hissed, turning the card face down once more. "Pirates become hanged. Ask again."

"There is mercy - sometimes." I struggled to give words to my hope. "Wives plead, sometimes, for their men, and there is mercy."

"For thieving a deer or a salmon, maybe." Her rank breath struck me as she laughed. "King George pardons no pirates, lass. John Gow will hang. Ask."

"How can I save him?" Not waiting for permission, I pointed to another card across the circle. A turf turned over, hissing in the fire as she smiled, and turned the second card. Tree, rope and hanged man again. I knew it was a trick, but could not fathom it.

"Twice, John Gow will hang."

"But-"

"Can she break the handfast, Lizzie?" My father still stooped by the door.

Darkness shifted in the crimson socket, as if something writhed beneath the scars. The tide of her sea grey eye turned on me.

"You linked though the stone? And swore?"

"Aye"

"Swore by Odin?"

"Aye"

Holding my gaze, she turned the first card up again. A man and woman, limbs twined in a clumsy embrace of ink lines.

"Hand-clasped oath is stronger than stone. Only hand-clasp can break it." The grimy yellow claw traced the lovers' limbs. "You must undo your oath or be wedded with a ghost who finds you every night. And what man will wed a haunted wife? You must go to him. Hand-clasp again. Unswear your oath."

"To London!" My father gasped. Neither he nor I had ever been further south than the three miles to Hamnavoe.

With a brisk movement the speywife swept the cards back into the darkness of her shawl. I tried to rise, unsteady, my ankles numb from kneeling, but the clawed hand clutched at my skirts.

"We are obliged to you, Lizzie." My father groped in his purse for a coin. The witch stared into the burning peats, but her scaly finger subtly stroked my gown, circling my belly, and her cracked lips stretched in a sly, slow smile.

"Keep your silver, Tam Gordon, for your passage south." Still she did not look at me, and the pale hand slyly stroked my belly. She knew, then, what I had only begun to hope. "Helen will bring me payment, won't you, lass? At Samhain." The fire hissed and flared, and the raven screamed in the darkness as her hand seized mine. Her thin, cold fingers gripped hard. "Find him. Hand-clasp. Swear. Tho you come too late, and he be hanged, hand-clasp and swear." She turned her sea-storm gaze full on me at last, and whispered, " And bring my payment come Samhain."

My mouth was dry as ashes. I snatched my hand from hers and stumbled to the door. My father steadied me, lifting the ragged canvas and bracing himself against the storm. Through chattering teeth I called back to the witch "Why would he haunt me? If I keep my oath, why would he haunt me every night?"

Her low bitter laugh came out of the smoke. "Why does any man come to his wife's bed at night? He'll lie with you, lassie, tho he be dead and rotten."

"John will not hang!" I spat at her. "I'll go to London. I'll plead for him, and win his life!"

"Come, lass" my father pulled me out into the night. Her laughter followed us, and filled my fevered dreams in the dark weeks that followed.

* * *

I had not known there were so many people in the whole world as I saw on the quayside when we docked in London. Or so many buildings! Wave upon wave of them, chimneys and spires and domes and towers, as far as could be seen on both banks of the great brown river. The crowds seethed along the wharfs and gangways in the June sunshine, carriages and carts and sedan chairs weaving through the throng. It was hours before noon, but already the heat was suffocating as I clutched the ship's rail, desperately searching the crowds for a glimpse of my brother.

Months of sickness and weeks at sea had weakened me and my legs buckled as I stumbled ashore into the great noisy reeking, mass of men and women.

"Helen!" Strong arms raised me. The world tipped and spun into darkness.

I came to myself again in the smoky stench of an inn. Tam was chaffing my hands and holding a beaker of brandy to my lips. A freckled boy slid onto the settle beside him. John's cabin boy, Jamie. He looked half-starved and frightened. The brandy tasted foul, but it woke me.

"John, " I said. "I must see John. And I must see the judge. I must plead for him".

Tam's face was pinched and pale. "Helen," His hand gripped mine too hard. "You come too late."

The room pitched as if I was still at sea. "They broke his hands," the boy said, eyes wide with the memory. "But he would not plead. Not even-"

"Hush!" Tam silenced him, still holding my hand. "Lands are forfeit if you plead. He tried to preserve such as was his for you. And for his bairn."

John. My John.

"But they came to press him." The wee lad's eyes were brimming. "And when he saw the board all bloody, and the great stones brought in...and... he did plead then." The tears fell, and he hid his face in his arms.

"He was hanged three days since," said Tam. "He died well, sister. He showed no fear, asked no mercy, faced the rope bravely."

"Twice," sobbed Jamie.

"What!"

"The rope broke." Tam winced at the memory. "We pulled on him, to hasten it. And the rope broke. He climbed up again, as bravely as before."

The brandy burned back into my throat like bile. I saw again the ink scratched lines of tree and rope and hanging man. 'Twice' the Speywife had said. And the raven said 'choose'. I swallowed the memory with the sour brandy as John's child turned in my belly. "Where Is he?" I said.

* * *

Jamie showed me how to dodge the night watchman, hunching low among barrels on the wharf. All about us the great city was restless in its sleep. When the footsteps and the swinging lantern had retreated, the lad beckoned me to the edge of the quay. Below us in the blackness the Thames sucked and slapped at the wall. Two yards down, the dead men hung in chains from great iron rings. The stench hit me in the same moment that my eyes saw through the gloom. The reek of seaweed, river sewage and the sickly rotten odour of dead flesh were all half-drowned by the sharp, hot stink of tar. The pitch-black shapes juddered and shifted in their clinking chains as the river swell lifted and butted them against the wall.

"The gallows are out there," whispered Jamie, pointing out into the dark. "At low tide. After three high tides they cut them down, and tarred them, and chained them here." He peered down at the dead, trembling tho the night was warm. "This is The Captain," he pointed.

"In daytime you can still see his red hair a bit, and some of his green coat."

My John. Here. Hanged and tarred, and just below my reach.

I held the shivering boy to me for a moment. "Go back now, Jamie. Tell no one where you brought me. Not even Tam." He scuttled away into the night, leaving me alone on the brink of the great river, with John's child twisting in my belly, and nothing but death before us.

I stepped to the very edge, and sat, shuddering as the cold stone chilled the backs of my knees. Lanterns glimmered here and there on the black water where eel nets were set. A few sleeping gulls bobbed on the swell. The drop was no more than a man's length, but perilous. Like most islanders, I could not swim. I tugged John's arrow-stone token from my bodice and kissed it. "Odin protect me".

Then I turned, hands flat on the wharf edge, letting myself down into the dark. My toes skidded down the wall, groping for a foot-hold. There was none. And there was no way back. I hung, heavily by my fingers, my growing belly pressed hard to the slimy wall. Suddenly, from the darkness came a harsh, guttural cry and something struck at me, beating about my head. I slipped, flailing desperately in panic, bruising my knees, grazing my cheek and choking back a scream. My fingers struck against the granite once, twice, and then grabbed – and held hard – to the iron ring. With all my strength I swung myself onto the pitch-black shape beside me. My skirts hampered me, but I kicked until I had one leg before and one aft, gripping fiercely with my knees, and wedging a toe into a link of chain. One-handed, I batted at the striking bird, driving it off, then clutched at the hanging body of my husband.

For a moment his shoulder was firm beneath my fingers. Then, like the crust on a summer cow shit, the tar broke, and the smell of graves and butchers' guts and fish-rot and fear broke over me and I wretched, gasping and twisting, like a fish on a hook. In the darkness I could just see the raven, perched on the dead man to our right. Head on one side, it studied me, then stabbed its powerful beak into the ruined face, and ate. Terror clenched my guts, and I knew that seven hundred miles away, the Speywife was watching.

John. Johnnie.

I clung to him. Tar and seaweed slithered between my fingers, and the sodden, rotting rags of his velvet coat. I had been so certain, through the months of sickness and sailing, that I would save him. Despair came at last, overwhelming even my terror. I laid my bloody cheek against the tarred breast, and sobbed. The river rocked us in our chains. The tide was turning, and dawn was not far off. Already the eastern sky was streaked with red. I would be discovered soon, if I remained.

"John," I whispered into the putrid wreckage. "I swore by Odin to love you always. And I will." My free hand groped over lumpen tar to where his hand should be, and tore the cloying mess until my fingers found finger bones, and we were hand-clasped once more. "She knew, Johnnie. She knew of the bairn. She knew you'd hang twice. If I break our vow she'll claim her price, and take the bairn."

The raven shook its great black wings and grumbled at me from his ghastly perch.

"If I honour our vow and keep our bairn you'll come every midnight, even as you are now, you'll come to my bed."

The cruel beak gaped as the bird hissed.

"I could let go, Johnnie, and let the river end me. Tho it's a sin. A sin to drown the bairn before its breathed." The river surged below us, rocking us against the wall. The smothered head lolled and turned, and the ruined face fell onto mine. I saw the wreckage of the empty eye. The livid pit of crimson and black, glistening, freshly ripped."Odin!" hand bones cracked as my fist clenched in terror.

Something writhed behind the long teeth as the black, rotting mouth covered mine, smothering my scream.

And the raven's rasping voice spoke. *"Choose."*

BACKGROUND ON THE HANDFAST WIFE
BY
ÁINE KING

The Odin Stone stood within sight of the 5,000 year old stone circles of Brodgar and Stenness, in what is now the World Heritage Site of Neolithic Orkney. This imposing monolith was over 8' tall and 3' wide, with a circular hole through it. Like many holed stones, the Odin Stone was a focus for folk rituals, most notably, 'hand-fasting'. No record exists of the exact words spoken by those who clasped hands through the stone to swear the oath, but this unofficial form of marriage was considered to be binding. Handfasting was not to be undertaken lightly, not least because it endured beyond the grave. The couple could clasp-hands again to unmake their oath, and avoid the fate of nocturnal ghostly visits if one died and the other married again. The Stone was smashed to pieces in 1814 by Captain W. Mackay, who objected to people crossing his land to reach the megalith. Some say he used the broken pieces to build a pig pen.

In January 1725, Captain John Smith sailed the *George Galley* into Hamnavoe (now Stromness). The young captain was handsome and charismatic, and oddly familiar to the locals. He was, in fact, John Gow, a local boy gone to sea and turned pirate. Hiding under a false name in the very small town where everyone had known him since he was a baby was not a great plan. Homecoming parties organised by his mother weren't very discreet, either. The ship, too was in disguise. The *George* was in fact The *Caroline*. Gow and his comrades were mutineers. A few months earlier, they had killed the *Caroline's* captain and three officers, renamed her the *Revenge*, and become pirates.

John fell in love with local girl, Helen Gordon, and they were handfasted at the Odin Stone. Meanwhile, several of John's crew changed their minds about being pirates, stole the longboat and headed for the Scottish mainland. Another 'borrowed' a horse and rode to Kirkwall to alert the authorities. The *Caroline* was a distinctive vessel, and had been recognised by other sailors in the port. John had time to flee, but instead he launched a couple of poorly-planned raids on local manses, during which he ran the ship aground on one of the smaller islands. He was captured, almost single-handedly, by one of his old school friends, and sent to London for trial.

Pirates were hanged, not at Tyburn, but at the Execution Dock, Wapping. The exact location of the Execution Dock is disputed. Gun Wharf and the Prospect Of Whitney pub are both plausible claimants. Wherever, it would have been a truly horrific hell-hole of suffering, torture and despair. Those brave enough to refuse to plea were 'pressed'. Rocks and weights were piled onto them until they died. Pirates were hanged with a short rope so that they died slowly by strangulation, rather than the quick neck-break promised by a longer rope and a drop. Their bodies were left on the gallows at the low water mark until three tides had covered them. Then they were cut down, covered in tar and hung in chains or cages from the Thames wall, where they slowly decomposed, as a warning to others.

John Gow was hanged twice. His friends pulled on his legs, hoping to hasten his end, but the rope broke and he had to face the noose a second time.

Local legend tells that Helen Gordon travelled to London to break her handfast vow, but arrived too late, and had to retract her oath clasping the dead, tarred hand of John Gow. Her courage is extraordinary. The journey alone would have been beyond most young women in the remote northern isles, let alone braving the horrors of the Execution Dock. Her fate beyond Wapping is not known.

The Speywife still haunts Brinkies Brae, selling winds to sailors

RING AROUND THE ROSIE
BY
BARRY McCANN

The pointed turret loomed into view like a spear in ancient Roman mist, a spectral candle of guiding light to the couple who stumbled upon it. Jan and Michael's pre-Christmas countryside ramble had gone amiss when a wrong turn had been taken at some point. Though armed with a map, the misty haze concealed landmarks from which positions could be plotted, conspiring to keep them lost.

The pair approached the churchyard's wrought iron gate, its sign declaring the Parish of St. Helens and Michael consulted his map. "Yes, here it is. Not far from the canal, so we'll head back there."

Jan was transfixed by a single light framed within one of the arch windows. "Why don't we have a look inside?"

He looked across the headstones and also detected the glow. "They usually keep these churches locked up."

"And leave a light on? Could be someone in there."

Glancing up at the dusky sky, he shrugged "Okay, but not too long. It will be getting dark and I'll be wanting my first beer."

They crossed through the deathly silence of slanting gravestones, not even hearing the token cry of a lonely crow. To his surprise and her delight, the church door was unlocked as Michael lifted the heavy handle and led her in.

It was a church lady that met them, initially startled as she was about to let herself out. He quickly apologised "Sorry, didn't mean to startle you."

She composed herself and smiled. "It's okay. Get a bit creeped out being in here on my own. Shouldn't really, being a house of God."

"But it is a very atmospheric one," Jan noted. "Are we able to look around?"

"Oh, certainly, but I'll have to leave you to it." She gestured to a switch. "If you can turn the light off when you leave, then the verger will know it's okay to lock up."

The door loudly clanked shut behind her, and the pair set about the musky, darkly cavernous interior.

As is usually the case with Norman churches, the structure was an assemblage of side chapels, font and choir space set around the main altar and pews. Michael took photos of every corner while Jan carefully read the names of deceased engraved into the slabs that formed part of the floor. She then found a calligraphic sign detailing the church's history.

"Hey, this place has been here since 803!"

He wandered over to join her. "You sure?"

"Ah, rebuilt 1393."

"Thought so. Awful lot of pre Norman churches were rebuilds."

"Shame. Wonder what the original was like?"

"Undoubtedly smaller." He then glanced at one of the windows. "Hey, it's gone dark outside. We better get going."

Heading to the entrance, he suggested "You open the door while I get the light," and waited by the switch as Jan struggled with the handle. After a few seconds she surmised "I think it's locked."

"What? Let me try."

Michael also struggled with it before coming to the same conclusion. 'Right, we've been locked in. Must be the verger she mentioned. Why didn't he check?"

Jan looked out through the side window. "No sign of anyone. We'll just have to ring the police."

Michael was ahead of her having retrieved his phone. "Guess what? No signal, great!"

Jan rubbed her eyes, feeling momentarily dizzy. "Well... Maybe someone will come along later?"

"Out here? At night? Wait, Evensong perhaps."

He strolled over to a table where mass sheets were kept and picked one up, examining it closely. "We can forget that. Next scheduled service is Christmas Eve, two days from now."

She joined and patted him on the arm. "But there will be people coming in and out before then, like that woman today?"

"Possibly, but we may be talking tomorrow at the earliest!"

Jan cast her eyes around the brooding interior. "Wait, there's got to be another way out, maybe one that can be unlocked from inside."

He smiled with realisation. "Such as the vestry. Why didn't I think of that?"

This time Michael followed as Jan took the lead, venturing between the choir stalls and onto the alter. To the side a door stood partially hidden by curtain. It was open and they entered the room behind.

As Jan's eyes adjusted to the darkness, her partner managed to find a switch and flicked it on. A low energy bulb came to semi life, but at least it highlighted the vestry, including a door to the outside.

Michael was straight over to try the handle, in the hope it had been left unlocked. With that dashed he looked around the wall in the event of a hanging key, while suggesting "Check the drawers."

She opened and examined every draw she could find but to no more avail. He began to breathe out with a heavy sigh when something alerted Jan's ears. "Shhh! Listen."

He did as instructed and began to pick up on the murmur from back within the church. They looked at each other with caution while trying to decipher the words, which became steadily more pronounced.

'Da, quaesumus Dominus, ut in hora mortis nostrae Sacramentis refecti et culpis omnibus expiati...'

"Perhaps it's the verger come back," Michael whispered, but Jan shook her head. "Praying in Latin? This is Church of England."

"Either way, let's let him know we're here."

He began to move but she grabbed his arm. "Why would an Anglican verger use papist language?"

"Well, let's go and ask him? What are you afraid of?"

She gripped his arm tighter, her palms sweating. "Did you hear the church door unlock and open?"

He shrugged "Now you mention it, no."

"Exactly, neither did I. That big heavy old door isn't exactly quiet."

"But we're in a vestry, removed from the rest of the building."

She pointed to the doorway leading back into the church. "But we can hear someone quietly praying in there."

"So let's go see who it is." Reluctantly she nodded and let him lead the way. Entering the altar, the murmur was more audible but its source not so apparent. They ventured back through the stalls and stood before the rows of pews. All empty, yet the sound continued.

"Hello?" Michael shouted, but the disembodied voice continued. He turned to Jan, an incredulous look on his face. "Where's it coming from? I can't tell."

She looked beyond him and pointed, her fear confirmed. He turned to see an alcove of side pews and the silhouettes they cast against the wall from the church's single light. Within these the figure kneeling in an attitude of penitence was a shadow without source.

Michael's head quickly darted round, looking desperately for a source but Jan's eyes remained fixed on the apparition. "It's some sort of trick."

"Played by who exactly? We're alone in here."

He looked back at her. "Are we? I reckon this is a sick joke. That woman's probably set it up."

Jan's fists shot up to the sides of her head, the murmur and shadow becoming too much. "I just wish it would stop!"

The wish was granted, though not the way hoped. The church's single light went out, extinguishing both the shadow and its sound. With the interior plunged into darkness, only the simmering of moonlight from the windows ensured some vision.

"Well that was on cue," Michael cynically suggested before shouting "You hiding in the dark now?" There was no response but the silence of the pews and Jan's heavier breathing.

"There are candles on that rack over there, why don't you light one and go looking for your intruder?" Her scepticism was deliberately obvious.

"Well, who else do you think it is?"

She wiped sweat from her now aching forehead, trying to remain focused. "Not who, what."

"You mean a ghost? Oh, come on. Centuries old building, creaky structure. Doesn't take much to convince the gullible its haunted. And that is what someone is playing on."

"Listen to yourself, Michael. You're more paranoid than I am. Why would anyone do that?"

Raising his voice, he addressed the pews once more. "Trying to give to the poor old townies a good scare. Have a laugh at our expense!"

The pair of them jumped at the sharp thud and they looked over at the windows. It had come from outside but very close. Then there was another. And another. Michael ran over to the nearest window as Jan painfully ambled behind. Side by side, they looked out upon the murkily lit church yard. There was no one apparently present, but Jan then pointed. "Look, those gravestones over there." Michael followed her direction and noticed a pair of them next to each other lying flat on the ground.

"Someone's obviously just pushed them over," he concluded. "Another scare tactic."

"To the point of vandalising their own cemetery? Do you still think that woman has anything to do with it?" Michael's search for an answer was interrupted when another adjoining gravestone tumbled over, apparently unaided. Then the next, and next, until an entire row had fallen like dominoes. And then they appeared. Tall, sinewy shadow figures grew from the darkness behind, each beside one another in a line stretching across the dim horizon and encircling the church. As they ambled forward, Jan and Michael perceived the figures to be of both differing heights and peripherals of attire. Male, female, adult, children, all as black as the night that conceived them. The figures halted several feet short of the building, remaining still and seemingly staring. But this was a feeling, as neither could make out any features on blackened out faces.

"They're not shadows," Jan observed. "There's a density to them."

"Then what the hell are they?"

Jan's weakening eyes tried focusing. "They look like husks. Blackened like charcoal." Her eyelids came down and she retreated to the pew behind, allowing herself to practically fall into it. Michael tried reassuring them both.

"Well, if they are solid husks, they can't get in. Not with that door locked."

With eyes closed and head in hand, Jan replied "I don't think they want to get in."

"Then, what are they waiting for?"

"For us to come out."

With that she leaned forward and began retching, crimson red splashing on the stone floor.

Michael leapt over and grabbed her by the shoulders, his fingertips black as the figures outside.

* * *

The following morning was heralded by figures of white haunting the church grounds; apparitions of investigators wrapped in hazardous material suits and breathing from oxygen masks.

The verger had found them when unlocking the church at first light. The sight of the dead couple slumped on a pew was horrendous enough, but it was the afflictions on their hands and faces that sent him into panic.

The police were initially on the scene and quickly had the area cordoned off. Before long, the medical team, also protectively dressed, set up an isolation tent into which the verger and first contact officers were ushered for examination.

Silently, the forensics entered the church and some later re-emerged with a pair of body bags, which were loaded on a van and taken away. The remainder continued investigating the building.

Later that day, a police car pulled up carrying the senior pathologist. In plain clothes and no mask, he entered the church and gestured to the team within to join him outside. Once assembled in the grounds, he then signalled it was safe to take off their protection before commencing the briefing.

"The official cause of death is still to be concluded, but there are a couple of strange aspects to the victims' condition."

"They looked horribly diseased," the lead investigator commented.

"Yes, and those physical ailments are symptomatic of *Yersinia pestis*." The team members looked at him quizzically. "Better known as Bubonic Plague."

His hand shot up to quell the looks of panic. "Don't worry, we're safe. Because that's the other mystery. There is no actual trace of the infection in their bodies. None whatsoever, they're clean."

It took a moment for the penny to drop before the investigator spoke again.

"So… all the symptoms of Black Death but none of the cause?"

The pathologist could do nothing but nod in agreement. Then another of the team piped up. "But Black Death is historic, isn't it?"

"Last outbreak in this area was in 1391, I checked." He pointed to the building they had just exited. "In fact the church that stood here at the time was used as a makeshift hospital. When it became hopelessly congested with dead and dying, they decided to sterilise."

"Sterilise?"

His expression turned solemn. "It was barricaded and burnt to the ground. With everyone inside."

BACKGROUND ON RING AROUND THE ROSIE
BY
BARRY McCANN

Like natural disaster, plague is as old as time and consequently enshrined in folklore. The Greek myths, for example, personified plague as the Nosoi, one of the evil spirits that escaped Pandora's Box. The Old Testament is noted for tales of pestilence sent down by a vengeful God as punishment, a belief still held by some in this era of HIV.

Plague epidemics were fairly common in medieval England. But the two outbreaks that cast the biggest shadow in both factual history and national folklore are the Black Death of 1348, and the Great Plague of 1665

Both centred on London, the epidemics are recorded as bubonic plague, spread not by rats as popularly believed but the fleas that fed off them. As each host rat died from plague, the fleas then had to find a new rat to feed on until they graduated to humans.

The symptoms of bubonic plague include painful swellings in the armpits and groin, often leading to gangrene. Other warning signs are high fever, rash, vomiting, and coughing up blood.

The Black Death of 1348 remains one of the deadliest plagues in history, having been carried from

Asia to the Crimea and then Europe by rats and their fellow traveller fleas on merchant ships. It hit Bristol in the summer of that year and took its grip on the city, reaching London by autumn where it also flourished in the unsanitary, slum conditions of the city.

The term 'Black Death' is popularly thought to originate in the blackened flesh of its victims, but actually comes from a poem by the Flemish astrologer, Simon de Covinus. Written around 1350, it describes the pestilence as 'mors atra', meaning black or terrible death. Sixteenth-century translations of the poem settled on the word 'black', rather than 'terrible', and it was then the phrase was established.

The actual bacterium that caused the plague, Yersinia Pestis, was not identified until 1894 by Swiss bacteriologist, Alexandre Yersin. And it was he who discovered it could be transmitted by flea bites.

So because the cause of the disease was unknown at the time, there was no way of knowing how to stop it. Most of those infected died, usually with a week of contamination. Consequently, the death rate quickly overtook the disposal of bodies and London churchyards could not meet the demand for burial space.

There was no other course but to mass bury victims in pits dug across the city and surrounding areas, a task undertaken as swiftly as possible for fear the infected corpses may spread the disease further. Records of these pits and their locations were either not taken, or not kept.

Even after the Black Death subsidised and the worst hit areas recovered themselves, plagues did continue to flare up over the centuries that followed. And the impact of the Black Death continued to be remembered through the iconography of skeletons preying on the living, poems and songs about the life destroying pestilence and the Danse Macabre – or Dance of the Dead – which became popular in the Middle Ages and portrayed disease as claiming anyone from knight to peasant, the victim pulled to their grave by a grinning skeleton.

Tragically, history was to repeat itself when in 1665 the pestilence struck back with a vengeance, again consuming the crowded and filthy streets of London with some 100,000 lives lost over several months.

As with the Black Death 300 years earlier, nobody knew what was causing this pandemic. Everything from bad air to dogs and cats were blamed, and many of these animals were slaughtered as an attempt at some crude form of sterilisation.

Red crosses were painted on the doors of plague victims as warning, while dead carts roamed the streets with the cry 'bring out your dead'. Again, the uncontainable death rate resulted in bodies thrown into in pits and buried across the city during, usually at night to keep out of public sight.

Once again, the recorded locations of these plague pits remained scarce. Most of them were built over, especially during the major rebuilding of central London following the Great Fire just a year later. Potentially there are hundreds of pits under the city's buildings and streets, some of which have already been uncovered during reconstruction projects.

Not surprisingly many of these are under or around churches. St. Mary's Church in Walthamstow is said to have two plague pits beneath its site, one from the 1348 outbreak and the other from 1665. The nearby Vinegar Alley is thought to have taken its name from ditches dug near the churchyard and filled with vinegar in the hope of stemming the spread of pestilence.

A pit fifty foot long pit dug in the churchyard of St. Botolph without Aldgate, is said to have contained over 1,000 bodies.

More recently in 2013, a mass Black Death burial ground in Charterhouse Square, Smithfield, was discovered during excavations for the Crossrail line serving London and the South East. The site had been undisturbed since the fourteenth century, and twenty five bodies were unearthed from two levels where they had been neatly arranged with a layer of clay between them and on top to seal in the disease.

DNA analysis from the skeletons' teeth indicated signs of malnutrition which means their immune system would be weakened. This suggests the bubonic plague may have developed into pneumonic plague, entering the victims' lungs and spread when expelled into the air by coughing, which could account for its massive acceleration.

Like the forbidding hidden cellar of an old dark house, the prospect of plague pits directly under the feet of modern Londoners is the stuff of modern folklore. And the further secrets their uncovering may reveal remains an intriguing prospect.

CHURCHGOING
BY
KEVIN PATRICK
McCANN

Joe had been driving around aimlessly for an hour in the rain and just wanted to get out of the car and stretch his legs for a while. But where to stop and what to do when he did? He'd seen quite a few pubs, all lit up and Festively welcoming and every one of them probably an exact clone of one original Authentic English Pub designed by somebody called Jason who lives in a converted windmill in Cheshire with his partner Tristessa and their two Shiatsu's Yin and Yang....

"Calm down!" he snapped at himself, "calm right down, find somewhere to park up and chill out."

The lane he was driving down was too narrow to just stop in. There was no other traffic but there were also no lay-bys and if he did stop now, dozens of cars would probably appear out of nowhere. At least it had stopped raining. He'd always hated it when there was rain over Christmas. It just seemed wrong. But of course it hardly ever snowed at Christmas – another lie – it was stuff your face spend a fortune get into a fight over the last bubble bath in the shop Happy Holidays... there was a church just up ahead – square tower and old looking.

He checked his mirror and then turned in through the open gate and into the empty car park. It was edged with dry stone walls and beyond that, there was nothing but fields and the beginnings of woodland.

He switched off the engine and got out of the car. It was cold but not unpleasantly so. What was that line out of 'A Christmas Carol?' Piping for the blood to dance to; beautiful metaphor. He breathed in deeply and felt his head clearing.

There were lights on in the church showing gold against the growing twilight. He glanced at his watch – four o'clock – and decided, on a whim, to have a look inside. It was better than standing outside in a carpark freezing. He hadn't set foot in a church since his Dad's funeral. A picture formed, unbidden but startlingly vivid - his Dad lying in a coffin holding a single long-stemmed rose and looking like he was about to open his eyes and ask if there was any chance of a brew.

He felt the world tilt and had the sensation of sliding slowly sideways. That settled it. He buttoned up his coat against the sudden cold gust that danced through him, went in through the lych gate and up the short path past tilting gravestones – they're always tilting – lifted the latch, pushed open the heavy oak door and walked in.

A man and woman, both in their sixties he'd guess, were sorting out piles of hymn books on a table right next to the door. The man glanced up.

"Welcome to St. Brigids," he said smiling.

Joe managed a smile back. He was hoping the place would be empty. Make an effort, he thought and said, "Lovely church you have here."

"We like it," the man replied extending his hand. "Graham Duckworth. I'm the Vicar here.

Joe shook the proffered hand, "Joe Sweeney."

The Vicar waved in the direction of the woman still stacking hymn books. "This is my wife, Marjorie."

Joe nodded towards the woman and even managed another smile. Oh god no! Not the bloody Vicar and Mrs. bloody Vicar to boot. They'll probably try and tap me for a donation to the roof fund or something...

The Vicar's wife finished sorting the last of the hymnals. "Sweeney: that's an Irish name isn't it?"

Joe sensed no hostility in her voice so smiled again; only this time there was nothing forced about it. "Yes, it is," he said. "My Dad always used to tell me we were named after Kings."

Marjorie turned to her husband. "Isn't there a story about him?"

The Vicar thought for a moment. "Yes, I believe there is. He went mad with grief after a battle so made himself a pair of wings and flew off into the woods where he lived in the trees." He paused, "I'm sorry; I expect you already know this one."

"No," said Joe, "no I don't."

The Vicar looked puzzled, "Hasn't your Dad ever told..."

"My Dad's dead!" Joe's vehemence echoed back at him from all round the church. Good manners demanded an immediate apology. "I'm sorry, it was only a couple of weeks ago and I'm still a bit raw."

There was an awkward silence and Joe was about to say a quick goodbye and leave when the Vicar and his wife exchanged a glance. In the few seconds it lasted an entire unspoken conversation took place.

"Perhaps you'd like to left alone with your thoughts for a while," said the Vicar. His voice was soft and sympathetic. Like his Dad's could be.

Joe nodded, "Is that alright?

The Vicar's wife pointed to a row of switches on the wall. "Would you mind turning off the lights before you leave?"

"Oh and make sure you're out by five o'clock. That's when the caretaker locks up so I'd make sure you're out by then."

"Thanks," he said, "I will be."

As they turned to go, the Vicar hesitated a moment and said, "I know how you feel."

As the door closed behind them, Joe turned and walked slowly up the central aisle. His footsteps echoed and he had the strange urge to try and walk quietly. He glanced up at the stained glass windows. Saint George, an assortment of apostles and Jesus as the Good Shepherd. The high altar was carpeted in red and there was a brass lectern in the shape of an eagle supporting a bible on its outstretched wings. A tall Christmas Tree at least twice Joe's height stood just to one side of the altar and next to that, there was a Nativity: Joseph, Mary, one cow, one donkey, one sheep, no shepherds and an empty crib. A votive candle, unlit, stood at the front. It'll be lit midnight on Christmas Eve...

He had a sudden flashback and he was maybe four or five. It's Christmas and he's standing looking up at the crib in church. He can't see it very well so Dad lifts him up...

He heard the church door open and close and turned round to look back down the aisle. He was half expecting to see the Vicar come back to pray with you but there didn't seem to be anyone there. There were pillars blocking his eye line so there might be someone behind one of those.

* * *

Thomas Caryngton, MA, Vicar of St. Brigids, enters his church, locks the door again behind him and looks around. It's cold and dark but he barely notices the chill and doesn't bother to light the candle, Mr. Adams, the Verger, has left on the table next to the hymnals. He prefers the dark as it reflects perfectly the dark night of his soul – if indeed I possess such a thing, he muses – just as the empty church reflects the emptiness in his heart.

* * *

"Hello," Joe called out. "Is that the caretaker?" His voice echoed back but other than that, there was no reply. But there was somebody there; had to be. Probably some deaf old sod of a caretaker who's forgotten to turn his hearing aid on. His Dad was always…no, don't think about that! "Hello," he called again only this time much louder.

* * *

Caryngton pauses. Was that a voice in the distance?

* * *

Joe felt the adrenalin beginning to pump. His legs suddenly felt weak and the hairs of his beard and on the back of his neck tingled sharply. Somebody playing silly buggers because…well because there was no other explanation. He didn't believe in ghosts anymore or God or everlasting life. That was all just so much wishful thinking. "Hello," he called again and this time, when there was still no reply, set off back down the aisle.

Halfway down he felt an icy chill pass through him. Someone's walking over my grave!

* * *

There are deep shadows everywhere that are spreading and linking like an incoming tide. Caryngton can see no one and yet, instinct tells him he's not alone. He dismisses the thought. He no more believes in ghosts than he does in mermaids. He's no longer even sure he still believes in God. There's no love in me, he thinks to himself. When I stand on that altar week in, week out spouting my homily, I'm just a sounding brass. He sets off up the aisle towards the altar. Halfway there he shudders with sudden cold and in his mind's eye catches a fleeting glimpse of a man with long hair and a beard. The man's face is drawn and pale, his eyes moist and sad. The picture is so sharp and clear, he gasps in shock and is suddenly brimming over with the most terrible grief. He sways and grips the end of one of the benches for support.

* * *

Joe decided to leave. It was getting dark, the church was creepy and …what was it Dad used to say? Just because you don't believe in ghosts doesn't mean they're not there. But when he got the door, it wouldn't open. It's locked! So it must have been the bloody caretaker after all. What to do now? He didn't have a mobile so couldn't ring the police for help. He could hardly smash a window. They were stained glass and knowing his luck, probably put in when the damn place was first built. He kicked the door with sheer frustration and the bang echoed and re-echoed round the church.

* * *

There's a distant clap of thunder and Caryngton's heart seems to leap in his chest.

* * *

All the lights suddenly went out. Joe ran over to the bank of switches and began flicking them up and down. Nothing, so the power must be on a time switch or something. He stood still and let his eyes adjust to the darkness. He could have closed them for a minute to speed things up a bit...but felt disinclined. A thought suddenly occurred: Candles! This is a church so there'll be candles. He felt in his jacket pocket. Tobacco tin, papers and yes, thank God, his lighter. And not just any old lighter – this one had a built in torch. It only gave off a small beam but it would be enough. He clicked it on and shone it round the church. Nothing this end but there must be candles on the altar. Focusing the beam on the floor just ahead, he began walking slowly back up the aisle.

* * *

Then Caryngton sees a light at the back of the church. It hovers by the door then begins moving slowly up the aisle towards him. He turns and runs, so terrified, he can no longer think. It is only when he reaches the altar that he stops himself with the thought, I'm a priest. This is a church. I'm safe no matter what I may see or hear.

* * *

Joe paused. He heard the sound of running just up ahead. "Hello," he called again. "Is there anybody there?" He flashed the torch beam around but as far as he could see, the place was still empty. Imagination, he thought to himself though he was no longer convinced; either that or the ghost of some choirboy trying to get away from some pervy vicar.

* * *

The light pauses for a moment and Caryngton does the only logical thing he can think of. He gets down on his knees and begins to pray.

* * *

Joe kept walking but now he could hear whispering and hesitated. He couldn't make out any words but he recognised the rhythm of prayer when he heard it. Sounds can't hurt you, he thought, and just up ahead are two rows of candles on the altar. There were in tall brass candlesticks but he was sure he'd be able to lift them down and get them lit. He flashed his torch towards the Nativity and the votive candle. That would do to begin with and besides which, the whispering had stopped as suddenly as it had started. "One-two-three, go!" he muttered firmly to himself then ran over to the votive candle and lit it. As its warm red glow spread out all around him, startled shadows ran for cover.

* * *

Caryngton watches as the light suddenly rushes past him and stops before the Nativity. The votive candle ignites and he is overwhelmed by a sense of peace. His vision becomes blurred and the tears well up like the stream Moses drew from the rock when he struck it with his staff. I am that rock, he thinks, an unfeeling lump of stone in the middle of the arid desert of my lack of faith...and now Almighty God, the loving and merciful, has given me a sign. And then he weeps and it is as if every pain he'd ever endured, every loss, every hurt he's ever felt is being purged from him.

* * *

Joe could hear the sound of sobbing, fierce and desperate. He looked around and there, just at the foot of the altar steps, was a shadow...but when he shone the torch beam full on it, there was no sudden disappearing act. It stayed exactly where it was, its outline familiar and he could see now that it was quivering. It was a man, dressed in black- so maybe in mourning- down on his knees, bent double and sobbing. Not a ghost then, he thought, just a man. But when he reached out and tried to touch the man on his shoulder, his fingertips met cold empty air.

* * *

Caryngton feels a gentle cooling touch on his shoulder and looks up. He is dazzled by light and raises one hand to cover his eyes. He hears a faint whisper. 'Sorry,' it seems to say. Caryngton presses his palms together. "Yes Lord," he says. "I am sorry, truly sorry." and then bows his head in reverence.

* * *

The shadow unbent and Joe could see a man who covered his eyes with one hand. Instinctively, he turned off his torch. "Sorry," he said and then realised he was apparently apologising to a ghost.

The man's lips began to move but his words were blurred and all Joe could make out, mainly by lip reading was 'I am sorry, truly sorry.' Joe's fear was gone. It had slipped away and been replaced by an odd kind of exhilaration. It's aware of me. It's not an echo from the past or a trick of the light. It's a ghost and it's got sentience...or I'm going crazy. There's always that possibility I suppose.

He suddenly had a vivid memory of his Grandad sitting in an armchair and saying, "Ghosts can't hurt you Joe."

"But they scare me Grandad," he'd said.

His Grandad had smiled, "No more than you probably scare them. Sure, half the time they don't even know they're dead. They'd probably think you were a ghost. At least, that's how they'd see you."

"But supposing I see one?" he'd persisted. "What'll I do then?"

Grandad had sat back in the chair, pressed his fingertips together and said patiently, "Ask it what it wants."

Joe looked down at the ghost. "What do you want?"

The ghost looked back up at him. "Forgiveness," it said – and now Joe could make out the words clearly - then bowed its head.

Joe couldn't believe he was actually doing this, "Forgiveness for what?"

The ghost looked up again, "For not believing in you."

It thinks I'm a ghost, he thought then corrected himself. No, he thinks I'm a ghost. What was it Father Kelley used to say when he was blessing the coffin at a funeral? Be at peace.

* * *

"What do you want?" Caryngton can hear the voice clearly and in it, he hears sympathy. He dares himself to look up and sees the face of a bearded man, thin and with hair curling at his shoulders.

"Forgiveness," he dares himself to say then bows his head again.

"Forgiveness for what?"

He looks up again, "For not believing in you."

"Be at peace," Joe said and with the edge of his hand made the sign of the cross in the air above the man's face. As he finished all the lights in the church came back on again and as the church door swung open, the ghost faded from translucent to transparent to gone.

* * *

"Be at peace," his saviour said – for Caryngton knew it was He – and blessed him. But before he could respond, there was blaze of light that filled the whole church, dazzling him. And that faded too and was gone. When his vision cleared, his Lord was gone. Gone from my sight, he thought, but not from my heart.

* * *

Joe walked over to the votive candle at the front of the Nativity before setting off quickly down the aisle. His heart was dancing in his chest and blood thundered in his ears. He felt like someone who's just woken up from a nightmare and being elated it was only a dream after all. And it was all true: there really is both magic and mercy in this world.

He'd expected to find an apologetic caretaker at the back of the church. But no-one came in and when he looked outside, the car park was empty. He looked back round the church one last time then flicked off the bank of switches to turn out the lights and left, closing the door firmly behind him.

* * *

As for the Reverend Carrygton, he's a changed man too. He gets up from his knees and looks around his church in time to see the votive light before their crib, blown out. He knows his vision has ended. He has an urge to run down onto the village, hammer on the doors of his apathetic flock shouting, "I've just seen Jesus!"

He kneels down, offers a prayer of thanks and leaves, re-locking the church behind him. Calmer now, he walks quickly home across fields silvered and shadowed by the rising moon: at one point he pauses, breathing in deeply, slowly exhaling, he smells a promise of snow on the air. Life is good and as he walks on towards the vicarage, he begins whistling an old song from his childhood. The words come back and he fades into the darkness singing.

BACKGROUND ON CHURCHGOING BY KEVIN PATRICK McCANN

My brother Barry and myself were driving aimlessly through the Lancashire countryside, saw an old church, parked up and went in. The vicar and his wife were just leaving and asked us to turn out the lights on our way out. It was late November and going dark and we were told to be out by five otherwise the caretaker might lock us in.

The church was Norman (though built on a Saxon site), cold and once we were alone, atmospheric. We strolled round for a while and then left. On the way back to Blackpool, Barry mentioned he had the beginnings of an idea. So did I and we decided to set ourselves the goal of writing a story each set in a church and have it ready by Christmas Eve [Barry's tale, 'Ring around the Rosie' is also featured in this collection].

It had been our Dad's funeral only a few days earlier and we both needed something else to think about. I spent the rest of the day thinking and by the morning, the story was pretty much fully formed in my mind. There's a myth that the inspiration for a story usually springs from one source alone. Mary Shelley had a nightmare; Bram Stoker had one: the results were

Frankenstein and Dracula respectively. The reality is usually more convoluted than that.

In my case, the story or poem comes first and I deduce the sources later.

Source one was a photograph I'd seen of a translucent vicar sitting on a bench in St. Nicholas Church, Arundel, Sussex. You'll find it on page 53 of *The Unexplained* by Jenny Randles.

I know Norman/Saxon churches were often built on the sites of old Pagan places of worship. I also know that stone circles were often seen as gateways between this and the other world – although these days they seem to be more associated with UFOs than Pagan Gods.

I'd also read *The Eagles Quest* by Dr. Fred Alan Wolf which examines the links between shamanism and quantum physics and came across the words "Without time...Matter would appear as ghosts." (page 205) so it must have occurred to me that people meeting as the result of a time slip (i.e. outside linear time) would perceive each other as ghosts.

I already knew about alleged time slips – there's even one incident that's supposed to have occurred five minutes' walk from my front door: although having checked the details of this one in which a man spends the night in a barn that he later discovered, had burnt down fifty years previously, I'm now convinced it was at best, a case of misremembered locations and at worst, a tall tale. You can find the account in *Supernatural Liverpool* by Billy Roberts under the heading of 'The Stable that Disappeared'.

And finally I remembered from my reading on shamanism and animistic religions that there is a widespread belief that when humans and spirits encounter each other, it's because there's a mutual need.

In 'Churchgoing', a vicar who's lost his faith encounters a man who's lost his Father. They perceive each other as spirits. The vicar thinks he's seeing Jesus and the man thinks he's getting proof of life after death. The encounter takes place in a Norman church that's probably built on a pagan site and involves a time slip.

So, all simple enough... apparently.

THE EAR
BY
JAKI McCARRICK

Christine knew that if everyone lamented the death of a patient the way in which she was doing, life in St. Joseph's would prove impossible. Yet, she could not stop herself weeping for the French-Canadian woman, who, for the past week, had occupied the bed beside her. So, when one of the orderlies, Dave, walked up to where Christine was sitting (on the bench outside the ward-office), rocking herself to and fro, and told her to *shut the hell up*, first with his brazen reptilian eyes, and then out loud, Christine wiped her tears and did as he asked.

Sondrine had had such faith. A devotee of the True Buddha Temple in Montreal, she'd described to Christine a detailed but accessible system of chants and blessing lights. Christine very much liked the sound of this: she'd longed for something simple yet immersive in which she too could hopefully lose (and paradoxically find) herself. She no longer held to the Catholic faith of her childhood, and was not at all tempted to return to it by the ubiquitous presence of crucifixes in the hospital, nor by the Virgins that lurched from the building's numerous reliquaries. She had no faith either (though wanted it) in the breezy optimism of the staff, and was especially suspicious of the nuns who continued to run various parts of St. Joseph's with their stiff and assured sense of belief, which, it seemed to Christine, was worn defensively, like body armour.

The following day, with a new and much less talkative neighbour already in Sondrine's bed, Christine commenced her physiotherapy in earnest: she began to walk, slowly (with the aid of a Zimmer frame), along the corridor that led from the ward-office and ended at the wide landscape painting in the older part of St. Joseph's, where many of the ward's supplies, drugs, boxes of bandages, commodes etc were stored. Christine often wondered why such a bucolic image – of a long hedgerow buttressed by whitethorn - had been placed in the least-used most baroque-looking part of the building, and thought that perhaps patients were being discouraged from lingering in such a place (to where they might come to indulge some sorrow or other) by the sentinel-like presence of this cheery landscape. Christine managed, however, to find another image upon which to deliberate that was not of this ilk: a print of Frederic Leighton's Nausicaa, hanging crookedly by the window that overlooked the car park. In the picture, the Greek princess is dressed like a slave – which chimed exactly with how Christine saw her life.

For Christine, the process of learning to walk again was rather like being an infant. Her steps were small and careful, eyes to the ground. So much so, she quickly came to know the difference between nurse and nun by the contrasting personalities of their feet. She had never before imagined feet to possess, in isolation, 'personality', but after a week of slow Zimmer-framing along the corridor outside her ward, Christine concluded that they very much did. The nurses *bounded* along, foot-punching the floor. They did not walk like the nurses Christine read about in newspapers: downtrodden, tired, overworked. In contrast, the nuns walked with a greater adherence to type: the nice ones with a certain humility; the more severe with a loud firmness (which chilled her and recalled her schooldays). The doctors usually wore black shoes; the males - loafers or moccasins or soft looking square-tipped shoes, Italian, she supposed, and the females kitten-heels - or flats. Most of the orderlies also wore black shoes, though these seemed to be chunkier, cheaper in design and quality.

As she gained in strength, Christine began to notice as many knees as feet, and was surprised to learn that most people had ugly knee-joints: bony, like the knees of river-wading birds, or thickly coated in fat like slabs of pork. By the time she was able to walk with a little more ease and confidence, having learned the knack of fluidly passing her weight back and forth onto the aluminum legs of the frame, her gaze rising accordingly, Christine felt she had emerged from some dark and viscose place, one that had felt strangely suspended in time, and was therefore glad of the brightness she began to see emanating from people's *faces*. This brightness, she supposed, was the 'inner light' of which she'd heard Sondrine speak. Christine had to admit she'd not before noticed another human being's 'inner light', which, she now observed, was *only* available on faces, via the eyes or mouth. This, she thought, was the best aspect of experiencing others in such a compartmentalized fashion: these surprising encounters with the sparkle of another's mind and heart. Christine realized that if she saw herself in the Nausicaa picture (she did), it was because, unlike Sondrine, she'd simply not been aware of her own 'inner light' – which, she thought, seemed like a strength, a power.

It was about ten days after Sondrine's death, around the time that she began to stop focusing on shoes, feet and knees, and was able to raise her gaze with ease as she walked, that Christine saw the ear. It startled her. She'd had to look several times, and from several different angles. She placed the Zimmer frame flush against the skirting board in order to lean in and examine: the exact likeness in shape and curvature of a human ear. The crumbling blue paint of the wall had exposed a small mound of flesh-coloured plaster - with wiry hairlines for the ear's bones, hollows and canals.

Each day, as her legs and hips grew stronger, Christine would find herself stopping by the ear, which was at eye-level on the wall opposite Nausicaa, between the drug storerooms and a life-size statue of the Virgin Mary that sometimes people would pray to. People further down the corridor might think Christine was before the statue, and people before the statue would usually be so involved with their prayers they would not notice the woman facing the wall and talking to it. Not that Christine (at first) would say much. But as the days went by and her strength returned (and her gaze ascended) and it looked like soon enough, in one or two weeks' time, she would be discharged and have to be sent home to the care of her husband, Christine began to speak more and more to the ear, as if she were running out of time and needed to offload her thoughts and feelings as quickly as possible. People who walked by her saw a woman muttering to herself. Considering the environment they would not have thought much of it. What they would not hear, of course, was what Christine heard. For by her third visit, she was convinced that not only had she (at last) found a portal to some kind of spiritual realm, or, if one does not mind the definition, God, a secret plain of infinite love, happiness and understanding (Christine had spent much of her life looking for its kind, like the mother she'd lost as a girl, whose 'replacement', Dr. Vaughn, her councilor, had said she'd been subconsciously seeking over the past three decades in her numerous career choices, degree programmes, the multiple lovers before her marriage, her various substance addictions, compulsive behaviours etc - and had, naturally, never found), but that she was also *being given advice.*

The first piece of advice Christine took from her daily colloquy with the ear was to procure a quantity of drugs from the storerooms. The two rooms, marked B24 and B25 on the outside with faded black and gold Letraset, were haphazardly manned by a young flocculent-haired nurse who was regularly distracted by Dave and his unerringly half-witted gags. The rooms were therefore often left unlocked, the stock spilling out in piles. Christine was given (by the ear) a detailed list of drugs to procure from the rooms. Some brand names were specified. These were: Dihydrocodeine Hydrogen Paracetemol, Aspirin – gastro resistant (Nu-Seal 75mg), a large quantity of any kind of sleeping pill so long as the pill-size was minute.

The second piece of advice was to call her husband and convincingly inform him that she'd forgiven him, just as she had done in the past, and that she would like to spend something of their anniversary day together. She had argued with the ear about this, for she'd no intention of forgiving her husband, and wished from the bottom of her heart she'd never *ever* laid eyes on him. Each day away from him was, for Christine, a day in which she grew exponentially in strength – and in awareness of her inner light. But then the ear explained, and so Christine made the call.

There was a caveat to the second piece of advice. Though by now, what the ear communicated to Christine sounded to her increasingly like *instruction*, and she was beginning to doubt the presence of what she alone seemed able to recognise, and to wonder if, perhaps, she was deeply deluded, affected unduly by the strong pain-relieving medication that had been prescribed to her. But, eventually, she complied with the ear's caveat. Which was to ensure there was a box of chocolates, preferably liqueurs (which, if she asked nicely enough, Dave might purchase for her in the hospital shop), placed as enticingly as possible on her bedside-table for when her husband came to visit. Christine explained to the ear that as her husband was gluttonous and thoughtless and a particular fan of liqueurs there would be no point in doing this as he would devour them all. This, the ear explained, was the point. Christine then received the ear's third and final piece of advice-slash-instruction, and that night, in her bed, she quietly placed the stolen pills on a saucer and crushed them with a teaspoon. She filled a syringe with a mixture of water and the crushed pills, and into the body of each chocolate carefully injected a tiny amount of the cloudy potion. She shook each piece lightly, so that the fluids within would blend, and was mindful to keep her finger over the lacerated part of the chocolate. She smoothed over all the punctured holes with her thumb. Later, she disposed of the excess pills and slabs of packaging into the sanitary-waste bin in the toilets.

As she lay in bed, eyes wide open, unable to sleep, going over in her mind how the following day might proceed, Christine began to consider that perhaps her husband had been right: perhaps she'd been difficult to love. She knew she'd been emotionally - and sexually - remote (hence her visits to Dr. Vaughn) and that, ultimately, she'd *made* herself this way in order to be safe, which in turn had only made her husband even more prone to his rages. She quickly interrupted this line of thinking when she saw how, once again, she was subtly shifting blame for another's actions onto herself.

The next day, during her husband's visit, Christine sat back while he spoke about the coriander growing wild in her absence, his Weight Watcher meetings, how much he missed her cooking, how he wished they could have been in a restaurant celebrating their big day rather than her wasting all this time 'recuperating from a few scratches'. He never once referred to the actual incident that had landed her in hospital. She realised as he yammered on about this and that, that he was a master of disassociation. He never seemed truly sorry for what he did. He moved on from such incidents much more easily than she did. She looked at her husband, sprawled out now on the chair beside her, gently stroking her hand, breathing heavily, his nasal passages making their familiar lazy crackling noises, and realised all of this in an instant. His infliction of suffering upon her rarely seemed to impact upon him. She realised she'd convinced herself he also suffered, that he possessed some great inner flaw that he was nobly fighting. She realized, too, that there would probably be more such 'incidents', and that she would grow old and he would grow old and he would continue to hurt her and she would continue to think (stupidly) that he was suffering too. It all came so clearly to her, this likely future of theirs, as he bounced each barrel-shaped liqueur into his mouth and swallowed with minimal chewing, as she knew he would. At no point during his long and anguished monologue of his weeks at home without her did Christine attempt to stop her husband eating the immolated liqueurs.

Three hours after her husband's departure from St. Joseph's, Christine received the terrible news: there had been a head-on collision. Her husband had fallen asleep at the wheel; his immense body crushed in the impact, so much so the paramedic on the scene said it had resembled a burst sloe. Also reported was the strange sickly smell in the car of fermentation, of spirits, whiskey or brandy, as if her husband had been drinking; it had been his wedding anniversary, after all. The matron sympathetically assured Christine that she would be well enough to attend the funeral, that soon it would be time for her to leave anyway.

The next morning Christine walked, slowly (without her Zimmer frame), towards the place of the ear. On her way down the corridor she could see men in white garments at the end, before the landscape painting and after the storerooms, their backs to Nausicaa. Dave was amongst them. Some of the men wore trainers and some black moccasins. They seemed to be in an intense discussion about something. By the storerooms she could smell fresh paint. When she got to the ear, the men moved out of her way, perhaps thinking she wanted to reach the statue of the Virgin just beyond. Christine looked hard - but the ear was gone. She saw it had been plastered over and repainted. She screamed loudly. She scratched at the wall. Dave called a nurse. She knew she had to hurry. She pulled at the wet paint and the newly-dried plaster and in no time her arms were blue and the pale plaster had come away in thick clumps and was pushing up under her fingernails. Within minutes she could hear the familiar low sound from deep within the ear, though she couldn't find its shape. She scraped and scraped, until she had dug a hole so big she could fit herself in. She went headfirst. She lifted her bruised and aching hips over the edge of the hole and pulled herself up and in. Then deep inside the ear she bellowed, "Sondrine, I'm coming, Sondrine" and disappeared into the wall.

BACKGROUND ON THE EAR
BY
JAKI McCARRICK

In his *Dictionary of Irish Mythology*, Peter Beresford Ellis states "the Celts were one of the first European peoples to evolve a doctrine of immortality of the soul" – and claims that the Greeks, specifically Sotion and Clement of Alexandria in the second century BC, attributed their own afterlife doctrines to the Celts. Hence, one of the most important tenets of many modern faith systems, the idea of a world after death, heaven etc, has its roots in the myths of Ireland and the British Isles. The Celtic "Otherworld" is a broad term that includes both the (afterlife) worlds of heaven and hell etc, but also parallel universes, or places that offer a more utopian *existence* – such as Tir na nOig (the Land of Youth), or Tir na tSamhraidh (the Land of Summer) or the Magh Mell (the Plain of Happiness) - amongst many others.

For my short story 'The Ear' I had in mind one of these Utopian lands of the Otherworld, a place very much like Magh Mell, one which, in contemporary everyday life, exists only in our imaginations, referred to sometimes as our 'happy place' – a place of the mind where children – and adults - go to when sad or when seeking some kind of personal protection; a place also often visited in meditations or dreams, or in various psychotic conditions.

The central image of the story came to me then just as the story's protagonist discovers it: in a hospital, on an occasion when visiting my father who was ill at the time. I saw an ear shape in the crumbling paintwork of the wall of my father's ward, and wondered what would happen if someone who needed comfort, a patient for instance, began to talk to this "ear". What would happen, indeed, if the ear spoke back? And what would it say?

So in my story, Christine, whose mind has been opened to a more interior, spiritual life after her friendship with Sondrine, the French-Canadian in the bed beside her – continues her growth and development after Sondrine's death via her contact with the ear shape (which, she believes, is a portal to a place very much like Magh Mell, the Plain of Happiness). It's quite possible her pain-relieving medication has persuaded her that the shape in the wall *is* a portal; or perhaps the drugs have merely helped her to see what was always there anyway. That's up to the reader to decide!

I also wanted to end the story with a fantastical, surreal image – to see how this would round off the story, give it a quirky end-note - and so couldn't resist the image of a physically better Christine climbing *into* the wall. Whether or not the reader actually believes Christine has entered this portal - to be reunited with her Canadian friend – or whether they think this is a crazy woman doing a crazy thing – is also up to them. I just wanted to try to collapse the reality of the situation a little, give some credence to the existence of the otherworld of Magh Mell.

The broad subject of the Otherworld is, when I think about it, an area I've visited before in my writing. In my play *The American Hotel*, two characters locate a time travelling portal in the bathroom of a hotel – and in my story "The Tribe" (featured in my debut collection of stories, *The Scattering*, published recently by Seren Books), the narrator travels 10,000 years back in time. So this is obviously an area I'm drawn to and hope to write more about.

CREATURES OF RATH AND BONE
BY
RACHEL STEINER

The rath stands at the center of the forest, the last vestige of a nation long dead left to ruin. After all this time, all of the research I'd done and the sacrifices I'd made to get here, it was real. And with a dread coiling around my throat like a noose, I know that Bridget is somewhere inside.

From the very beginning, something about the forest set me on edge, and I couldn't say why. It was just a feeling, a nagging instinct that every animal knew well: the feeling of being hunted down. I ignored it. After all, I was accustomed to hiking and camping trips like this one. The forests of the Britain and Ireland boasted no extant predators large enough to endanger a person. The wilderness didn't scare me, and even if it did, I wasn't alone. I was with my best friend, former roommate, and camping partner Bridget Galloway. We'd spent over a year planning the trip to Carterhaugh forest. It was supposed to be a week of camping in the forest, spending our days hiking and searching for some ancient ruins I'd heard were in the area, but had never been officially discovered. This was our last trip together before I went away to grad school, and if everything went well, it could change the course of my career.

"It should be around here somewhere, east of us," Bridget muttered, more to herself than me as she pointed vaguely to the right. I shrugged, giving up on finding the rath at this point. We'd already been wandering for three days, and the longer we walked northeast, the thicker the forest became. We seemed to be walking *away* from any sign of a man-made trail. Underbrush and dead leaves turned into brambles and sharp thicket. Trees turned from young, thin trunks into primeval giants. The canopy above us grew thicker, bathing everything in a blue-grey light. We had left the young, new forest and were nearly at the heart of the ancient woodland, a territory so foreign that it made paranoia slowly invade every part of my consciousness, strangling my rational mind. It was as if the forest was alive, a conscious entity. And it was playing with us.

"Didn't we pass that tree an hour ago?" I asked, pointing to an enormous beech tree. It had to be at least ten feet in diameter and probably over three hundred years old. Frowning, I grabbed my camera and clicked through picture after picture until I found a frame of that exact tree and showed it to Bridget.

Her eyes wide, Bridget snatched the camera from my hands and stared at the photograph, enlarging the image on the screen to make sure she was seeing the truth.

"This isn't possible," she murmured, staring at the tree before her eyes flickered over to me. I shrugged and took the camera, looping the strap back over my neck.

"It's fine, Bri, we're just lost. We'll find our way," I said, trying to remain positive. Bridget didn't answer, instead pulling her compass out of her pocket. Her eyes went wide and she held it out to me, her hand trembling. The needle kept spinning, even when I grabbed her wrist to stabilize her hand.

"There's probably a... magnetic field around here or something. It's not your fault, Bri," I said, and she visibly calmed at my simple, scientific reaction and deliberately ignored the shaking in my voice.

"Yeah," she said, taking the compass back. "So how do we find where we're going now?" I bit my lip, thinking. Any method of finding north without a magnet required a view of the sky or sunlight, but the trees blocked too much light.

"I guess we just keep moving, and maybe we'll move out of the field eventually," I said, allowing Bridget to take the lead again.

It started raining, turning the air cold and damp, making the ground muddy and even harder to walk through. The long trek was wearing on both of us. Every step felt like I was walking with a boot full of pebbles. And we were shivering, clutching our arms for warmth. The British Isles were colder than the Midwest in early summer, and neither of us were accustomed to the damp weather. There had to be somewhere to make camp.

So we kept walking, and with every step I could feel Bridget's ire growing. It was becoming clear that this had been a mistake. We shouldn't have come.

"Excuse me?" Bridget snapped. Shit, I hadn't meant to say that out loud.

"I just...you know how dangerous this is, Bri. We've both heard stories of hikers dying of exposure twenty feet from a major trail. No one even knows where we are." Bridget rolled her eyes.

"It was *your* idea. This was all just some plot to find that stupid ring fort you've been talking about. Well guess what, it's not fucking here, and no one cares! So it's your damn fault we're lost!"

"You're the one who couldn't read the damn map!"

"Don't you dare start blaming this on me! It was your idea to come here, Jennifer! 'Oh, I want to find this stupid fucking hill. It'll be the greatest discovery since King Tut!'" she mocked, imitating my voice with a whiny, pathetic tone. "Well guess what, you're not going to find a damn thing because we're going to die out here."

"Could you, for once in your life, not turn everything into a catastrophe?" I demanded. "You want to be immature, fine. I'll just be the responsible one—like I always am—and keep us alive." I turned away from her, ready to keep walking.

"Don't you dare try to pull that bullshit!" Bridget screamed, picking up a pine cone and hurling it at my back. It thumped against my shoulder and fell to the ground. Anger boiled in my veins and I whirled, but she kept yelling. "You always make me feel so fucking stupid! It's always' 'Oh Bridget, you can't do that.' And 'Oh, Bridget, actually, you're wrong!"

"Well maybe if you actually did some research before we went places, I wouldn't have to correct you all of the damn time!" I yelled back.

"Oh fuck off! You think you're *soo* smart with your double majors and your Ivy League grad schools. Well guess what, we all know you're nothing more than an insecure bitch!" I blinked, burying the rage bubbling beneath my skin as I gave Bridget my coldest smile.

"At least I'm not the actress who's terrified of being washed-up and broke by the time I'm thirty."

The sound of her palm meeting my flesh rang out in the otherwise silent woods. I raised my hand to my stinging cheek and stared at my best friend. Bridget was gaping at me with her hands covering her mouth in horror, her pale blue eyes wet with tears.

"Oh my God," she gasped. "Oh my God, Jen, I'm so sorry. I don't know what came over me." She sounded so horrified.

"It's okay," I sighed, running a hand through my hair. "It's this place, it's…not right," I murmured, the adrenaline in my system dissipated, leaving me exhausted and empty. Bri nodded, shrinking into herself.

"I love you, Jen," she said, tears in her eyes as she hugged me.

"I love you too. We'll get out of here, I promise," I responded, praying that I wasn't wrong.

We wandered for another hour, and Bridget's demeanor betrayed the growing fear she was trying so hard to hide. Meanwhile, I focused on the survival instincts telling me to flee. Those instincts began screaming when the forest finally began to thin, turning into a large clearing of barren earth. The only sign of life in the clearing was a ring of death cap mushrooms. A fairy ring, they were sometimes called. Entering one was said to be a lethal mistake. The dread pooling in my gut told me that something about that folktale had to be true. Before I could warn her, Bridget stepped inside the ring.

"No!" I yelled out, and she looked at me like I was crazy. Maybe I was. "We can't camp here," I said, the panic making my heart race and my voice rise and octave.

"I'm not leaving until you tell me why," she said, folding her arms and staring at me in a way that reminded me of my mother when she caught me trying to sneak out as a teenager.

"I… I just have a bad feeling about it," I mumbled. Bri raised an eyebrow and snorted.

"You have a bad feeling? Really? Of all the things you could have a 'bad feeling' about and you choose the circle of mushrooms?" When she put it that way, I sounded like a complete idiot. "You're the scientist. You're the rational one. Come on, Jen, what happened to that crazy logic of yours? Now come here and help." I blushed, rubbing the back of my neck in embarrassment.

"At least I'm not the one who won't say 'Macbeth' during a show," I muttered, stepping into the circle despite my better judgment.

"I heard that," she said with a wry smile, handing me a tent stake. Well, at least our friendship was back to normal, even if the dread rising from my stomach and into my chest was making it hard to breathe.

As night fell, it grew cold and silent. No animals stalking through the underbrush. All I could hear was the sound of my breathing and Bridget's beside me as we lay in the tent. The only thing keeping me awake was fear.

The wind began around midnight, creating a shrill howl as it blew through the trees. Through it all, I told myself it was only the wind, but the sound grew louder, turning to the deafening thunder of hoof beats and baying hounds. The tent began to shake and terror blossoming in my chest. I laid flat on my back as the sound changed, becoming the screaming, high-pitched keening of inhuman voices and a resounding echo that made the ground itself tremble.

I tried to tell myself it was an animal, but the keening grew louder, until it was right outside the tent. Terror kept me frozen in place. I could make out the vague shape of Bridget's sleeping body in my periphery as the shadows around me seemed to shift and grow. The keening crescendoed to a deafening volume, a noise overwhelming enough to liquefy my organs and turn my bones to dust. A heavy weight crushed my chest, paralysing me as the shadows came alive in a swirling vortex around us, ripping the tent to shreds as they landed.

One humanoid figure emerged from the horde. His skeletal body solidified as he walked with a slow, steady gait to the remains of our tent and I could see the shine of slick blood over his white, exposed ribs. I looked into the creature's eyes, eyes that reflected an eerie green in the darkness, conveying an animalistic hunger as he stared at me. Antlers grew from the creature's head, clawing towards the sky. He carried a bow with arrows on his back. Shadow hounds followed his every step, baying and snapping like rabid beasts, their eyes the glowing red of dying embers.

The creature pointed with one too-long finger to Bridget's sleeping form. I opened my mouth but no sound came out. The shadows began to creep across my vision as the creatures surrounded Bridget, reaching out to touch her, pet her, smell her hair. One of them licked her exposed neck with its long black tongue but she didn't stir. With a grin of terrible, too-white teeth, the horned man grabbed Bridget's prone body as if she weighed nothing, and the shadows began to swirl around my vision, blinding me. I screamed, turning my throat raw as my voice blended in with that of the horde, until I could no longer differentiate between my keening and theirs.

I woke with a start, my chest heaving as I stared down at my sleeping back, wiggling my fingers just to prove that I could. I was afraid to look up, to see a horned man waiting to kill me. Laughing at my fear, I wiped the sweat from my brow.

"Ugh, Bri, You won't believe the dream I just had," I groaned, hoping that my voice would wake her. The forest might not have been full of strange creatures, but that didn't mean I wanted to be awake by myself.

Bridget didn't answer. I turned to look at her, hoping that at least seeing her sleeping body would ground me in reality. But Bridget was gone, and in her place was a ripped, bloody sleeping bag.

Scrambling to my feet, I swore under my breath, eyes searching my surroundings. The tent was torn to shreds. Clawing at my hair while panic bubbled up in my throat and lungs, I struggled to think of what to do. Those creatures, the things I saw were real. It was impossible, it had to be, but Bridget was gone. Bridget was gone and those *things* had her. They had her and God only knew what they were doing to her. I had to find her.

I scoured the ground, praying for some sign of Bridget, a drop of blood, a button, anything. My flashlight saved me. A glint of gold on a pine branch, a strand of her hair illuminated by the beam. I clung to it like a lifeline. The forest ahead of me was dark, older than anything I'd encountered before. It was almost impassable, but my flashlight revealed another strand of hair. Slashing through thickets and brambles with my knife, I grabbed it. There was more hair ahead of me. Breadcrumbs.

I didn't want to imagine the ways those creatures could be hurting her, but my mind kept jumping to them, more and more as the shadows grew darker, the trees more twisted. I don't know how long I searched those woods, hacking and slashing my way forward. My body screamed at me to give up, and I wondered if I would ever see the sun again. Then, the trees finally broke, revealing the clearing at the center of the forest and the location that had been my original location for taking this trip: the rath.

* * *

The rath stands at the center of the forest, the last vestige of a nation left to ruin. It's real.

After all this time, all of the research I'd done and the sacrifices I'd made to get here, it's real. And with a dread coiling around my throat like a noose, I know Bridget is somewhere inside.

Taking a deep breath, I ignore the pounding of my heart and run up the side of the hill to the crumbling ruins of a once great fort. At the center of the ring fort stands one monolith, carved with spirals and a horned figure. In front of it lies a dark, stone-lined hole. I run to it, almost too afraid to breathe.

The hole is lined in stone, built into the hill with a staircase leading down, deep into darkness. I flinch at the sight of fresh blood on the steps. Below is cave darkness. I can't see beyond the beam of my flashlight and my heartbeat pounds in my ears, the only noise I can hear as I begin the slow descent into the earth.

The rath is cold; goosebumps form along my arms and I shiver, the flashlight shaking in my hand as I descend. The walls take on a vaulted shape that has to be man-made. Strange mosaics made of shells and bone cover every inch of space, forming intricate and strange pagan patterns. I've never heard of anything like it and my heart longs to photograph and record it, if only to prove that it exists. It's too complex to be primitive, but ring forts were at least a thousand years old. I want to study it, but Bridget's absence makes the darkness unbearable. I can't linger, not if I ever want to find her. Besides, as I descend, I start to hear things, strange murmurings I can't understand, but still make me want to bolt back to the surface. I'm not alone anymore, and my pace down the steps quickens.

Finally, my feet meet solid, flat ground. A tunnel stretches before me, its winding walls still covered with the strange mosaics. The whispering grows louder, to the din of many voices as I run toward a flickering light at the end of the tunnel.

The light comes from a large, circular room filled with creatures that look human but aren't. Their forms are humanoid, but something about them is just...wrong. Some are too tall and thin, their backs nearly hollow. Some have wings, some bear animalistic or plant-like characteristics. They are fey, wild, monstrous creatures that have no place in the modern world.

The horde's attention is turned toward a dais at the front of the chamber. There, a creature resembling a human female sits in a throne wrought from tree roots. Her beauty is a thing of nightmares, of bone cut sharp enough to kill. Her skin is white and poreless in a way that no animal's could be. She wears a sheer white gown of gossamer cobwebs, and atop her white hair sits a crown of antlers. Her fingers curl with an extra joint, and her limbs are too long. And her eyes, her eyes contain no iris, no sclera, only a void-like pupil. My throat, constricts in a whimper at the sight of her, the Queen of nightmares.

Before the Queen's throne lies an altar, and presiding over it is the horned man who'd taken Bridget. He wields a knife made of glass, poising it over the prone body of my bruised and bloodied best friend. Without thinking, I shout her name, fighting through the crowd to get her. The queen gestures and they part for me, allowing me to run, pocket knife in hand, to the stone where Bridget is tied.

Her hair is matted down with dried blood and her ankle looks purple. She isn't conscious. I flip open the blade of my knife, sawing through the ropes that bind her while the creatures watch, waiting for me to entertain them.

"Do you wish to take your friend's place in our Tithe?" the Queen asks, speaking modern English. My head jerks up and I shudder as I meet her oil-slick gaze.

Her grin is a trap. I grab Bridget's limp hand and squeeze it.

"L-let her go," I stammer, trying to hide the shaking in my voice and the Queen laughs.

"That won't be happening, my dear," she croons in her spider-silk voice. "You trespassed and there is a price to pay."

"What price? Whatever it is, I'll pay it."

The Queen rises, her gossamer gown draping about her body like shimmering moonlight. It would have been breathtaking if the sight of her didn't make me want to scream.

"We are of the forest, the earth. These lands are of our flesh. We have been here before your kind was in its infancy, and we will endure long after your demise. You and yours are simply...vermin."

"Just tell me what the fuck you want!"

"Once every seven years, we require a sacrifice, a Tithe. You have trespassed on our lands. One of you must die to compete the Tithe."

"You want to kill us," I said, horror making my stomach roil as Bridget stirs, groaning and blinking.

"The Tithe only requires one."

"Take her! Take her and let me go! I don't want to die!" Bridget wails, struggling against her bonds. I stare at her in shock. I'd brought myself into near certain death to save her, and she was willing to throw me to them! Maybe the Queen was right, we are nothing but vermin. There is no friendship or love where survival is concerned.

"You have your sacrifice, take her," I growl, tempted to plunge my knife into Bridget myself, but dread twists my stomach into an aching knot as I look into the queen's black eyes. I will not be leaving this rath alive.

"I think not. My court needs fresh blood, and there are not many of you humans so willing to sacrifice your own." The queen grins, a wicked minefield of a smile that is all teeth.

I try to back away, only to meet the point of the horned man's knife. This is a dream, I try to convince myself, but the scene keeps unfolding before my unblinking eyes. The hunter stabs out Bridget's eyes while she screams and I do nothing. He slashes her throat and her scream is cut short, turning into a gurgle as she chokes on her own blood. I am numb as Bridget's head lolls back, her mutilated eyes accusing me, blaming me for everything.

The hunter takes a bone chalice from another creature's gnarled hands, allowing Bridget's blood to flow off the table and into the cup. He presents it to his queen, kneeling at her feet. She slits her own wrist with one talon, allowing her blood to mix with Bridget's before the hunter does the same to himself.

He walks toward me, cup in hand. My lips close against the chalice's rim. With one strong hand he forces it to my lips and yanks my jaw open, pouring in the blood. It tastes of copper and salt. I nearly gag choking it down. He stares into my eyes, drawing his knife again. It's the same knife he used to kill Bridget, still wet with her blood. He slices the knife across my throat and I am triumphant as I stare into the face of the friend I betrayed. I got the better end of the deal. Bridget is dead, like the rest of the humans will be. I will outlast them all. When I wake, it is with the call of the hunt and the horde in my veins. I know not what I once was, only what I am now.

I am one of them, a creature of rath and bone.

BACKGROUND ON CREATURES OF RATH AND BONE
BY
RACHEL STEINER

The Faeries of the Britain and Ireland are not the small, sprightly beings we think of today. Faeries are powerful nature spirits, and even the more benevolent of these creatures were known to play cruel tricks on humans. Though stories of the Fair Folk are found throughout Britain and Ireland, they are most prominent in Ireland and Scotland. Among the Irish, they are known as the Aos Sidhe, a supernatural race that lives beneath the earth and came from a world parallel to our own. In Scotland, they are known as the Sith (both words are pronounced the same, and have the same translation). The word Sidhe translates as "the mounds," and thus they became known as the People of the Mounds. These mounds were often ancient ring forts, known as raths. Even today, many locals will refuse to venture near the raths at night, just in case something lingers there.

People living in areas where the Fae were supposed to frequent were known for employing various superstitions to keep them happy and away from human settlements. This included offerings of milk to appease the Fae, using certain plants to ward them off and hanging cold iron above the doors of a house. Cold iron was said to be one of the Fae's only weaknesses. People would not call the Sidhe "faeries," believing it could anger them. Instead, they were referred to as "the Good People," "the Fair Folk," "the Good Neighbors," and "the Little Folk," among other names. Their powers included the ability to bestow or take away good fortune, the ability to cause or cure illness, control over the weather, influence fertility, and fly. One of the Sidhe's most important powers was glamour, a magical illusion that made people see whatever the Faery wanted them to. This ability extended into shapeshifting, with many Fae taking several forms. Faeries could also make travelers become lost, changing the appearance of the wilderness around them and leading them astray, a phenomenon known as being fairy-led. In literature, this behavior is seen by Puck in Shakespeare's *A Midsummer Night's Dream.*

Legend states that the Fae are tricky and easy to displease. Angering them could be caused by something as simple as picking the wrong flower. They do not like trespassers, and entering into one of their sacred places, such as an old forest or a fairy ring could earn their displeasure. These places were often considered gateways into the Otherworld, and as such were avoided. For mortals invited into the Fae realm, eating Faery food would either trap them, keeping them in the Otherworld forever, or cause them to never be satisfied by human food and drink and starve, as occurs in pre-Raphaelite poet Christina Rosetti's *Goblin Market*, which uses this folklore as an allegory for the dangers of sexuality.

Different sources claim different origins for the Fae. These theories can be divided into pre- and post-Christian influences over British folklore. One pre-Christian explanation for faeries claims that they are an older race of people, the first inhabitants of Ireland and Great Britain. Another theory claims that the Faeries are a form of ancestor worship and that faeries themselves were spirits of the dead. In this line of thought, the Otherworld ruled by the Fae is considered the afterlife. Other scholars postulate that faeries are ancient Celtic gods who dwindled in influence with the coming of Christianity, turning from deities into demons and nature spirits.

Theories concerning the origin of faeries that clearly come from a Christian tradition often involve the ideas of demons and hell. Some of these ideas come from folklorist Robert Kirk, author of *The Secret Commonwealth of Elves, Fauns and Fairies*. One idea claims that the Fae are fallen angels, whose sin was that of indecision. They did not follow Lucifer's prideful fall, but did not choose to remain in Heaven either. For their lack of conviction, God cursed them to remain on earth for eternity. Another theory states that the Faeries were spirits too wicked to get into Heaven but too good for Hell, and thus were left in a limbo state. This sometimes earns more chaotic denizens of Faerie lore the name "the Unforgiven Dead."

Faerie society is divided between what Irish author, poet, and mystic W.B Yeats termed the Solitary and Trooping Fae. Solitary faeries are often attached to a particular area, a stream or tree for example, and are usually seen alone. Their disposition is unpredictable, as they can either be helpful domestic spirits, such as a Brownie, a spirit that will help care for a household so long as it is acknowledged; or they can be hostile, such as the river spirit Jenny Greenteeth, who drowns unsuspecting humans. Solitary Fae, while powerful and often fearsome, are usually considered to be on the lower end of Faerie society. The true power lies with the Trooping Faeries, who are akin to aristocracy.

Trooping Faeries are so named because they could be sighted traveling in large processions. Their hierarchy resembles that of human noble courts, complete with knights, lords, ladies, and a leader in the form of a king or queen. Trooping Faeries are said to appear like extraordinarily beautiful humans.

According to Scottish lore, the Trooping Fae can be divided into two courts: Seelie and Unseelie. The two words translate as roughly "holy" and "unholy," and the Seelie Court is generally seen as benevolent and kinder to humans than the Unseelie Court, which is said to be malicious and deadly. The Seelie Court may occasionally steal away a mortal or play tricks on humans, but they are neutral towards mankind as a whole. The Unseelie Court, however, is considered evil by human standards, targeting humans to harm and kill them simply because they have the power to do so.

Connected to the Unseelie Court is a malicious force known as the Sluagh, translated as "the horde." Said to be the spirits of the restless dead, they formed a flying crowd sweeping up people in their path. They are often associated with the Wild Hunt. Some legends insinuate that because the Fae cannot reproduce, the Sluagh kidnap souls to add to their number.

Faeries were often known to kidnap humans, either children or adults. Sometimes, they would replace them with a replica known as a Changeling, and other times the person would simply disappear. The kidnapping of adults happens in such well known tales as "La Belle Dame Sans Merci" by John Keats and "The Ballad of Tam Lin." Both of these stories insinuate that the men kidnapped will die by the Faeries' hands.

'The Ballad of Tam Lin', which comes from the Scottish borderlands, contains the idea of a 'Tithe to Hell' that Faeries must pay once every seven years. In order to spare one of their own, they sacrifice a human. 'Tam Lin' dates back to at least 1549, and it is thought that the tithe to Hell is a post-Christian addition to faery lore. 'Creatures of Rath and Bone', while heavily inspired by general Faerie lore, was particularly influenced by this ballad.

The Faerie legends have been adapted here to fit the pre-Christian conception of Faeries as a lost race, or possibly, a species undiscovered by humans. I liked the idea that two humans, alone in the forest, would be vulnerable to these creatures. Unprepared and lost in the wild, humans are not the apex predators we believe ourselves to be. The two girls trespass on ancient rules they are unfamiliar with, reminding the reader that we are no longer suited to live in the natural world. Faeries, as nature spirits, control this domain and violating their laws brings consequences. By setting foot inside a fairy ring, they summon the Unseelie Sluagh, led by the Welsh figure of Gwyn Ap Nudd, one of the leaders of the Wild Hunt. The Faeries' home, the rath, was inspired both by the ancient ring forts that Faeries supposedly inhabit in Ireland, and structures like the Glastonbury Tor, a Neolithic hill in southern England that is supposedly the hill where Gwyn Ap Nudd rules the Faerie Underworld. In my tale, Gwyn is not the Faerie's leader, rather an unnamed queen is. She is based on the Queen of Elphame in 'The Ballad of Young Tam Lin.' At the end of some versions of the ballad, she bemoans not plucking out Tam Lin's eyes when she had the chance, a common punishment for those who have seen the Fae and lived. This is the reason for Bridget's gruesome death. Jennifer's fate is connected to the idea of the Sluagh, the Unforgiven Dead. For betraying her friend, she both figuratively and literally becomes the monster she once feared.

THE FINAL ANSWER
BY
WILL GRAHAM

"Fuck him", Melissa Purcell thought as she pressed on the accelerator. "And his wife, and fuck his promises. Fuck him. Sideways. With a broken hockey stick." She downshifted and took the curve a little too sharply, bringing her back from her mental rant.

'Now, darling',' her grandfather's voice whispered in her mind. 'What did you expect from a relationship with a married man?' As always, she thought, Pa had a point. What did she expect? Had she really fallen for the empty promises, the romantic dinners, the secret of their relationship? Yes. Did she really believe his promises were true? Did she really deep down inside think there was a happily ever after for them? Well.... yes.

'Even the best of us get fooled', she thought. 'Even the best of the best. And I'm supposed to be at least pretty good, dammit. But when you get right down to it, we can all be fooled when we want to be, and this is all on me, dammit. I made my choices.'

An ugly row at her apartment that very morning. He stomping out and slamming the door, she sitting on the couch, refusing to give in to the tears that lurked just under her eyelids. Thinking to herself this was the second time her heart had been firmly broken, the first being her ex-husband who turned out to be a degenerate gambler. 'You sure know how to pick your men, don't you?' she lashed herself mentally again. Before her tears erupted, she packed two bags, threw out all the perishables, jumped into her convertible, and took off for parts unknown.

How long had it been since she'd taken a break, much less an actual vacation? Melissa honestly tried to remember and could not; her work kept her busy to an extreme; another airport, another temporary office, another exhausting consultation, then off to the next. She was fortunate in that her services were in high demand on a global level, and even more fortunate that her admittedly outrageous fees were even higher.

Not quite forty, pretty in a serious yet stunning way, and blessed with a mind so sharp she once overheard a man mutter to the rest of his group, "she's so goddamned smart she'd scare Carl Sagan." She walked past as if she hadn't heard it, taking it as the compliment it was intended and hiding a slight smile as she moved past them.

She got off the motorway and wandered where she chose. She'd deliberately left her cellphone behind, as well as her iPad. No phone calls, no emails, no nothing. Not for a few days at least.

Melissa had absolutely no idea where she was heading or when she'd end up but, wherever it was, it would be cut off from the outside world as much as possible. There would be absolutely none of today's instant communication methods or gadgets anywhere near her.

She was free.

For the first time in forever, she was free of any responsibility, any commitment, any anything. Her business issues were currently resolved, there was nothing pending (though it was only a matter of days most likely, before that changed and, in her current frame of mind, whatever it was could wait), she had no children, no pets to hold her back. Nothing at all between her and a well-deserved rest and relaxation. For a weekend or a week, it didn't matter. She didn't owe anyone anything and intended to savor every single moment of it.

She drove aimlessly, seeing everything and looking for nothing, eventually stopping for lunch at a tearoom. "How many, miss?" asked the waitress as she walked in.

"Just me," Melissa replied with a smile.

She received a smile in return and the waitress said, "Very good, miss. Table or booth?"

"Booth if you have one."

"That we do," the waitress said. "That we do indeed."

Melissa was led to a beautifully inlaid booth in the far left corner. Force of habit made her choose the side with her back to the wall and she could clearly see the entrance.

"Cup o' tea, miss?"

"Do you have Lapsang Souchong?"

The waitress smiled at her. "Of course we do, miss."

"That would be perfect, then. A pot, please."

"Of course," came the reply. The waitress handed her a one-sheet menu. "Take your time, please. We're not exactly overrun at the moment."

Again, out of habit, Melissa swept the room with her eyes. The three couples in the room were simply there, enjoying the food and each other. She bit her lip when she remembered this morning, fighting back a touch of jealousy over the apparently happy couples.

The waitress came back with a teapot and one cup. Carefully pouring, she set the cup in front of Melissa. "Have you decided what you'd like, miss?"

Melissa only glanced at the menu. "What's your soup of the day?"

"Tomato and basil."

"Perfect," Melissa replied. "With a toasted cheese sandwich and a small order of chips, please."

"Just a few minutes, miss, and we'll have you all tucked up and cosy." She bustled off as Melissa took her first sip of the piping hot tea and raised her eyebrows in quiet approval.

Her food was in front of her shortly. After making certain she had all she needed, the waitress sauntered away to greet a new customer coming in the door.

Melissa ate slowly, savouring every bite and sip. The sandwich was perfect, the chips thick, crispy and perfectly soft inside, the soup was magnificent, obviously made fresh in the kitchen. When she was finished, she politely raised one finger to the waitress, signaling for the cheque. Melissa paid in cash, leaving a sizable tip. Waving to the waitress as she left, she got back into her car, started the engine, and drove off.

Deciding on a whim, Melissa drove back to the M4. According to her GPS, she was in for about a four hour drive, so she sat back in the driver's seat, slipped in a CD of some of her favorite American rock tunes, and settled in.

She followed the M4 and then - as directed by her GPS system, took Junction 32. Her GPS guided her the rest of the way, and she simply relaxed, letting the sounds of Bruce Springsteen and his glory days wash over her at almost full volume.

Realising she was getting tired and most likely needed to stop for the night, see noted an exit up ahead and, after turning off, kept her eyes open for a town or village. Smothering a creaking yawn, she was pleasantly surprised to quickly see a sign that read 'Gweneglys'.

Lowering her speed to the legal posted limit, she passed a snow-white church and a cluster of buildings. She read the signs as she passed; 'Fresh Meats Daily! Alexander Konrath, Prop.' Right next to that storefront was another with a sign that read 'Turritt's Baked Goods. M. Turritt, Owner.'

'Butcher and Baker,' she thought. 'Where's the Candlestick Maker?' She drove deeper into the small village, smiling to herself at the weak joke. Keeping an eye open for an inn or perhaps even a bed and breakfast, she made a right turn and - as if by magic - there it was right in front of her: 'The Welcome In(n).'

The name appealed to her, a gentle pun that made her smile, and she pulled in. Walking through the front door, she heard a voice say, "Good Evening, Miss!"

She turned to see a balding slightly chubby man at the front desk. "My name is George Smalls. Welcome!"

Melissa stepped over to the desk. "Do you have a room for the evening?"

"We most certainly do," he said. He turned to the pegboard behind him. "Are you a superstitious lass?"

Melissa laughed. "Hardly. Why?"

"Room 13 is open, and it's one of our nicer rooms. With the windows open, a most lovely breeze comes in."

"Sounds perfect," she replied.

Smalls turned the large, leather-bound register to her. "If you'll just sign in, please."

"I assume you take American Express?" she asked as she picked up the pen.

"Of course we do," he said. She handed him her Platinum Card, and he ran it through, returning it with a small flourish. He handed over the key to Room 13.

"Am I too late for dinner?" she asked. "Something cold will be fine."

"Oh, I believe we can do a little better than that, Miss, uh," he glanced at the register. "Purcell. Let me speak to my wife while you get settled. Do you need any help with your luggage?"

"Thank you, but no. I can handle it."

She went back outside and took her overnight bag from the backseat; no need for the suitcase locked in the boot. Going back inside, she was met again by Smalls and his equally chubby wife.

"Good evening, ma'am," Mrs. Smalls said in greeting. "How about a nice bit of roast and Yorkshire pudding?"

"That," Melissa said, "sounds perfect. Just let me put my bag in my room and I'll be right back."

She found her room easily enough. Pausing long enough to put her bag inside the room and wash her face after the long day, she went back downstairs and into the small dining room where she ordered a drink to accompany her meal.

There was only one man in the room, alternating sips of coffee and what looked to be cognac. Smalls directed her to a table on the opposite side of the room.

In what seemed like less than a moment later, a waiter appeared carrying a tray. He looked vaguely familiar to Melissa, but she couldn't quite place him. He laid the food out, finishing with a large glass of crystal-clear lager that beckoned Melissa's taste buds.

"Will there be anything else, madam?"

"Not for now, thank you."

"Just let me know. I'll check back on you in a bit."

"Thank you."

Hungrier than she thought she was, Melissa dove into the meal. Midway through, the man across the room picked up his coffee and cognac and approached her.

"May I join you?" he asked politely. "I've been sitting here alone for most of the evening."

Melissa arched an eyebrow. "Are you married?" she asked immediately.

He laughed. "Good heavens, no. My name is Turritt, Michael Turritt. I own the bakery down the street."

He too rang a faint bell in her memory, but again she was too tired and emotionally wrung-out to place him. She considered a moment, deciding a little conversation wouldn't hurt. "Please," she said, indicating the chair across from her.

He sat down gracefully. "You're Melis...?"

She gently interrupted him, used to being recognised. "Yes, I am."

He nodded. "I thought I recognised you. I've seen you interviewed several times, and of course, there's your books. A genuine pleasure to meet you."

"And you, Mr. Turritt." She continued to eat her dinner.

"A fascinating career you've had," he said. "May I ask how you got started in it?"

Dabbing her lips with a napkin before replying, Melissa took a sip of her lager. "How does anyone get into anything? I guess it started when I was young, maybe around twelve or so. My father had a book about famous British crimes, and I slipped it out of his library and read it. Something about it all lit a spark in me, and I decided then and there to make the subject of criminality my life's work."

"Interesting, in one so young," he said. "Please go on. I've read all your books, except your latest. I own it, but have not had the chance to read it yet. Perhaps you'd sign it for me before you leave."

"I'd be happy to," she said. "Once that spark or whatever you want to call it turned into a quest for knowledge, I read anything and everything I could get my hands on. Constantly studying, trying to understand what made people do some kinds of things."

"You mean like serial killers?"

"Especially serial killers," she said. "No apparent motive, no connection to the victims, simply random. For whatever reason, it fascinated me."

He nodded. "And of course, the most famous one of all..."

She shrugged. "I don't believe we'll ever know the truth on that," she said. "Too much time has passed, the history too muddled. No," she said as she shook her head firmly. "We'll never know the answer on that one."

"Isn't that what you new book is about?" he asked.

"Yes, but it's more a collection of theories and possibilities than actual evidence."

"Sounds intriguing," he said, encouraging her. "Tell me more."

"Thank you, Mr. Turritt, but perhaps another time. It's been a very long day."

"Of course," he said, standing. "I beg your pardon, I should have realised. Perhaps tomorrow morning you could come to my bakery down the street? We could continue this conversation over coffee and croissants."

"Perhaps so," she said, standing up herself. "But right now, all I'm interested in is the bed that's calling my name."

"Of course," he said with an easy smile. "Good night, Ms. Purcell. And please do try and stop in tomorrow. I'd dearly love to have you sign my copy of your book."

"Good night, Mr. Turritt. I'll try and stop in before I leave."

They shook hands politely as strangers do, and Melissa turned and headed up the stairs to her room.

She was asleep almost instantly after turning off the light by the bed.

* * *

Melissa awoke with a start. Four strong hands pinned her limbs to the bed. A shadow moved in the room, lighting candles. When the room was awash in candlelight, the shadowy figure stepped forward. She gasped when she recognized Michael Turritt.

"Ah, you're awake," he said.

'Don't panic,' she told herself. 'You've talked yourself out of worse situations.' Aloud, she asked, "What the Hell is going on here?"

"Well, that's a bit complicated," Turritt said.

Melissa craned her neck enough to see the two men holding her down. One of them was the waiter from downstairs. "It would appear we have time," she said aloud, trying hard to keep the fear from her voice.

"I'll give you the short version," Turritt said. "Contrary to popular belief, there really is a Gateway to Hell. It actually exists, just outside of Nevada, in the States. It opened only once in all of history, during a violent storm, and briefly at that. Some of us managed to escape. We made our way home, so to speak, and decided to start over. London itself would have been a bit too obvious, so we simply relocated. I can't explain it myself, but every once in a while we - and our village - pop up, so to speak. The rest of the time we spend in.... oh, I suppose you would call it 'Limbo'."

"'We'?"

"Oh, yes. You see, the three of us share a common bond."

"And what bond is that?" she asked. "Aside from scaring the Hell out of women in the middle of the night?"

"You shall see, my dear," Turritt replied. He lifted the surgeon's bag into view. "Allow me to introduce myself; 'Michael Turritt' is a convenient alias. My real name is Montague. Montague John Druitt."

'This cannot be happening!' Melissa's mind shrieked.

"The gentleman on your left, who is known as 'Alex Konrath' the local butcher is really Aaron Kosminski. And finally, the man on your right, your waiter for the evening, Francis Tumblety."

Melissa's stomach twisted as she recognized the names.

"I'm sure you noticed the name of our little village," Turritt/Druitt went on. "'Gwyneglwys' It translates quite easily." He smiled and waved his left arm in a semi-circle, ending with his palm upturned. "'White Church. I'm sure you saw the building as you drove in. It's actually not so much a church as it is a.... chapel." He made the same motion with his right hand, his eyes turning to ice. "Or, as we prefer to call it, 'Whitechapel.' I'm surprised you didn't make the connection."

'This cannot be happening,' she screamed in her mind. 'It just can't be.'

"Every great once in a while, someone perfect comes along," Druitt said. "Someone just like you. You're about to know the answer you've been seeking your entire adult life."

"What do you mean?" She struggled against the hands that held her down. She may as well have tried to wrestle a brick wall.

Druitt reached into the small bag and pulled out a butcher's knife. "As you admitted to me, you've wondered since the age of twelve who Jack the Ripper was."

He twirled the knife absently between his fingers, the candlelight flashing from it.

Melissa opened her mouth to scream, and Druitt shoved a rough gag into her mouth. "The answer, my dear, is quite simple...."

He paused dramatically.

"We all are...."

"I get her cunny," Kosminski whispered.

"Of course, dear fellow," Druitt said. "You always do...."

Shortly after that, Melissa started screaming into the gag.

Just before dawn, she stopped.

* * *

One year later
The Times
November 8

Today marks one year since the disappearance of internationally renowned criminologist and author Melissa Jennifer Purcell. Ms. Purcell disappeared after last being seen in a village café outside London. The last known CCTV footage of her vehicle, which has never been found, shows her heading towards the M4.

New Scotland Yard, the Federal Bureau of Investigation, and the United States Secret Service have used her criminology consultation services. All three agencies, in addition to the London Metropolitan Police Force are still bringing all possible manpower to bear as the investigation continues.

Sales of Ms. Purcell's latest non-fiction book, 'Who Was Jack the Ripper?' (published under her maiden/professional name 'M.J. Kelly') have skyrocketed since she vanished, leading some skeptics to believe her disappearance is nothing more than a publicity stunt.

Police authorities do not agree with this line of thought, and the search continues.

BACKGROUND ON THE FINAL ANSWER
BY
WILL GRAHAM

Back in the now ancient year of 1967, my father was transferred from Chicago to Las Vegas, the city I still consider home.

Behind the school I was attending at the time was the back of a wondrous place called Charleston Plaza Mall. A grocery store, a drug store, a newsstand, a bookstore, record shop, chain stores with racks and racks and racks of paperback books (remember, this was 1967).

One day, for no real reason, my brother and I wandered over to the mall after school before heading home. Going into the record store first, I saw an album that caught my attention instantly: the RCA Camden recording of the 1959 Joseph E. Levine film 'Jack the Ripper'. A crude illustration of a top-hatted man in an alley as a woman approached beckoned me. Priced at a budget busting $0.99, I went through my pockets and came up a bit short. Fortunately, my brother was kind enough to let me borrow a quarter, and the transaction was done. (I'm not sure, but I believe I still owe him that quarter.) A combination of film dialogue, with additional narration by Sir Cedric Hardwicke filling in the gaps due to time constraints, the album had me mesmerised. The idea of a killer prowling a city and remaining undetected fascinated me.

Flash forward to 1968 and we went to Indiana to visit my mother's family. Her sister - my aunt - was the local librarian and when I mentioned Jack, she held up one finger and disappeared into the stacks.

When she came back, she handed me a copy of Tom Cullen's 'Autumn of Terror', one of the few books about the Ripper case at the time.

By the end of that summer, I had the book memorised.

Jump to 1976, and the arrival of the Holy Grail: Donald Rumbelow's 'The Complete Jack the Ripper'. I asked for it as a birthday present and, as she loved to tease me about it for years, my mother was mortified but she bought it anyway.

With the self-confidence that comes from being nineteen years old, I wrote a letter to Mr. Rumbelow, care of his publisher. Said letter contained possibly a million and one questions about the case. Surprisingly, stunningly, Mr. Rumbelow had the grace and courtesy to actually reply to my letter, trying to answer as many questions as he could.

I still have that first edition. And I still have that letter.

Today, of course, there are hundreds of books on the investigation, from Patricia Cornwell's massive personal investigation to the computer generated 'CSI: Whitechapel' by John G. Bennett and Paul Begg. Jack has inspired many fictional works too. From short stories (Robert Bloch's immortal 'Yours Truly, Jack the Ripper', adapted into a terrifying episode of 'Boris Karloff's 'Thriller' television series being my personal favorite) to novels such as 'Prince Jack' (speculating on the supposed guilt of Edward, Duke of Clarence, who was a popular suspect at the time) to movies ('Murder By Decree' is - for me - the single best Sherlock Holmes movie and Jack the

Ripper story ever done) to the flawless first season of BBC series 'Whitechapel' starring Rupert Penry-Jones, Phil Davis, and Steve Pemberton as a most unlikely and eccentric trio investigating a modern day 'Jack'.

The two part mini-series 'Jack the Ripper' starring Michael Caine and the late Lewis Collins is a stand-out in every sense of the word. Although more than slightly fictionalised, it is none the less a fascinating look into 1888, when Jack prowled the back alleys of Whitechapel and how law enforcement did everything possible and available to them at the time to end the reign of terror.

For some reason, the last 'official' victim, Mary Jane Kelly, seems the most fascinating. The single most savage of the murders, there are people who visit her grave annually on the date of her death, leaving flowers for her, saying prayers, and giving the poor woman the attention and affection she never had in real life.

Computer games, board games, the recently and massively detailed table-top game 'Whitechapel' and the supplement 'Dear Boss' all sit on the 'Ripper Bookcase', along with far too many others to list.

Like Melissa Purcell in my story, I don't believe we'll ever know the real truth. We can research and speculate and theorize, but I doubt seriously we will ever know the real identity of Jack. A private joke among myself and some friends is 'I just bought a new book about Jack the Ripper.... they've positively identified him and, this time, they MEAN it!"

As to why Jack continues to fascinate us.... I don't have an answer for that question, either. I can only speak for myself and say there is something darkly intriguing, fascinating, and puzzling about the entire matter.

Who was Jack? How did he elude the massive manhunt for him? Why did he choose the victims he did?

Was there a connection we don't know about between them or were his choices entirely random, victims of convenience, simply being in the wrong place at the wrong time?

We'll never know.

Over the years, however, it certainly has been interesting to try and figure it out....

CAMP 46
BY
PETULA MITCHELL

Jacob Jupp had spent his whole life living in a shack in the woods. He owned the shack and his family had owned the woods for generations. They had made a living coppicing, bodging and making charcoal. Sometimes the living had been meagre and sometimes good according to the prevailing fashions of the day. Old Jupp, as the villagers called him even though he was barely 55, had had enough of living there though. So when an offer came from developers to buy the woods and build thirty houses and flats on the land he took it. His one proviso was that he should have the biggest house in the development. On the plans it looked splendid. A four bedroom country home fit for a man of new-found substance and wealth.

It was a long wait for the planning permission to be granted and was kicked around the planning authorities for several years, but finally the go ahead was given. Jacob Jupp knew he'd finally weathered his last winter in the shack by a wood-fired boiler. He dared to dream he might finally be warm and dry, the pains in his bones would not be so acute and he would gradually wash the ground-in charcoal out of his black hands. He even fancied he would find himself a wife. Perhaps a Thai or Filipino lady would consent to live with him and brighten up his later years. Perhaps he might even have a little family of his own. The local women would barely acknowledge him. If he ventured to the pubs in the village they would recoil from the smell of wood smoke and his black charcoal-stained fingers. Old Jupp the Woodsie was never going to find a local girl.

A deep sense of loneliness had afflicted Jacob Jupp for many years. He had known love just once in his life when a family of travellers had pitched up on his land for a summer. They had helped him in his work and had made good money between them. The travellers' daughter, Ruby, was as pretty as the wild flowers and as sweet as the summer rain. On hot summer nights he had held her close as her sighs rose up to meet the moonlight. He still remembered the softness of her face against his neck and the sweet taste of her lips against his own. However , as travellers must, she moved on. The call of the road was greater than her love for him. Also, the family were superstitious and swore the woods were haunted. The figure of a man in grey regularly appeared from nowhere and just as quickly melted back into the trees. Jupp tried to tell them it was just an old tramp that frequented the woods and had done so for many years. The locals weren't keen on venturing far into the woods because of the same story. His lovely Ruby had started to think there may be something in these tales and told him about disturbing dreams that were haunting her nights. Jupp blamed her father for putting nonsense into her head and decided to have it out with the old man who was un-swervable in his belief there was a presence in the woods; one of intense evil that was gradually getting stronger. Even Jupp himself had started to imagine things and one night as he lay down to sleep with Ruby in his arms he saw the tramp standing over them. The face was covered by a scarf but he clearly saw round spectacles with icy blue eyes staring out from behind the lenses. He woke with a start and the vision had gone. Ruby woke at the same time and put her finger to Jupp's lips. "He's gone for now Jacob, but he will come back. Be careful of him," she said. Jupp told her it was just a crazy dream and they had both been listening to her father for too long.

Nonetheless strange things had started to happen at the pond on the site of an old prisoner of war camp in the woods. Dogs swam in the water and then went home to lay down and die. The sound of a man's plaintive cries for help had been heard on foggy nights. Jupp put it down to the peacocks at the big house just half a mile away and everything else to too much local Hepworths ale being consumed. He didn't believe in superstitious nonsense. He knew those woods down to the last twig and had never seen or heard anything that made him think anything sinister was afoot. Foxes, peacocks, pheasants and even grey squirrels could make unearthly noises when they had a mind to. People from the village just didn't understand. Once the trees had been ripped from the earth and the greedy diggers had gobbled up tons of soil the wildlife had fled anyway.

From his hut in the woods, Jupp had listened to the drone of the building site for months on end. The unrelenting march of the diggers and rasping of chainsaws had drawn ever closer and more ferocious. Even though he could have afforded to move into a rented house for a while, he stayed put. Moving once would be enough, he thought. He looked forward to a new life of comfort and ease in his modern home but the upheaval of the coming move seemed to be playing on his mind. For a man who rarely, if ever, remembered his dreams he had spent weeks leading up to his last night in the shack plagued by them. It was always Ruby. He hadn't thought much about her in years. It was too painful to think of her leaving. He'd watched helplessly as she drove away from him with her family, knowing she would never return. Now she came to him in the night looking anxious but the half-formed words on her lips never made any sense. As he began to pack up his few belongings, he became aware of the old grey tramp watching him.

Partial glimpses of him through the trees and un-thinned coppices were now more frequent. He was there and just as quickly melted away in to the undergrowth. Jupp presumed that once he had moved out of the old wooden shack, the tramp would move in. He almost pitied the old man. This parcel of land was the next one in line for development and an access road would soon be driven through it. No doubt a bulldozer would make short work of the little wooden building that had been a home for so long.

The day finally came where Jupp stood watching as the builders put the final finishing touches to his new home. It was the first house on the estate to be handed over. A grand portico stood over the front door and two huge bay windows jutted out on either side. At the top of a slope, he had a commanding view down the road; a good choice he thought as he would not suffer any flooding. Now his new life could begin.

Jupp felt a little uncomfortable in the smart new shirts and jeans he had bought the previous day , but felt he should look presentable and clean for the handing over of the keys. As Jupp let himself into the front door he felt he had finally found a way to be happy and an included member of local society. Perhaps as a man of wealth he should join the local Lions Club and give some time and money to the community that could no longer ignore him. He stood looking out of his new kitchen window, the garden still surrounded by the few remaining trees. He planned in his mind's eye the decking and sun house he fancied he'd install. Suddenly he saw the figure of the old tramp melt out of the undergrowth and stand facing him from the end of the lawn. Jupp was surprised as he had only ever seen him from a distance. The same grey ragged coat and black boots that he had worn for years were topped by a surprisingly youthful face. What should have been grey hair was dark and slicked down with immense care, the bespectacled face that by rights should have been wrinkled and rheumy-eyed was clear and bright, free of lines and probably no more than thirty-five. Cold blue eyes stared at him through the glass. Jupp blinked and shook his head. By the time he looked up again the tramp was gone. He had melted away as fast as he had appeared. Jupp scratched his head and presumed he must just be imagining things. It had been a whirlwind few days and he was tired. He decided to head for the pristine new bathroom and have a hot, wonderful shower with all the new products he had bought for himself in the local pharmacy. He would never smell of woodsmoke again.

After the shower he went to his new bedroom, got dry, and slipped under the soft new duvet. His head nestled into down-filled pillows and he looked forward to a nice afternoon nap. He was soon asleep, but was tormented with dreams. The tramp was there again in the garden, and Jupp, annoyed at the trespasser chased him back into the woods along paths and trails he knew well. Soon he stood by the rancid water of the old pond and watched as the figure of the tramp walked into the water and kept going, up to his knees, then his waist, then up over his head. Jupp felt himself trying to shout, but words refused to leave his mouth. The water boiled and bubbled in a fury and where the one man had walked into the water, he returned with two companions and headed straight for Jupp. Again, the ragged clothes and ancient boots belied the faces of the young men inside them. Their blue tinged complexions were inhuman and as they opened their mouths they spat and spewed out stagnant mud. A horrendous smell came with it that made Jupp gag, and he turned and ran.

He woke up in his new bed soaked in sweat and panting, his mind still filled with the horrible image of their faces and the stench of them lodged in his nostrils. He pushed the sodden covers back and felt the cool air from the window pass over his skin. It smelt sweet and the awful stench began to fade. 'Dear God! What was all that about?' he thought. He got up and pulled on a dressing gown and headed to the kitchen. He checked the garden and was relieved to see it was empty. A bottle of scotch stood on the worktop and he reached for it, not even bothering to find one of his new crystal glasses. The glow of the liquid in his stomach reminded him he hadn't eaten since breakfast and it was now nearly six o'clock in the evening. It was almost dark, autumn drawing the days to an ever-earlier close. A chill passed through him and he switched on the central heating. It was the first time he had ever lived with such a luxury. Jupp returned to his master bedroom and into his bathroom. He turned on the tap to splash his face with water, but instead of warm, clear water coming from the tap a green foul smelling stream started to fill the sink. He jumped back, revolted by the stench, his heart hammering in his chest once more. His rational mind tried to take over. It was simply dirt in the pipes. It just needed to be flushed through. The dream had unsettled him and he needed to pull himself together.

When he looked in the sink again the water was indeed clean and clear. He admonished himself for being so jumpy over nothing. A bad dream, just a weird, bad dream. He found a clean shirt and new jacket he had never been out in before and returned to the kitchen to pick up his keys. He found the bottle of whisky he had taken a drink from on a tray with two of the new crystal glasses next to it. He didn't remember doing this and he certainly wasn't expecting guests. He needed to get out and clear his addled brain. The stress of moving had clearly not been good for him. He locked the door and headed for the village.

A ten minute walk brought him out on to the High Street. There weren't too many people about, but the large pub that laid back from the road served decent food. He settled himself down in the restaurant area and ordered their best steak. He was hungry and the smell of good meat and a couple of pints of beer soon made him forget the nightmare that had haunted his afternoon. Meal finished, he moved to the main bar and sunk some more beer with a couple of old friends. Jupp paid for all the drinks. He had been bought many a beer by the two men he drank with when he had been on hard times. It only seemed fair to share his good fortune now.

By closing time the night air was chilly and he rang for a taxi to take him home. After opening the front door of the house, he slipped off his jacket and luxuriated in the feeling of warmth. As he turned the lounge light on he was met by the sight of a grey coat standing with its back to him. Jupp froze, and the figure turned around.

"Guten abend Herr Jupp" the figure said "You have a much better house for yourself now. I really must congratulate you on your good fortune."

"Who the hell are you? And how did you get in here?" Jupp replied.

"I must apologise Herr Jupp, for arriving unannounced. I know it is not the British way of doing things, but I do need to speak to you with utmost urgency. My name is Hans Jaeger and I am, or should I say was, the highest ranking Waffen SS officer at Camp 46. Pleased to finally make your acquaintance".

The man held out a gloved hand and Jupp felt compelled to take it. It was like holding a lump of frozen meat. The tray with the whisky and two glasses was on the low coffee table between them and Jaeger sat down and lifted one of the glasses to his lips. He indicated that Jupp should sit opposite and do the same.

A sensible man, Jupp tried to make some sense of an entirely irrational conversation. "Mr Jaeger, the camp closed in 1948. You aren't old enough to have been there".

"I know it is a bizarre concept is it not. I am still in my prime but I assure you Herr Jupp I have been here for seventy long years and now it is time for me to complete my task as commanding officer. I must rally my troops once more and carry on with the fight for our Fuhrer!"

"Mr Jaeger, the war ended. It ended a very long time ago. You appear to be the only one left".

"Not so! You see under this very fine house you live in is a gateway. There were two ways back into this world. There is the old pond or this, much easier route in here. Only a few of my men can survive the transit through the water and those that do are weakened by it. When they demolished the camp, tonnes and tonnes of debris, rocks and soil were deposited on it. But now your builders have moved all of that and we can open the gateway again. There are hundreds of us simply waiting for the chance to return and achieve what we didn't do in the past. Take England!"

Jupp stood in stunned silence and looked at the serious expression his visitors face. He wasn't sure if he was in the presence of a spectre or a madman, but either way, he wanted him gone "And you think you and all your Nazi mates can just march in over my new house? I don't think so! Now get out and go tell them your invasion is off. This is my land!" The beer had made Jupp quick-tempered and he tried to punch the ghastly apparition. He missed and stumbled forward.

Jaeger dissolved into thin air and reappeared in the kitchen. He raised his arms into the air and started to mutter an incantation. Jupp ran to the kitchen to try to stop him but by the time he reached the room the floor was starting to move and the smart stone tiles began to lift. As the floor bulged he could hear in the distance the thud of marching feet, quiet, but becaming louder and louder. The floor lifted, groaned and snapped under his feet as the supernatural soldier continued to chant louder and louder. There was a bang, and the unmistakable smell of gas as one of the pipes ruptured. Jupp felt something touch his shoulder and turned to find Ruby standing beside him.

"Don't be afraid Jacob. You must stop him. I'm with you and after tonight I will always be with you". He knew then what he had to do. He reached for a box of matches he had kept out to light his new wood burning stove. He had taken a little bit of his old life with him into the new house and had been looking forward to winter evenings by the fire, football on his large screen TV and a few beers by his side. He closed his eyes and imagined himself back in the woods with the sun rippling through the trees and the sound of a dawn chorus all around. The chanting and the sound of marching faded away. Ruby put her arms around his neck and pressed her lips against his face. She felt cold and he wanted to wrap her up in a blanket to warm her.

He struck the match.

The explosion rocked the new housing estate to its core. Jupp's house and the two nearest dwellings were completely destroyed, swallowed by a mysterious sink hole. Luckily the estate was as yet unoccupied. Broken glass and ripped off roof tiles littered the new streets and the gas supply to a large part of the village was cut off. It took months to clear up all the mess and the body of poor Jacob Jupp was never found. His house was never rebuilt. An underground spring had filled the large sink hole with water almost immediately and created a new pond. Surveyors deemed the surrounding ground far too unstable to build on so it was turned into a green space and planted with trees. Jacob Jupp's friends, the ones who had known him all his life, erected a seat in his memory next to the water. A faulty boiler was blamed for the explosion and the whole thing declared a tragic accident. 'Thank goodness the other houses weren't lived in.' the locals all said.

Later, on summer nights a man could be seen walking hand-in-hand by the lake with a pretty dark haired girl, who stopped to reach up and kiss him and then nuzzled into his neck. The man looked very much like Jupp the Woodsie but no one recognised the girl. They sat on the bench for hours, holding hands, looking out across the water in a contented silence. When anyone spoke to them they just smiled and never replied. In the meantime, at the old stagnant pond the old tramp was still seen on cold foggy nights, weeping and calling for help. No one knew who he was or where he had come from. Only Jacob Jupp, and he had taken the secret to his grave.

BACKGROUND ON CAMP 46
BY
PETULA MITCHELL

The small town of Billingshurst in West Sussex has a long history dating back to Roman times. It was an interchange in the 18th century between the Wey and Arun canal connecting London and Chichester and the A272 which is the main road towards Winchester one way and Haywards Heath and East Sussex the other. The old Roman Road of Stane Street cuts through the village centre connecting the coast to Dorking in Surrey and eventually London. During and after the Second World War many prisoners of war were housed in this area.

German prisoners of war had, before D-day (the Normandy landings of June 6th 1944) generally been sent to other parts of the British Empire. Many were held in Canada. The belief was that, held so far away, they would be unable to escape and rejoin the German war effort. However once the Americans landed in large numbers in mainland Europe the volume of prisoners increased dramatically and an agreement was made to hold the greater proportion of them in the United States as resources were so tight in Britain.

In 1946 America took the decision to repatriate its POWs and it is reported that all the detainees were told they were going back to Germany. However, the prisoners who were part of the deal to relieve pressure on the British were still classed as British POWs and sent back to Liverpool where they then found themselves incarcerated in British camps. At one point, there were 40,000 men in the UK. They were used mainly as a work force, but as restrictions on their movement gradually relaxed there was significant interaction with local communities and eventually 25,000 German ex-prisoners settled in this country.

However some were undoubtedly left feeling embittered by their experiences. Being paid one shilling a day for their work and repatriated with very little money in their pockets they felt was a poor return for years of arduous labour here. The death rate among the detainees here was very low, running at 0.003%. Compared with a death rate of over 30% among those detained in Russia and South East Europe, Britain was by far the safer place for enemy combatants.

On a local level, Camp 46 at Kingsfold is just a short distance outside of Billingshurst; it opened in 1945 and used to house 900 German prisoners of war. One ex inmate described it as a dismal place, surrounded by barbed wire and watch towers. The men were categorised from A to C and colour coded grey to black depending on their political views. 'Category A Grey' prisoners would be pro-British or at least pro-democracy and 'C Black' would be a hardened National Socialists who held loyalty to the Reich above all else.

The men were held at Camp 46 for re-education and 'de-Nazification' before release and also to work on local farms and brickyards. It is recorded that some of the men felt they were overworked and one is quoted as saying, "we are worked like animals from dawn to dusk, and as animals need no politics why bother us with it?" Many of the men hoped that going along with the education programme would lead to an early release, but as hopes of this faded many became bitter. A small number of them emerged as vocal and committed Communists, but this was passed over as just a way of trying to annoy the British in charge of their care.

In my story I have taken a few liberties. The grey tramp legend actually comes from a few miles away at Buck Barn crossroads where he is seen walking in front of the traffic; a somewhat dangerous pastime as the main A24 is dual carriageway and this section is the main road towards Worthing and is controlled by a complex set of traffic signals. Perhaps our tramp would prefer the peace and quiet of the woods? Maybe he is the spirit of one of three Germans who escaped from Billingshurst and weren't recaptured until they crashed their car onto Worthing beach?

This part of Sussex is undergoing an unprecedented amount of development. In the past five years whole new towns have sprung up from nothing and areas that were previously held as sacrosanct green spaces have come under the developers cosh. As thousands of tonnes of soil are dug up, moved around and scraped off the fields who can tell what or who is being disturbed? The layers of history run deep in this part of the world. Will we regret disturbing them one day?

STRANGER THAN BEFORE
BY
BARRY McCANN

The cobblestone streets of old Lancaster echo with footsteps of the past, replaying moments from lives that have no end in death. But on this evening the ghost was a man, aimlessly wandering under the streetlights and haunted by one who touched his soul, an ethereal mistress inhabiting every living thought and feeding a sense of loss.

Paul Harkness encountered her some evenings earlier while visiting the Student Union. Entering the venue, he looked for a familiar face and his photographic eyes zoomed in on her presence. Sat in the shadows with only a cocktail for company, she shone in the frame of a low cut, long black dress and a curious looking gold necklace radiating above an ample cleavage. Evidently more mature than the usual crowd and with an air of glowing sensuality, her gaze caught his and held him in a stare. Feeling invited, he approached with an offer to replenish her glass.

"Let's dance," she suggested, her gloved hand taking his and leading him onto the floor. Waltzing silently, only their eyes spoke. There was something piercing in the woman's look, yet guarded about her aura. She then leaned forward and whispered "walk with me."

Leading her to the door, he was distracted by the shout of "Hey, Paul!" They both turned and it belonged to his friend, Clara. Reading the situation, she grinned. "Sorry, speak another time." The new companion pulled his arm firmly and the pair escaped into the night.

Behind them the moon shone as they quietly walked across the empty grey streets. Paul took a clearer look the gold necklace, which bore a name in strange, Gaelic lettering.

"Ruthven? Is that you?" Her head turned slightly and she looked at him with hooded eyes. "Just Ruth will do," she said, adding "I'm not trespassing, am I?"

"In what way?"

"That's not your woman back there?"

"No, just a friend. We're both history students."

"History? Very close to my heart," she mused, but said no more. Whatever else Ruth may have added was continued in silent thought.

They quietly strolled arm in arm, until Paul tried breaking the ice again. "You seem a bit of a closed book." Her lips slightly curved into a smile. "The truest words are those unspoken." She pulled his arm reassuringly, adding "But I shall speak beneath your dreams." He didn't quite understand her words but remained in quiet awe of them.

Eventually, they arrived at a bridge over the canal and Ruth stopped at the stone steps that led to the embankment below. She pulled Paul into an embrace and pressed her passionate lips onto his. Then she drew back announcing, "I have to go. Thank you for your company."

"Already? Nothing I said was it?" Her soft-gloved hand patted his cheek. "Now is not the time. But you may see me again."

"How do I find you?"

"You will, if you really wish it. I'm just a blown kiss away." Smiling, she descended the steps down to the water's side, turned and disappeared under the bridge.

He crossed the road to see her come out the other side, but no one appeared. He went back over and down the steps she had taken, expecting to see her waiting under the bridge. But, reaching the bottom, there was no one there or further down the bank. Assuming there must be another exit somewhere, Paul reluctantly turned and took himself home.

Throughout the days that followed, he was unable to drive the enigmatic Ruth out of his head. He tried to dismiss it as a silly crush, the fascination for a mature woman by a younger man. But, in his heart of hearts, instinct told him it was deeper than that. He had to see her again.

As evening beckoned, Paul walked the route they had taken that night in a vague hope that replaying the conditions of their previous encounter will somehow invoke the woman herself. The grieving of a deserted lover keeping the nest frozen in time, and hoping she would return.

Eventually, he found himself back at the bridge where they had parted company and hesitantly looked over to the canal below. To his relief, the figure of Ruth was stood there facing the water with arms raised and head staring up at the sky. The moon was full and her attitude was one of drawing from its eminence.

He watched her for a while, until suddenly she turned her head and looked straight up, smiling with a mischievous glint in her eyes. Paul got the feeling that she knew or sensed he was there all the time and kept him in suspense. He wanted to speak, but words escaped him. She lowered her arms, turned her head from his gaze and went back under the bridge.

Paul raced down the steps to the canal side but, again, she had completely disappeared. Slowly venturing in her footsteps, he carefully examined the wall of centuries old stone masonry for signs of a concealed exit. There was none evident and he felt troubled by her actions. Was she toying with him? Why didn't she speak? When they had conversed, he hung onto her every word, and continued to hang on since, yet now she was elusive. It was time to seek a second opinion.

Next morning, he called to see Clara at her flat on the city outskirts. As the two shared coffee, he told her everything. "She's a tease," his friend concluded. "Though I've heard that name before." She got up and extracted a volume on local folklore from her bookcase, flicking through the pages until arriving at the one sought. "Here we are, the Water Witch. Early 1800s. Quite the celebrity around here."

"Who was she?"

"A woman known as the Lady Ruthven who, according to testimony, would be seen by the canal performing, quote, 'infernal rituals.' Renowned for luring young men at full moon and engaging them in 'unholy acts.' The magistrate ordered her arrested for witchcraft and it's said she took refuge under a canal bridge, disappearing without trace."

"But a canal bridge is where I saw Ruth last night. And where she left me those nights before."

"Seems your friend has a role model, look" Clara passed the open book to Paul, the page bearing an illustration of the Water Witch. The resemblance to Ruth was unmistakable.

"She certainly looks the part," Paul confirmed, before reading a further paragraph to himself. "Says here she's since been seen on a number of occasions since, and each time someone in the area has disappeared without trace."

"Yes, I've read that bit," Clara said dismissively. "People disappear over time and blaming Ruthven is the locals' way of rationalising such things. If rationalising is the right word."

Paul continued to recite from the book. "It's believed she can be summoned back from the waters by drawing the moon under the bridge." Clara laughed. "And how you going to get the moon under a bridge?"

"Don't know, but I'm going to try and find out." Her face dropped. "What? You're not serious!"

Paul nodded to himself. "I have to be, I need to get hold of her, speak with her."

Clara frowned. "Question is what's got hold of you?"

"She has. Since I first met Ruth, I can't get her out of my head. Every waking hour, she's there. In my dreams, she's there. No one has ever affected me like that before."

Clara's expression turned into concern. She took the book back from Paul and turned back a page. "Listen to this account from 1805. 'Ruthven be attendant at many dances and other merry makings to snare her prey. She bewitches a man by becoming one with his thoughts, thus he be unable to dispel her from his mind. That be the lure to then seek her out, the net by which she pulls her catch in. Once in her power, the victim serves his mistress and doeth her every bidding.'" Clara raised her head, adding "I think we can guess what sort of favours they were."

Paul looked his friend straight in the face. "But that's exactly what's happened to me!"

She raised a hand up to cut him short. "Wait, let's get a grip here. Your Ruth, somehow, has learnt the trick her predecessor used." Clara thought for a second, before continuing "did you accept anything from her?"

"Only a kiss. There's just something beguiling about her. Hypnotic, even."

"A hypnotic kiss, perhaps? Or something intoxicating she managed to pass with her lips."

Paul breathed deeply at the suggestion. "She did say something very strange. Something about speaking beneath my dreams."

Clara's eyes narrowed. "Sounds like she was giving you a hint. In a very eloquent way."

"Well, hopefully I'll find that out tonight. Now I know where to find her."

Clara glared at him. "You really believe that?"

"I've got to try. Whatever she's done to me, I think only she can undo."

"I'll come with you."

"No! I've a feeling she won't show unless I'm alone. She seems to sense presence without even looking." Clara pondered his point for a moment. "Alright then. But even if she is just a nutter, be careful all the same."

Evening fell and Paul made his way to the appointed place. He may have told Clara he knew where to find Ruth, but no idea as to how. Would she be stood by the bank again or muddy the waters with further teasing? Approaching the bridge, he would soon have an answer one way or the other.

Meanwhile, Clara was on the internet researching a catalogue of papers when a thought occurred. She typed 'Ruthven Water Witch' into the

243

search engine and a small list of references came up. The one bearing the title 'Regarding the Lancaster Water Witch by Dr. John Polidori' caught her eye, the abstract reporting he came to Lancaster in 1809 to investigate the stories and disappearance of Lady Ruthven. She clicked on the link and began to read.

Paul stood under the bridge, wondering what to do next. The moon was full, but hidden from his eyes by the structure above. Then he noticed it reflecting on the water's surface before him and something occurred about what the instruction meant. Not drawing on the moon itself, but its reflection. He placed himself in alignment to the image with arms raised, eyes closed and began to concentrate.

Clara hurriedly hunted down her phone, even though she was unsure what to make of the claims in Polidori's journal. But if there was a chance of even some truth in them, he needed to be warned. Clicking on Paul's number, an automated message responded. 'Sorry, we are unable to connect you. Please try later.' She reasoned he must be under the bridge, hence the blocked signal, and raced off to her car.

Patiently waiting, Paul opened his eyes and looked down at the moon's presence when something else struck him. Recalling her words 'I'm only a blown kiss away', he realised they may been intended as a clue. With nothing to lose, he blew a kiss down at the watery moon and imagined it penetrating deep.

Seconds passed and then came a sound of bubbling, the moon's reflection shimmering as the water appeared to boil. He stepped back as a shape began to surface, breaking through the skin of the water. It was a coffin, and an unusually wide one from what he could see. The water calmed as the casket floated up to the canal side, and he jolted as the lid swung outwardly open of its own accord. Within the object, she lay.

Ruth's eyes opened, looking straight up before fixing on Paul. Smiling, she levitated up into a standing position. Her hand held out in invitation and Paul took it, raising her as she stepped out of the floating casket. They stood face to face, Ruth taking him by both hands. "I knew you would come," she said.

"Yes," he affirmed. "But why so elusive?"

"You have to learn how to find me, a test of your dedication."

"I had to come, you were calling me. Constantly, inside my head!"

She calmed him with a gentle 'husssh', then her grip tightened slightly. "I called and you answered. Now be proud, you've done well."

He hesitated before asking the question. "Are you really her? The Ruthven? Clara reckons you're just some sort of disciple?'

She leaned closer to his face. "Oh, yes. I be Ruthven who danced her infernal dance and invited menfolk to come play."

Her hand lightly caressed Paul's arm as he tried to make sense of the situation. The woman's claims were impossible, yet she sounded convincing. "You then disappeared."

"When I was hunted my masters granted me new sanctuary, well beyond the eyes of others." She drew a finger down his cheek. "Now I emerge when need arises, and remain cloaked when in sanctum. I sense you are learned of my activities since."

"And what need is this? What is it you want?"

She patted the side of his face and whispered. "To sow the seed and reap my harvest."

"But how can a witch live so long and never age?"

245

Ruth laughed and shook her head. "Witches are not immortal. They be as human as you are, and I was." Gently, she rubbed her index finger back up his cheek. "I attained a higher state of being, that be my instrument." Drawing her hand under Paul's chin, she pulled him forward as their lips connected.

It was the echoing sound of running footsteps that interrupted the pair and their heads turned in unison. Clara stood several feet away with alarm written large on her face. "Get away from her!"

Ruth glared at the woman, as Paul tried to reassure his friend, "it's okay. I know who she is."

"No you don't! You don't know what she became!"

Ruth grinned widley. "I was just getting around to that." She looked back at Paul as a pair of fangs protruded into view like claws from a feline paw. Before he could speak, she lunged forward and sank them into his jugular, causing him to cry out in pain.

Clara instinctively launched herself onto the vampire, but the creature withdrew from her victim's neck and lashed out with superhuman strength. Her sheer force sent Clara crashing against the wall, leaving her stunned and breathless. Ruth then grabbed the rigid Paul and threw him into the casket, his back crashing onto the hard wood surface. She jumped on top of her catch, wrapping herself around him like a cocoon and continued to feast.

Within moments, Clara regained herself and struggled over to the bank's edge. Ruthven lifted her head, her blood dripping mouth hissing "too late, detective!" The casket lid swung shut and it began to submerge, away from the mortal world until time for the next harvest.

"Is this how it ends?" Clara whispered to herself. What could she could do? Who she could tell? Who would believe her? Collapsing to her knees, Clara's incohate scream reverberated around the tunnel walls.

BACKGROUND ON STRANGER THAN BEFORE
BY
BARRY McCANN

The vampire has come a long way from their earliest tales in the ancient cultures of the Mesopotamians, Hebrews, Ancient Greeks, and Romans. These hideous creatures, usually bloated rotting corpses, were the remnants of suicide victims or witches. They may be created by a malevolent spirit possessing a corpse or bitten by an existing vampire. The term *vampire* itself was not popularised until the early 18th century, after an influx of vampire superstition from Eastern Europe.

During this time there had been an epidemic of alleged vampire sightings in Eastern European countries, with frequent staking and grave diggings to destroy potential revenants. It began with an The westward outbreak of reported vampire activity began in East Prussia in 1721 and in the Habsburg Empire from 1725 to 1734, before spreading to other localities.

Based on a 1746 treatise by French theologian Dom Augustine Calmet concerning the outbreak, Voltaire wrote in chapter 463 of his *'Dictionnaire Philosophique':*

> *These vampires were corpses, who went out of their graves at night to suck the blood of the living, either at their throats or stomachs, after which they returned to their cemeteries. The persons so sucked waned, grew pale, and fell into consumption; while the sucking corpses grew fat, got rosy, and enjoyed an excellent appetite. It was in Poland, Hungary, Silesia, Moravia, Austria, and Lorraine, that the dead made this good cheer.*

The hysteria quelled when Gerhard van Swieten, personal physician to Empress Maria Theresa of Austria, investigated claims of vampire activity and concluded they did not exist. The Empress subsequently passed laws prohibiting the opening of graves and desecration of bodies, but the vampire lived on in superstition

British folklore tradition is comparatively thin on vampire myths but not without them altogether. William of Newburgh, Canon of an Augustinian Priory in Yorkshire, recorded accounts of undead activity in 1197. This included an occurrence in Buckinghamshire, where the cadaver of a recently deceased man returned and appeared before his widow, then began walk in the daylight hours. The Bishop of Lincoln ordered the body to be exhumed, which was found to be still fresh. When the body was cremated the haunting ceased.

Newburgh also related a similar event from Melrose, Scotland, where a friar serving as chaplain to the household of a noble woman died and was buried in the local cemetery. However, he rose from his grave each night and returned, appearing in the woman's bedchamber to mutter and moan.

She alerted the friars of Melrose Abbey and a group of them decided to keep overnight vigil at the graveyard. One friar was on watch while his companions had gone to warm themselves, when the deceased man rose from his grave and rushed at him menacingly. The friar retaliated with an axe and chased the creature back to its grave, which opened of its own accord to allow its owner to return and closed up again.

Next day, the friar and his companions exhumed the corpse and took it to Melrose Abbey, where it was cremated and the ashes spread to the winds. And that was the last of the undead friar.

These stories may lack the bloodsucking element we normally associate with vampire tales, but there is one from 1874 centering on Croglin Manor in the Vale of Eden, which was rented by Australian siblings Michael, Edward and Amelia Cranswell.

One evening, Amelia was awakened by a shrouded figure at her window, with flaming eyes. Roused by her screams, the two brothers rushed to her room and found their sister crumpled on the floor with blood dripping from fang marks on her neck.

Fortunately the wounds were superficial and she recovered, but some months later the creature struck again, smashing through the shutters on her window. Armed with a gun, Edward rushed outside and shot at the wraithlike figure which stumbled but kept on running away.

He pursued it to Croglin Churchyard, where it disappeared among the graves. He returned with a party the next day and found a family vault opened, the coffins inside strewn open except one. It was opened and the body inside found to have a bullet wound in its leg. Consequently it was taken away and burnt.

So how did the vampire evolve from the hideous smelly bloated creature it had been to the modern, often sexy figure of today? Look no further than Victorian gothic and the revamping effect of increasing technology.

They were a haunted lot, the Victorians. With the reassurance of religious patriarchy challenged by Darwinism, Freud and psycho-analysis, people began to examine themselves. Human beings were more complex creatures than previously thought, with a primal base still carried deep within. Thus evolved the spectre of the past still being very much a part of the present, ready to rise and take hold again in environments of degeneration.

And if this fear for the human condition was not enough, there were also the concerns about it becoming lost or rendered alien in an increasingly mechanised society were the worker's role is little more than an automaton. Mass industrial expansionism not only changed the social and geographical landscape, but transformed the working class into something neither human nor machine.

Even the natural cycles by which people once worked (sunrise, sunset, the seasons, etc) became replaced by the clock, time itself now mechanised and controlled. In a sense, life was becoming "vamped" by mechanisation and this would have profound implications on human perception as reshaped by the machine.

Gothic literature of the period became full of things that appear human but not quite human, thus vampires that were previously the stuff of ancient myth made their return in nineteenth century literature. John Polidori's 1819 novella 'The Vampyre' established the archetype of charismatic, Byronic vampire, inspiring such works as 'Varney the Vampire', 'Carmilla' and eventually 'Dracula'.

The British vampire had well and truly been revamped.

THE PIED PIPER OF ESSEX
BY
RA GOLI

Fifty Years Ago...

Rain pelted against the brickwork of the underpass. Murray shivered against the inside wall and pulled his thin, ratty blanket tighter around his freezing body. The tunnel reeked of urine and he was starting to stink of it too; it'd been months since he'd last bathed. He briefly considered going out in the rain for a wash, but it was coming down too hard and to do so in the middle of winter was risking hypothermia. Instead he gulped down the last of the cheap whisky he had in an effort to warm his belly and forget his life, if only for a few hours. It did neither as the cold wind surged through the tunnel, as if to remind him of his place in the world. At the bottom. A pestilence on society. He thought about all the rich people who'd walk by him during the day, to and from work. Few actually looked at him, even fewer gave him money. They'd be sitting in their warm homes now, perhaps settling down to watch television with a hot cup of something, their bellies full from a hearty meal. His stomach growled audibly and he tried to think about something else.

His thoughts were interrupted by the sounds of laughter and footsteps slapping concrete. He peered towards the end of the underpass tunnel and saw two young men running inside for cover. They swayed slightly and slapped each other on the back as they laughed. Drunk, he thought. Murray closed his eyes and pulled the blanket over his head in the hopes they'd ignore him and keep walking. He was out of luck.

"Would ya look at this Charlie."

"You there."

Murray felt a kick to his thigh. He tried to ignore it, then there was a tug at his blanket and he clutched his gnarled fingers around it and pulled it back. He looked at the men, his heart thumped against his ribcage and his whole body tensed.

"Hey you bum, don't snatch," one of the men said. The other laughed and kicked Murray in the side of his ribcage. He winced from the pain and gasped for breath. The first man squatted down so they were eye-level and slapped Murray hard across the face.

"Please," he said. Before he could say any more, the man snatched the blanket and tossed it aside. He grabbed Murray by his collar and pulled him to his feet.

"Did I say you could speak to me?" he said, then spat in the homeless man's face.

His companion laughed and punched Murray in the side of the head. The first man released his grip and Murray fell to the ground with a heavy thud. He pressed his hand against his cheek and felt warm blood ooze from the cut. His head pounded. He tried to crawl away but one of the men grabbed his ankles and pulled him back. His hands flailed as he tried to find purchase on the cold cement.

"Help," he called out, his voice reverberating around the tunnel.

"Aint no one around to help you old man, it's near on midnight," the first man laughed, then started kicking him in his side. A wheezy scream clawed its way out of

Murray's throat. A foot rolled him onto his side. He covered his head with his hands as the man kicked him hard in the belly. The air was forced out of him and vomit rumbled up his gullet. He hadn't eaten for days, so threw up nothing but alcohol and bile.

"Gross," said the second attacker, then kicked him between his legs. Murray curled into a ball, his hands clutched his aching jewels as the pain spread through his body. His nose crunched under a boot heel and blood spurted across the concrete. His vision blurred and he fell in and out of consciousness as the assailants continued to kick him until he was almost dead. Eventually they grew tired, or simply bored enough to stop. He managed to open one swollen eye and saw the men walk away, carrying the blanket he'd fought hard to keep.

"It stinks of piss," one said, holding it aloft as protection from the rain as they exited the tunnel.

Murray winced, every harsh, gasping breath a fresh agony. His whole body ached and his breath sounded weak and raspy. Rats poked their heads out of golf-ball sized holes along the tunnel walls. Cautiously at first, but when they saw he wasn't getting up, they became braver and approached. He was still alive as they started chewing on his fingertips and swollen face. He couldn't blame them. They were starving too.

* * *

Present Day...

"You really think this will work?" Derek asked.

Carly was crouched on the cold concrete drawing a second large pentagram on the ground with chalk.

"Sure, if we concentrate." She placed four red candles around one of the symbols, sat inside the other and placed the Ouija board in its centre. Derek sat across from her and looked down at the wooden board, a small plastic skull with a window for a mouth, sat on top. She lit two more candles and placed them on either side of her, illuminating the board further. She opened the book on the occult in her lap and her eyes scanned the page. Derek read the upside-down title: 'Summoning Spell', but the rest was in Latin and he couldn't understand it. She steadied her breathing and concentrated her focus.

"Why do you want to summon him anyway?"

She let out a huff and frowned, her concentration blown.

"Sorry," he smiled. "You may as well answer me, I've already interrupted you."

"I told you, I'm writing a paper on the supernatural."

"Yes, I know that, but why this guy?"

"His story is so sad and interesting. He was beaten to death and when they found him, half his face and fingers were missing."

"That's gross," said Derek.

"They never found who killed him. Imagine if we could find out that information?" Her eyes twinkled with morbid fascination.

"Whatever floats your boat."

"Can we concentrate now please? No more talking."

"Okay, okay." He mimicked zippering up his mouth and placed his fingertips on the planchette. She smiled at him, then began reading from the book. The witching hour was almost upon them and an inky gloom cloaked the pair as Carly's chanting became louder and faster. Derek kept his fingers on the planchette, acting as a conduit should the ghost wish to communicate. His eyes flitted to the other circle sporadically but nothing had been conjured yet. Carly was shouting now, the same repeated phrase. When she switched to English, Derek joined in.

"We invoke thee. We invoke thee. We invoke thee".

A thunderous wind surged through the tunnel, blowing out the candles and sweeping the planchette from the board. Derek swore and Carly quickly retrieved it and relit the candles beside them as the wind died down to an icy breeze. The gloom that'd descended around them like a fog, now swirled like a cyclone in the centre of the other five-pointed star. They stared wide eyed as the stygian twister grew in size and intensity, then suddenly dissipated like ghostly dandelion spores in a sickly cold breeze. Their attention was drawn to the board when they heard the plastic skull scrape against the wood.

"Who's there?" It felt like a beetle was crawling up Carly's spine and she shivered.

The planchette moved until the letter 'R' was visible inside the skull's mouth. She swallowed hard and watched unblinking as it continued to spell out the word she knew it would. R-A-T-M-A-N. When the planchette stopped moving, the tunnel was as silent as a crypt. Then the scraping began, like claws along a stone wall. Carly screamed when a figure emerged at the end of the tunnel, hunched over and snarling like an animal. They sat frozen, rooted in terror as the creature came closer. Other sounds joined the symphony of scrapes; numerous rat-like squeaks and a slow drip, like that of a leaky tap.

When the ratman came into the candlelight, she saw what made the dripping sound. His fingertips had been gnawed off, the fresh wet plops stained the concrete as he approached them. She tore her eyes away from the ground to look at his face. It was a putrid red mess. Where his nose should have been, were two skeletal holes, his lips, eyelids and half his skin had been chewed away by tiny teeth. A hollow, wretched scream escaped her throat and she scrambled to her feet. She wanted to run but Derek sat frozen as the thing moved closer.

"Derek, get up!" She backed away, wanting to put distance between her and the ratman, even if it meant sacrificing her boyfriend. The squeaks became deafening, reverberating around the tunnel as a flood of rats ran towards them, their red eyes glowing like tiny hellfires. The deluge of rodents swarmed over Derek in an instant and he jerked into action, waving his arms and kicking his legs, his body twisted on the ground as the rats started feasting. Carly could hear him screaming and the cacophony of tiny footsteps behind her as she ran out of the tunnel.

She headed for the car, her escape. Only when she was almost there did she realize Derek had the keys. She skidded to a halt and turned and eyed the rats exiting the tunnel after her. If they were following her, maybe she could circle back for the keys, but what if the ratman was still there? She had to make a decision, there were no houses nearby, no one to help her and they'd left their phones in the car, not wanting any electrical items to interfere with the summoning.

Adrenalin-laced fear gnawed at her belly and she bolted away from the car, heading for an abandoned building. Surely, she could hide until morning, she felt if she could hold out until daylight, she'd be safe. She climbed an old wire fence and almost twisted her ankle when she landed on the hard dirt on the other side. Her lungs burned with the effort of running and a savage cramp bit at her side, but she kept moving. She hobbled around the back of the building until she found a door ajar, snuck inside and gently pulled it closed behind her.

She found a room and hid in a closet, trying to quiet her breathing. Moonlight penetrated the gloom from a nearby window and shadows wiggled like fingers against the walls. She thought about Derek and choked back a sob. She couldn't fall apart now.

She heard the scraping noise again and let out a whimper, then covered her mouth with her hand, taking shallow, silent breaths through her nose. Her eyes were squeezed shut and her pulse thumped thunderously in her ears, but she still heard the footsteps coming closer.

The door was yanked open and she sagged with relief when she saw Derek's face in the dappled half-light. She frowned. It was all wrong. His clothes were ragged and his eyes were sunken. Through blurry tears she realized what she was looking at: the ratman was wearing Derek's face. She saw his rodent minions gather behind him. She opened her mouth to scream but the rats were upon her before she could emit even a squeak.

* * *

They walked quietly towards the city, the man and his friends. Determined. There would be more rats to collect along the way, millions of them. He smiled. After all these years, he would finally have his revenge against the cruel city that'd treated him like vermin

BACKGROUND ON THE PIED PIPER OF ESSEX
by
RA GOLI

The Ratman of Southend is the urban legend of a homeless man, seeking shelter from the biting wind in an underpass at the Queensway and Southchurch road in Southend-on-sea, Essex.

The man was attacked by a group of bullies who beat him nearly to death, then stole his blanket. He later died of hypothermia and afterwards, rats gnawed at his fingers and face. Another version names the perpetrators as a gang of teenagers and claims the homeless man was still alive when the rats started feasting.

The legend says that he haunts the subway underpass as a disfigured creature; a ratman, hunched over and snarling with a mouthful of yellow teeth. People had reported hearing screams at night and the sounds of scraping nails against stone. Some versions claim squeals and moans can be heard at night in addition to the scrape of claws.

Another version of the story claims that the Ratman is the deformed son of the town's mayor. The Essex mayor was a serial adulterer and his son was allegedly born as a grotesque rat-like cryptid as punishment for the man's sins. Other versions of the story say the son was born with a rat face, tail and carnivorous appetite and that the mayor built the underpass, including the addition of a secret cell, where his son lived in isolation, hidden from the world.

There is no mention of who exacted the punishment, perhaps a mythical god, or vengeful wife with a penchant for witchcraft. Again, the sound of scraping nails is a warning that the ratman is coming. The Southend underpass is featured on several ghost tours of Essex, for those who wish to see if the legend that the ratman escaping his cell at night to feast on human flesh is true.

Urban legends are usually the retelling of stories that are supposed to be true and often happened to a friend of a friend, or rooted in the 'don't go out at night because the bogeyman might get you', fear people have. Often the stories are at least partially believable, and the teller is convinced that it really happened.

Most urban legends, myths and lore have similar stories around the world. You could draw comparisons to a similar urban legend from Melbourne, Australia called The Cat Man of Altona Homestead.

In this story, the homeless man named Edward Goodson had a liking for fish and often carried some around in his pockets, making his odour attractive to cats who would follow him around. In 1909 Edward was found murdered in the toilets outside the homestead, though there is no mention of who the killer or killers were. The legend says that if you were to sit on the toilet, you'd hear the sound of cats meowing and feel as though the felines were scratching at your legs as they avenge the death of Edward.

Another similar cryptid urban legend is that of the Goatman, usually hailing from Texas, Maryland or Louisiana. In one version, this half-man half-goat seeks revenge against the teens who killed his flock of goats. The Bunnyman, a crazed axe-wielding half-man half-bunny, is said to lurk under a dark bridge in Virginia and slaughters victims at Halloween if they hang around the bridge, gutting them like rabbits.

The Ratman has even shown up in the videogame Grand Theft Auto IV. He can be found in various areas including the subway, maintenance tunnels and abandoned buildings in the game. Several large cities all over the world have urban legends regarding giant mutant rats that live beneath the city within the sewage system, some claiming the rats to be three feet tall. Legends of various haunted subway tunnels appear from major cities also, people claiming to have heard strange noises or seen ghostly spectres. Whether the Ratman is a ghost or a half-rat, half-man depends on the story, but the message is the same, don't go into the Southend underpass alone at night.

In my story, The Pied Piper of Essex, I focused on the violent treatment of the homeless man and his equally violent revenge against the people who summon him in the underpass. The years of cruelty Murray was subjected to and his gruesome murder, shaped the monster he became in the afterlife. Befriending the rats is symbolic in the sense that he himself was treated like the scum of the earth and perhaps felt more of a kinship to the rodents, then the rest of society.

SPOOR
BY
DC MERRYWEATHER

The reporter sat and gazed from the car's passenger-side window and into the dense patch of woodland that pressed close against the road. As they passed, she caught glimpses of its gloomy interior: the ramshackle, twisting branches, the beds of soft bracken, and the indistinct forms of things half-concealed within its hushed stillness.

They neared their destination and the reporter folded away the local newspaper on her lap. She had been studying the photograph printed on its front page which showed the unfocused, silhouetted blur of something moving across a twilit school playing field. The picture accompanied the latest story the paper had ran about sightings of a large unidentified animal which some claimed was prowling the farmland, meadows, as well as the narrow strip of woodland they were now passing, on the town's outskirts. The long, high belt of hawthorn, hazel, and beech that rose dramatically just inches from her window pulled her attention back. Past the knot of the trees' limbs nothing stirred. Certainly not what was provincially known as 'The Beast', which eyewitnesses were divided over whether it was a big cat or some kind of feral dog.

More recently, a local farmer claimed to have wounded an animal responsible for leaving the eviscerated corpses of his calves at the fringes of his fields. The farmer was quoted in the paper as having shot at what resembled a huge black hound and then watched as it sloped away into the woods.

When the story ran on the newspaper's website, it received the largest amount of traffic in the site's history, and, it appeared, even the most ardent sceptic couldn't resist clicking and commenting on the story. Consequently, the reporter and photographer were dispatched to take photographs of the Beast's supposed woodland lair and to interview residents of the nearby housing estate.

The car turned off onto an exit ramp, followed the road around, and pulled into a layby. To the reporter's bewilderment, the photographer seemed genuinely eager to explore the woods. He talked earnestly about obtaining photographic evidence of the evasive animal's spoor: footprints, markings, maybe even its den. Anything which would support claims that there was indeed something 'beastly' skulking within the normally genteel patches of the local scenery.

She had considered staying in the car while the photographer went about clambering through the weeds taking his dynamic pictures of twigs, but, with a sigh, she unfastened her seatbelt.

With the beige block of 1960s Brutalism that was the town's High School squatting in the distance, they both cut their way across its football pitch and on towards an underpass which sneaked beneath a dual-carriageway. On the other side stood the beckoning woods.

Something crunched beneath their feet as they carefully made their way through the dim, grey canyon of the underpass. The reporter looked down and saw the ground was scattered with stones and mud, broken glass, and even small hunks of ragged concrete torn from somewhere. Despite the proximity of the school, the walls were virtually free of graffiti, and the little amount of ineligible scrawl there had now faded.

As they were about to emerge, however, the reporter noticed a small set of elaborate symbols and shapes, sketched on the wall in black, possibly charcoal. They examined a couple of crude drawings which looked reminiscent of Neolithic cave paintings; one showed a circle of stick figures surrounding a large dog-like animal. The other reminded her of something. She tried to remember what. Romulus and Remus suckling on their wolf-mother? Yes, that was it.

She then noticed the photographer had stopped and was pointing his lens at something balanced on the top of a wooden post just outside the underpass. She walked over for a closer look. The object had swirling patterns, similar to the ones she had just looked at, lightly etched all the way across it. Otherwise, it was a normal sheep's skull. The first bit of evidence already, she thought to herself. But of what, exactly?

A scurrying wind swept across the meadow and shook the trees. Woodpigeons bolted from the grove then swooped upward into the pale Autumnal sky, as if spooked by something.

The reporter pulled her red woollen coat tighter about her against the wind, feeling something in the pocket as she did. She dipped her hand in and withdrew a couple of oatcakes wrapped in cling-film. She remembered placing them there now - compensation for a missed breakfast.

The photographer was forging ahead towards the trees, hands in pockets and kicking a path through a thick growth of bitter green nettles. She followed after and gazed up to where, above the centre of the forest, birds wheeled in the sky like leaves in a slow whirlpool.

Soon the thickness of the woods enclosed around them, and they followed a muddy trail, still partially hidden by thick summer growth. Within this concealed world it was as if time had paused. Aside from the occasional piercing caw of a lingering blackbird, and the leaves on the uppermost boughs shivering and hissing in the sharp breeze, the dark trees stood in silence. A silence of something being withheld.

They progressed deeper in, the photographer occasionally snapping away at the lush greenery and up at the deeply contorted branches of the trees, though the reporter knew not why; she presumed for his enjoyment alone. With little enthusiasm, she tagged along, concerned her boots were gathering mud.

To take her mind off things, the reporter cheerfully anticipated the advancement of the diggers and bulldozers that she knew would arrive in the next year or so. Even so, she still found it difficult to imagine the rows of houses that would eventually be standing here, instead of this old and haunted place.

After a short while, the photographer stopped dead and pointed out the trace of a kill. There, half-hidden in the dark green were shiny specks of viscera, and some tufts of long-haired fur, maybe that of a badger. The reporter grazed her finger over a dark patch on a nearby leaf. It was blood, and still wet. The two looked about, studying the surrounding undergrowth. If crackpots and simple-minded yokels were to be believed, the reporter mused, it concealed the dark beast of local legend.

They ploughed on along the subtle labyrinth of pathways that led deeper into the wood, cast acorn cups crunching underfoot.

The reporter suddenly stopped in her tracks. She noticed just in time that she was about to walk into a spider's web which spanned the side-path she had decided to follow. The spider sat there in the centre of its vibrating web; it jolted into skittish life as it sensed prey.

The photographer called her back and pointed out more bloodied leaves he had found. The reporter began to feel as if they were being lured into following a trail that had been left for them.

The photographer attempted to clamber up a steeply sloped area but slipped over on the damp, leafy surface. He got to his feet, complaining and trying to wipe the mud from his jeans and the camera lens. In frustration and embarrassment, he kicked at some foxgloves in frustration, sending the brightly coloured spikes flying. The reporter suppressed a laugh but was comforted by the fact that she wasn't the only one who wasn't enjoying this fly-ridden, rank-smelling hole.

She was about to ask him if they should go when she sensed movement somewhere to the right of her. When she looked, there was nothing to see. The foliage stood motionless. She listened intently but heard nothing except for the plaintive, fluting chorus of birds in their treetop territories, and the conspiratorial whisper of leaves.

She decided to take a less treacherous path up the slope than the photographer, but she too managed to stumble. Wrong-footed by a collapsing lump of wet and rotten wood, her suddenly faltering step was enough to send the oatcakes tumbling from her pocket. They burst from their wrappings as they hit the ground and then went rolling back down the path and into the undergrowth. She cursed under her breath and went to retrieve them. One had laid to rest in a small hollow in the soft earth. When the reporter picked up the oatcake, she looked down at the roundish indentation in the mud where it had come to rest.

She was no expert, and the shape of the depression was indistinct, but she could swear it would have been a human footprint if it wasn't for the indentations at the front of each toe, like claw marks. It seemed freshly made, too. She knew she hadn't noticed it the first time; had something crossed the path behind her?

When the reporter's eyes searched the foreboding and claustrophobic depths of the woods for any other tell-tale sign or movement, she had an uneasy feeling that something was gazing back at her.

She caught up with the photographer, and they continued along a wider path in a welcome open patch of woodland. Even so, when she craned her neck and gazed up to the canopy of trees that formed overhead, she realised she still couldn't even see the sky. The feeling of being removed from the rest of the world was most unwelcome, and she could also feel the telltale itchiness of an oncoming attack of hayfever building in her throat. The desire to return to the city was strong; she was yearning to return to its comfort and familiarity.

As they wandered past a thicket, some ripe-looking berries caught her eye, and she couldn't resist picking some. She could take back a pocketful as a reward. She began to imagine the picture she would later upload to Instagram - the fruit placed in an olive wood breakfast bowl, perhaps with some pumpkin and chia seed Bircher, and topped with mashed raspberries and raw agave syrup.

As she daydreamed, the reporter reached carelessly into the blackthorn where clusters of sloe berries hung. Almost instantly her finger was pricked on one of the long dark spines that guarded them. She flinched her hand away. A bead of blood formed on the fingertip; a shiny red berry of her own. She sucked on the blood, sampling its metallic taste on her tongue.

She turned to tell the photographer he had taken more than enough photos of leaves and whatever else to accompany the silly story she would dash off, and they really should get out of this dreadful place. The photographer, though, was now stooping over something else he had found. He called her over.

A pair of dead hares were laid out side by side, nice and neat at the base of a wild cherry tree. The lifeless eyes of the creatures stared wide into nothing as if still transfixed on their killer. Their pelts sagged slack and empty from disembowelling, yet were otherwise unmarked aside from a clean slit along their underside. No sign of blood or innards. The reporter grimaced as she gazed at the forlorn sight. Her eyes then went to where the photographer was pointing. On the tree was carved the very same swirling pattern they had seen before.

The photographer looked up at her with a puzzled expression but said nothing. From off in the distance they then heard what sounded like twigs snapping underfoot. Someone walking their dog, the reporter thought? In any case, she realised, they weren't alone.

She recalled a story her paper printed some years back of a homeless ex-squaddie camping out in the countryside, poaching chickens from local farms and things like that. Such a scenario would explain the hares, hunted and killed on their warren in the adjacent meadow and brought and laid out here.

The reporter sensed she might have a real story to break here, and began to feel slightly more enthusiastic as well as at ease. No beasties were lurking in the undergrowth after all, just some drop-out with a Bear Grylls fixation.

She headed off, leading the photographer in the direction of the sound.

They pushed through an entanglement of branches, their muddied shoes pressing windfall crab apples into the dirt and the reporter's coat leaving tufts of red wool snagged on clawing thorns. As they waded through, they did not hear the dry rustling of a tawny, patterned adder as it slithered through the litter of dead leaves, nor catch sight of it before it vanished beneath the russet bracken.

They stepped out into a quiet clearing dappled in hazy amber sunlight. The only sign of life, a snail inching its way along the lichen-covered trunk of a long-fallen oak, its dead roots twisting up like the antlers of a great stag.

The reporter gazed up through a gap in the covering of trees at the welcome sight of a gleaming pearl sky. Roosting blackbirds peered down at her from high boughs, as if expectantly watching.

The two strode to the centre of the clearing to where a small campfire smouldered, pale smoke still curling lazily above the charred wood. Someone had recently extinguished the fire. Above the camp, suspended from a tripod of sticks, hung a large copper pot. Empty.

The photographer kicked soil over the smoking ashes and scanned the surrounding vegetation which seemed undisturbed and at peace. In the air, there was a thickly pungent and musky aroma, as from a river-wet stray dog.

The reporter noticed a slight knoll of soft black dirt near her feet. She swung a desultory foot over it. The top layer displaced to reveal something stark white beneath the black soil.

Puzzled, she knelt and stroked away dirt from the object, and soon unearthed the skull of some large animal. She managed to pry the thing from the ground and examined its gnashing form. Once again, the reporter and the photographer exchanged bewildered glances. It was evident that this skull hadn't belonged to any farm animal or pet. It wasn't fox or badger, either - nor big cat, for that matter. A dog, perhaps? A wolf, claimed the photographer. And what sharp teeth it had!

The camera clicked, and the reporter thought of headlines. They wondered if they should stay and wait for the camper to return to his fire. It turned out they didn't have to.

Out of the surrounding undergrowth, from where they had been crouching, arose a small group of children; noiselessly emerging en masse at some secret signal. Half a dozen or more, all aged about eight or nine, and sandy-haired. Their bare torsos daubed in what might have been brownish paint, or mud, or blood. The markings were in the shapes of that familiar swirling pattern. And what green eyes they had! The reporter and the photographer spun around and saw that the gang of young boys and girls had them encircled.

The children did not answer when the reporter spoke to them. Instead, they stood and stared at the intruders with what felt like an annihilating vehemence in their eyes. They did not make a sound.

The photographer lifted his camera to take a shot. His head then jerked forward, and a confused and alarmed expression showed on his face. It was then the reporter saw, with horror, that an arrow had penetrated his head just behind the jaw on the left-hand side. The arrowhead protruding from the photographer's gaping mouth resembled a Devilish forked tongue.

The reporter turned to face the culprit; slightly taller than the rest; he was draped in an animal skin of long black fur and was in the process of pulling back on his longbow once more, and this time he was taking aim at her.

As the photographer dropped to his knees, gurgling and choking on his blood, she darted for the bushes. The boys there let her pass, and she managed to stumble through the undergrowth for a few yards before the arrow slammed into her right thigh with sudden, violent force, embedding deep.

The reporter screamed as she staggered on through the branches that clawed at her face and attempted to ensnare her, and across the uneven and treacherous mud. She heard the pack howl as they began to give chase, and she sensed just how quickly they were closing in on their quarry.

The reporter then realised she would never make it out of the ever-enclosing wood.

BACKGROUND ON SPOOR
BY
DC MERRYWEATHER

An eerie quiet had descended on the desolate Cornish moor when Steve Parkyn made his way home through the gorse bushes in the early hours of one dark morning. The midnight rambler stopped in his tracks, however, when he caught sight of The Beast.

It was perched on a nearby fencepost, glowering at him with the steady gaze of its luminous eyes. After letting out an unearthly squeal, the creature then bounded away into the safety of a forest. Steve, and his friend who was accompanying him on the nocturnal sojourn, decided to follow after.

"Well it seemed like a good idea at the time," he told 'The Independent' newspaper in 1995. "We shone the lamp around, crouched down and caught its eyes. They were sort of bright white. Then it went off at a fair old rate, and we saw it was about 3ft long, with a tail of 18 inches and was a pinky brown colour."

This encounter with The Beast of Bodmin Moor in the early 1980s is one of many such reported sightings of phantom wild animals in the British countryside. Rumours of non-native creatures lurking somewhere out in Britain's otherwise gentle landscape have grabbed the media's attention and the public's imagination since the 1960s.

Sightings of the more famous 'Beasts' said to prowl the sparsely inhabited stretches of Bodmin and Exmoor occasionally make the national news, but many regions around the country have their own stories of farmers complaining about mysteriously mauled livestock and bewildered dog walkers catching fleeting glimpses of strangely large animals dashing away into darkened undergrowth.

The elusive creatures are frequently given nicknames by local journalists, inspired by having found a source of copy more colourful than the usual underwhelming stories about pot holes in roads and the opening of supermarkets.

One particular news story in the Spring of 2016 that stood out to me was a couple's sighting of the 'Werewolf of Worcester' – a creature blamed for attacking roe deer on parkland at Earl's Croome in Worcestershire.

The pair were driving through the National Trust property at 1 a.m. when they spotted something on the road ahead of them. Robert Ingram and wife Nicola told 'The Daily Mail': "It was petrifying. It looked like it was on steroids. "It was getting dark, but I saw its eyes reflect in my headlights. We stopped the car, and it was just standing there. We'd heard rumours about an escaped panther in the area, but we'd thought it was a load of nonsense. But when I saw this animal with my own eyes, I was stunned. It was enormous, far too big for a fox or a dog. It must have weighed about nine stone - about the same as a slim adult."

The paper dubbed the animal a 'werewolf' because of a sketch of the sighting that the couple drew which more resembled a lycanthrope than a big cat. The tongue-in-cheek lurid headline also helped expose the attitude newspapers have in what they consider slow-news-day filler.

274

Pumas and panthers are the most common alleged sightings in the woods and pastureland of Britain, but there have also been lynx, wolves, and, in one bizarre instance I found, a bear. Often, though, the creatures are only identified as being a 'black beast': a vague, dark, elusive shape shifting across dusk fields.

Theories as to why big feral animals should be stalking the rural corners of England are varied. Many cite The Dangerous Wild Animals Act of 1976 which prohibited people from keeping any large exotic predators except under the authority of a licence, which led to owners releasing their 'pets' into the wild. Similarly, the 1981 Zoo Licensing Act which clamped down on 'ramshackle zoos'.

Sceptics point out that the sightings are merely misidentified domestic cats and dogs, or foxes and badgers. Or, that they are figments of the imagination, tall tales.

Despite the numerous stories over the years, there has been little conclusive evidence of alien big cats, or 'Beasts' roaming the countryside. Following the 'Worcester Werewolf' story, some locals speculated that the cat-like creature responsible for the mangled deer corpses could be the descendant of a menagerie of big cats kept by Black Country eccentric Lew Foley in his Cradley Heath council house from the late-1960s. After the Dangerous Wild Animals Act had come into force, Mr Foley was said to have set loose his pride of furry felines out onto the Malvern Hills. No one knows what became of them, but the handful of sightings of beasties slinking about Worcestershire woodlands and fields since then has set people thinking.

Around about the same time of the 'Werewolf' piece, I came across another news story online about an actual wild wolf caught on film running through a Netherlands town. The accompanying video showed the huge grey wolf bounding along the pathway through a quiet suburban street. Wolves had not been seen in the country for 150 years. It is thought this one had travelled almost 200 miles from Germany.

What resonates with us about stories like this, and why all of the sightings of phantom animals are such favourites with the local press and its readership, is the possibility of an intrusion of the wild into – or, at least, existing on the fringes of - our cosy urban spaces.

It's as if the earthy, primitive past that we've long lost all connection with is haunting our consciousness, and is threatening to intrude once more into the security of our developed world of brick and concrete. The paw-prints of a savage beast leading across a manicured lawn to our window.

Our fascination with such myths has a base with both a yearning for what's lost, and a fear of the untamed. We have successfully kept the wolf from the door, but part of us still strains to hear its distant howl when the wilderness calls.

COME AWAY
BY
TRACY FAHEY

After what happened, they closed it down. One day it was full of women walking with their children, gently guiding them around the decorated trees, the next day there was a high fence around it. 'CLOSED TILL FUTURE NOTICE' the sign said in big red letters. And so the days went by. The paint peeled in the wind and rain. The red letters faded to a warm pink.

Now the boards themselves slope away, revealing complicated fissures and cracks; a hint of a way back in. No one talks about it anymore, or if they do, it's in whispers, away from us. They don't think we remember. But I do.

* * *

We spent every day that summer playing down by the river. It was – and still is – a pretty place. But back then it was beautiful. The river swept by, smooth and muscular as a fish, boiling with white froth whenever the sky turned grey and the winds started up. There was an abandoned ruined castle on the far side of the river, and on the near side a little, concrete bird hide on the slope down to the bank. Every morning we'd go there to play and our first stop was the fairy village. Earlier that year we'd gone down with our class to help set it up. The men from the local estate had mowed the grass down into a tight little buzz-cut that smelled green and fresh. All that was left was a clump of trees and a neat little hillock.

"You can adorn it how you want," our teacher, Miss Brook told us. It wasn't true, of course. We'd spent days beforehand with her, laboriously drawing fairies and houses and working out elaborate decorative schemes for the village. We'd all gotten a door each to christen with our names, and we painted them carefully; all neat letters, bright colours and sticky glitter. It was exciting to see the doors all lined up neatly at the base of the trees. The tiny doorways shone like spots of colour against the rough grey bark.

"Now go on, decorate around them." We stood for a few moments, unsure where to start. Our bags were full of different things, pretty stones, dolls, bits of toys. We looked to Miss Brook for guidance.

"Here. Watch me." She dipped her hand into her satchel and brought out a little feathery dreamcatcher which she tied onto a branch. "Use the branches. Or make arrangements on the ground." She smiled at us, her springy curls glowing in the sun. Miss Brook loved fairies. She told us stories about them in the afternoons, just before the bell would ring for the end of class. The tales were always about magic little beings that granted wishes and brought good luck.

That summer we were all fairy-obsessed. The village grew from bare beginnings into a tiny colony. Each day we'd check on it, and each day brought a new addition to the little clearing. Annmarie went to the beach and brought back shells which she carefully arranged in complicated swirling lines around her tiny red door. Jane's tree was decorated with plastic butterflies which she'd carefully painted at home. Her mother came down with her to attach them up high in the branches. Shelagh and her little brother built a tiny Lego village around hers, with tiny Lego people standing outside their houses, each one with an arm lifted in a miniscule wave. Lynda's fairy house was the prettiest of all. She'd collected all her mother's old, discarded costume jewellery, and her tree twinkled and sparkled in the summer sun, mock-pearls winking in the light, the sun-dazzle of diamante flashing signals from the branches.

And the long summer went on, hot day after endless hot day. We continued to decorate the village. Clusters of stones and pebbles delineated our different territories. The adults joined in. A tiny wishing well appeared. A local man, a sculptor, created a handsome wooden board, sanded down and smooth to touch, with letters poker-stained into the surface. We stood in front of it, spelling it out to each other.

> 'Come away, O human child!
> To the waters and the wild
> With a faery, hand in hand,
> For the world's more weeping
> than you understand.'

I recognised it from Miss Brook's class. As I read it I could smell the dusty warmth of the classroom, a scent made up equally of chalk and felt and plastic chairs. I saw her fizz of curls bowed over a book, reading the poem aloud in the sleepy hush of the afternoon.

"Come away." I repeated aloud. I traced the letters with my finger, absorbed.

"Come away where?" Lynda ran up behind me, laughing, with her blonde hair falling over her shoulders.

"Nowhere." I grabbed her hand. "Let's go collect some pretty stones."

* * *

I spent more time there than anywhere. A safe place to play, the parents told each other. Fences all around, a contained space. All the parents loved it. All that is, except mine. That was the summer my mother was sick, you see. While the summer hummed outside, all bees and running water and green light, she was inside in her room. I didn't like going in to her room. It felt tight and huddled and smothery; her curtains stayed drawn, the air smelled warm and spent. She stayed under the bedclothes, a hump of flesh, her eyes staring at me as if she'd forgotten who I was.

"She's just tired," my father said. I wasn't so sure. She'd come back from the hospital like that, as if they'd lifted something out of her, some crucial cog that she needed to keep working. Now she lay in bed, the delicate, precise mechanisms of her run down, faltering, stopped. When he was home, my father hovered anxiously outside her door; his hands always full with trays and hot drinks and medicine. I ran wild. I ate random things at random times. My hair grew tangled, my hands were cracked with dirt, little spider-webs of grime spreading across my palms. No one at home noticed.

Lynda's mother tried to tame me. She lent me some of Lynda's pretty smocked dressed. She even tried to brush out my tangled hair once or twice, but it hurt like a nettle-sting and I pulled away impatiently. After a while she gave up.

* * *

We played lots of games that summer. Our dolls were dressed as fairies and we added wings to their backs and swooped them around the village. We made them swim in the little stream that flowed down to the river. There was a fairy school that we played at for a bit, but that was too boring. Some of us made wishes at the wishing well. But there was one game we kept returning to. It centred around the little hill that the men from the estate had built up from leftover dirt of their digging. As summer went on the dirt formed solid into a glossy, grassy bump, taller than us. One of the dads added a wooden set of painted blue eyes to it. He set them deep in the hillock, so it looked like a surprised giant, surfacing into a strange world.

We gave him a name. Pook, we called him. We started adding things around him. Paper windmills. Little lanterns. Wilted bunches of flowers. We played around the mound and told each other stories about him. He was a fairy king in some of them, but mostly he was an enemy.

"Pook will get you," we told each other, daring each other to climb the hill. Only the bravest would do it, and when we got to the top, we'd jump off, shrieking. Just to scare him away in case he *did* come for us.

He got out at night, Annmarie said. He got out and walked around, looking for us. At night, when the shadows drew in and the sound of the river grew wilder it seemed more likely.

The adults didn't like this story as much. Especially not when Shelagh's brother, Mike fell off the hill after trying to dig out one of the blue wooden eyes. He twisted his ankle badly and spent the rest of the summer hobbling around with a metal crutch. '*He tried to harm Pook,*' we said, shaking our heads wisely. '*That's what happens if you do.*'

When we went there one morning, one of the parents had painted a sign and stuck it on the hillock. 'DON'T CLIMB ON MY HEAD' it read. We pretended Pook had written it, and though we knew we were joking, we didn't climb there anymore.

But we still played there. More toys appeared there, trucks, farm animals, pieces of string with baubles attached. No one said it, but it felt safer that way, to keep adding to the store of treasures around the tiny doors.

***

I went there today.

You can see it now if you squint through a crack in the fence. It's another world in there. The grass is dark green, waist-high. It's grown up over the painted toadstools and the fairy doors. The dreamcatchers are tangled up in leaves, the tin ornaments are rusted a dull brown. Pook is missing an eye. *Did Mike go back and dig it out this time?* I wondered. The board with the poem on it has fallen down. I can just see one edge of it sticking up.

'Come away' it says.

***

That summer the days slipped by, bright and blue-skied, like beads on a string. Every morning smelled like a fresh promise, of coconutty gorse and the heavy, secret scent of honeysuckle. And as the summer went by, the village began to change. Just a little at first.

One morning we arrived down to find Shelagh's Lego tableau demolished. Someone had taken the roofs off the houses, and meticulously pulled out the windows and doors. Outside the tiny ruins lay the carefully dissected bodies of the Lego people, their yellow faces frozen in rictus expressions of shock. *Other kids*, we said, but the dismemberment was so precise that it felt...purposeful. Not an act of destruction, more like a planned attack. The next thing to change were Annmarie's shells. We stood in silence looking down at them. They were laid out neatly to read 'GO AWAY.' Lynda's mum was with us, I remember.

"Someone's playing a silly joke," she said loudly, shuffling the shells with the toe of her pink Converse sneaker. The letters tangled and fell apart. We started playing again, but it was oddly subdued. I went home early that evening.

The next day I got there first. My Barbie, abandoned the day before, was hanging from a branch. A twist of blue baling twine was knotted tight around her neck. She swung gently in the breeze, her large eyes wide with reproach. I took her down and didn't say anything. But from then on the place didn't feel quite the same. The trees seemed a shade darker, the air a fraction colder. And the rustle of leaves in the air sounded a little – just a little – like whispers.

Getting down to the village first became an obsession. I would get there just as the light was lifting off the river, when the pinkish streaks in the sky were fading into blue. I'd make a private wish at the wishing well, and then wander around, noting any tiny changes. I wasn't the only one. Sometimes I'd see grown-ups there, with dogs, or joggers in their running gear. It was a magical place, one that demanded attention. Most often I would see a man there. I noticed him because he always wore a heavy tweed coat despite the warmth of the mornings. Like me, he would trace his way around the trees, stopping briefly beside each one, as if he were making the Stations of the Cross. I thought – I couldn't be sure, but I thought it – that he was checking the fairy doors.

It was sometime around then that I got the idea to re-decorate my door. I took my little door home to paint it; I covered the bright red paint with a dark charcoal and went looking for the old box of Halloween decorations.

"What are you doing?" It was my father, his kind face knotted in a permanent expression of worry.

"Doing my door for the village," I said proudly. I started to sift out little ornaments from the box, delighted with his attention. He stooped with a grunt to unload the dishwasher.

"Just don't make a mess."

"I won't. Can I go upstairs to show Mum?" I'd started asking since the last time when the sight of me had made her shudder with heavy, noiseless sobs. He straightened up and looked at me. My hands were streaked grey with paint.

"Better not. Just play quietly, OK?" I shrugged and nodded, shaping the brush in my mouth. It tasted bitter, almost salty, gritty with particles.

I was so proud of my tree. I put everything in place carefully and waited. It was something different, something to make everyone notice. In the faint, pink light of dawn, the tiny tombstones stood lopsided at the base of the tree. The dark grey door was open at an angle, one skeleton hand clasped around it. Each grave marker had the name of a dead fairy lettered on it— mostly flower names like Lily, Rose and Bluebell. The largest was one for Pook. I nodded at it in satisfaction, then wandered over to the wishing well to close my eyes and wish my usual wish. *Make Mum better.*

"Did you do this?" It was the man in the tweed coat. I hadn't seen him arrive. He crouched down beside me. The tweed coat smelled of damp and grass, a heavy, slightly unpleasant smell. Glasses flashed opaque over his eyes.

"Yes."

"It's beautiful." He examined it closely, peering at each tombstone. His hair fell over his forehead as he stooped. For a moment we stayed in silence as he traced a finger over the lettering, until a goose flew low beside us, skimming down on the river with a series of low honks. Then he stood up, buttoned his coat, and was gone.

When the others arrived, they loved my arrangement. "Let's play fairy funerals!" said Shelagh excitedly. And we did, weaving tiny daisy chains into wreaths, as Annmarie's Barbie was carried into the clearing by our other dolls, all wearing clothes made of black bin-liners. It was the most popular game of the day, and we all joined in, all except Lynda, who had brought down more sparkling ornaments to decorate her shining tree. Instead of playing she watched us over her shoulder.

"Your tree looks so pretty," I said. It was true. The gold costume jewellery now filled all the lower branches so it flashed in the sun like a Christmas tree.

"Yeah," she said, fitting the last ornament in place, a broken bangle. "My mum says it's the nicest one." There was a touch of defiance in her voice. I stood there for a moment, uncertain, and then turned back to my game.

The next day was the day that everything changed.

I stood in front of my tree that morning. I could see what had happened, but I couldn't take it in. The tiny graveyard was scattered, the tombstones upended with the lettered sides mashed into the ground. Someone had stamped on them to make sure they were broken. I could even see the outline of footprints. The skeleton hand I'd carefully glued to the door was gone, and the door itself lay face-down at the foot of the tree.

"What happened?" It was the man again. This time he wore a scarf twisted around his neck. I turned to answer, but to my horror, felt my mouth turn down with overpowering misery. A smothering sob rose hard in my chest. It was ruined. It was all ruined.

"Now then." His voice was gentle. "Tell me what happened."

He took off his glasses and smiled at me.

* * *

The next day, Lynda disappeared. She left her house early that morning, before breakfast, to go and play, but she never came back. The police and all the parents searched for her, up and down the riverbank, shouting her name. We all had to stay home for days. She was just gone. For weeks afterwards I'd see her mother, her hair tangled as mine, wandering around the roads, her pretty face red and swollen, her hands clasping and unclasping by her sides as she walked. The last place Lynda had been seen was in the fairy village, by a jogger passing by. He was held and questioned, but there was nothing else he could tell them except that he'd seen a little girl with blonde hair among the trees.

After that we didn't want to go there anymore. Someone boarded up the little copse. We didn't even take the decorations away. Sometimes when I walked by, I would imagine them, rotting and swaying in the breeze.

I thought of Lynda all the time. I changed my wish. My mother wasn't getting any better anyway. She just lay inside, growing light as thistledown, her sharp bones poking through her face. No. I wished instead for Lynda to come back. though deep down I knew it wouldn't work. I couldn't wish on the little wishing well anymore, you see; it was hidden away, growing mossy and abandoned behind the fence.

* * *

I still think about Lynda. Wherever she went to, I still feel her here. Still ten, still beautiful. When I close my eyes I see the sun blaze down on her golden hair as she sits surrounded by the sparkling glass and metal of her tree.

I sit and remember.

When he took off his glasses, I could see his eyes were blue.

"Did one of the others do this?"

I nodded, still unable to speak.

"Which one?" His face was drawn into fierce lines. His mouth was a pale slash on his stubbled face. I pointed dumbly at Lynda's tree. The rising sun caught the iridescent beads of a broken rosary, flashing tiny arcs of light on the tree trunk.

He nodded once, and then looked at me again. His eyes were a startling blue, like the sky, like the cobalt blue colour in my paintbox. I looked at him, mesmerised. I'd only seen one other pair of eyes as blue as that.

"Are you Pook?"

He didn't reply, just straightened up, gathered his coat around him and walked away.

* * *

There was no Pook, I know that now. He was just a man. But that doesn't make it any easier to live with.

I'm sitting beside the gap in the fence, looking out at the river. Midges cloud the brown water; rising fierce and massed from the dark green weeds. A boat, moored, drifts lengthways, admiring itself in the crinkled reflections of the river. Seabirds dip past, tip-tilted to one side.

Someone's scored the bird hide with savage letters in black paint. 'It's never over.'

It never is.

BACKGROUND ON COME AWAY BY TRACY FAHEY

'Come Away' was born out of an amalgamation of several Irish folkloric strands and practices, both past and present. All of these relate to the Irish fairies, or *na Sidhe*. One is the trope of the changeling, the other the contemporary practice of creating fairy villages. Together these illustrate the contradictory beliefs about the Good People that exist in Ireland; the darker, older legends juxtaposed with the sanitised, Disneyfied versions that lend themselves to touristic attractions today.

Na Sidhe are not your average Shakespearean or Victorian conceptions of tiny, artless creatures that grant wishes. In Irish folklore they are reputed to be the original settlers of Ireland, the Tuatha de Danann, gradually driven into hiding in the fairy-forts, those islands of trees and bushes that festoon the Irish countryside. These are actually ring-forts, remnants of much earlier settlements which often have a double use as burial cairns. *Na Sidhe* exist as oddities within the global fairy pantheon; they are pale, almost full-sized creatures who can pass as human. They are to be crossed at your peril; many legends tell of the dangers of situating a home on a fairy path or warn of the repercussions of accidentally straying into a fairy funeral. *Na Sidhe* are warriors, dangerous and cunning folk who may grant wishes, but there is nearly always a terrible price to pay.

One of the most famous tales about *na Sidhe* is their propensity to steal human children and human women; women for breeding (one of the legends in relation to Irish fairies is that they are angels who have lost their souls and who seek to interbreed with human women to have children who possess souls) and children, who they often substitute with their own. They are popularly believed to target the most beautiful children; that's why it is the prettiest girl in 'Come Away' who is targeted.

The idea of fairy villages is therefore anathema to these dark legends. Fairy villages are a cute, touristic translation of Irish fairy lore, characterised by tiny doors attached to trees which are then decorated by children. These pretty little playgrounds stand in stark contrast to the 'real' homes of the fairy forts, which are still left undisturbed by farmers. The fairy forts are never decorated; it is believed to be extremely bad luck to interfere with them in any way. However the idea of decorating the trees does relate to the syncretic tradition of the rag-tree, still visible at many Catholic outdoor shrines in Ireland that are based on older, pagan, holy wells. These trees, believed to mark the sites of miracles, are decorated with rags and ribbons as testimonies to the curative power of the wells.

As children we played in the local fairy fort, we decorated the whitethorn on our lane, and my grandmother told us cautionary tales about farmers who transgressed fairy boundaries. One was the tale of a farmer who ploughed up a fairy fort only to find a selection of miniature clothes underneath the trees. We were brought up to appreciate the idea that these stories and the unwritten rules that governed them were rooted in the landscape, like the trees of the forts themselves.

The idea of these colourful, fun fairy villages runs counter to this tradition of fairy homes being places to respect. 'Come Away' was born out of a certain unease occasioned by these fairy villages. I walk my dog beside the river Shannon every day, where I pass one of these little villages, created by a committee of residents as an attraction for local children. I've been watching and photographing it now for over a year, noting the strange, incremental additions of everything from carved rabbits to miniature caravans to car tyres piled and painted to represent the Minions from 'Despicable Me'. And something about it felt...not quite right. If *Na Sidhe* are as vengeful as legends have them, would they be insulted by these colourful, childlike re-imaginings? What if they were to wreak a terrible revenge? And so, slowly, bit by bit, the idea of writing on that theme grew.

However, when it comes to folklore, I'm a firm believer in writing with an honest, contemporary voice rather than simply trying to re-tell old stories. The best and most original folk horror mingles the past and present to create something unique and horrifying. I'm reminded of Peader O'Guilin's superb 'The Call', which effortlessly translates the terror and beauty of *na Sidhe* within the genre of young adult dystopian fiction.

In 'Come Away', I wanted to touch on these old stories, but to mix in with them one of the true horrors of contemporary culture; the idea of child abduction. Therefore the plot is designed to be read both ways, either as a story of fairy wrath, or a story of simple human evil.

Either way, it's a story of quiet horror. I hope it haunts you as it haunted me in its gestation, as I walked by the river and dreamt of malignant fairy revenge.

ABOUT THE AUTHORS

Andrew Garvey

Andrew Garvey began somewhat seriously writing short stories in 2012. He has been published in several collections in the UK and the US. While he focuses on horror he also writes a little historical fiction, fantasy, sci-fi and political satire, contributing in 2016 to 'We've Been Trumped' a speculative collection on what a Trump presidency might be like. In 2015, he co-wrote (with author/musician Mike Staples) a critically well-received but thoroughly unprofitable flash fiction collection, 'Little Penny Dreadfuls: A Collection of 99 Stories of 99 Words.' He has written and edited work for museum exhibitions, disability charities, local authorities and the NHS and *Fighters Only* magazine. This is his first full length collection as editor. He lives in Staffordshire, England with his wife, son, bull terriers and books

David Saunderson

David Saunderson is the founder and managing editor of Spooky Isles website. An Australian-born writer and event promoter, he lives in London with his wife and has a fascination with the paranormal, horror and macabre.

Michael Connon

Michael Connon is a native of the North East of England where he currently resides following sojourns in London and Ireland. His fiction has won various awards in the UK and United States and has been published in several anthologies. He has written comedy for television, radio and the stage but his first love is speculative fiction, citing Ray Bradbury and Philip K Dick as early influences. Michael has had an unhealthy fascination with the paranormal from an early age following a premature exposure to 'The Unexplained magazine. He read Modern History at Oxford University and maintains an interest in current affairs, exopolitics and the conspirasphere. He is currently looking to develop some of his short stories for radio and television.

Tracy Fahey

Tracy Fahey is a Gothic fiction writer. Her short fiction is published in fifteen US and UK anthologies. In 2017 her first collection, *The Unheimlich Manoeuvre* was nominated for a British Fantasy Award. Two of her short stories, 'Walking The Borderlines' and 'Under The Whitethorn' were long listed for Honourable Mentions in *The Best Horror of the Year Volume 8*. Her first novel, *The Girl In The Fort* was released in October 2017 by Fennec, an imprint of Fox Spirit Press. Her second collection, *New Music For Old Rituals* is forthcoming from Black Shuck Press in 2018.

Ed Burkley

Ed Burkley received his PhD in Psychology in 2006.By day he works as a professor and researcher studying human behavior. By night he writes about the darker side of the human condition. His other short fiction appears in 2017's edition of *Year's Best Body Horror Anthology* (Gehenna & Hinnom), *Uncommon Pet Tales* (Smoking Pen Press), and *Night Shades* (Firth Books). He enjoys travel, photography, and spending lazy afternoons drinking hot cocoa in the backyard with his wife and Norwich terrier. His website is *www.edwardburkley.com*

Chris Rush

Arklow native **Chris Rush** has been writing about horror and the supernatural for several years. His debut novel 'Folklore' was an overnight hit, terrifying readers across the globe. Based on Irish lore, it became an International bestseller and remains in the Amazon bestsellers lists. His follow up 'All Shall Suffer' has been received with widespread critical and commercial success. Chris is also a lead paranormal investigator and team historian for Paranormal Researchers Ireland. His upcoming work includes two (co-written) non-fiction books and he is currently writing his third horror novel, '13 Dead'. With a lifelong fascination of the horror genre, Chris is continuing to build a portfolio of horror and supernatural works that will put Ireland and himself firmly on the map as a formidable force in the world of horror.

Catherine Shingler

Catherine Shingler was born in Blackpool but grew up around London so has a footeither side of the north/south divide. Originally a librarian, she managed to escape and ended up working in museums. She would have liked to have been a proper writer but was not prepared to put in the necessary effort, although she has produced a book for children about the Staffordshire Hoard. Her horror heroes are M R James and J Sheridan Le Fanu. She is married with two grown-up children and a large cat, and lives in Stoke-on-Trent.

Ann O' Regan

Ann O' Regan is the Spooky Isles' Ireland editor and has been writing articles on Irish dark history, hauntings, folklore and mythology for many years. She is an Irish folklore and monster expert and provides Irish translations, consultation and back matter essays for the very successful comic *Wayward*. Ann is a writer of horror fiction inspired by her research and favours Gothic horror. She has been published in the anthologies *Zombie Bites* from Red Rattle Books and *The Christmas Book of Ghosts* from Michael S Collins and has her own internationally popular blog, *Dark Emerald Tales*. Ann lives in the west of Ireland and is a paranormal enthusiast who loves to explore and research the dark and supernatural histories of Ireland's spookiest places, as well as collecting folklore tales from the four provinces of Ireland.

Phil Davies

Philip Davies is a Funeral Celebrant and scriptwriter for children's television writing for shows such as *Go-Jetters* and *The Furchester Hotel*. When he isn't writing, Philip acts as curator over a collection of miscellaneous esoteric items that were left to him by his late Great Uncle Islwyn which he is in the process of cataloguing and presenting to the unsuspecting public. A keen player of modern board games, and reader of comic books, he lives near the Welsh border in the mediaeval market town of Shrewsbury.

Hannah Kate

Hannah Kate is an editor and writer based in North Manchester, UK. She has had stories and poetry published in a number of anthologies and magazines, including *The New Writer*, *Noir Carnival* (Fox Spirit), *Dark Chaucer: An Assortment* (Punctum Books), *Werewolves Versus the 1990s* an *European Monsters* (Fox Spirit). She's also the founder and editor-in-chief of Hic Dragones micropress. Hannah presents weekly literature (Hannah's Bookshelf) and local history (A Helping of History) radio shows on North Manchester FM, and is currently the treasurer of the Friends of Crumpsall Park and the secretary of Friends of Bailey's Wood. When she's not writing creepy horror stories, Hannah enjoys reading creepy horror stories. Under the name Hannah Priest, she is an academic writer and lecturer with a PhD in medieval literature and numerous academic publications. Her current academic work mostly revolves around creepy horror stories.

Kevin Williams

Kevin Williams is a short story writer, currently based in the West Midlands. His writing is influenced both by a lifelong love of the supernatural and his ongoing study in the field of psychology. Through serving in the military, Kevin has lived throughout the UK and visited many diverse places across the globe; his experiences can often be found woven throughout his stories. His work has been published by the Birmingham Mail and as part of the Birmingham Literature Festival. Kevin lives with his wife and daughter and often writes accompanied by his black cat, Nell; mainly for atmosphere.

Áine King

Áine King is an Irish EastEnder. She studied fine art and theatre at St Martin's School Of Art, Brighton and Sussex universities and RADA. Her work as a dramaturg, designer and director includes adapting Nick Burbridge's short stories *Hard Chairs* for Shakespeare's original theatre, the Rose on London's Bankside. She was one of six invited directors for the Old Vic 24 Hour Plays at the Komedia, Brighton. She won Fringe Report's 'Best Auteur : writer, director, designer' award in 2011 for her production of *Dracula*. Áine was recently diagnosed with a rare photosensitive disorder which makes her allergic to light, and now lives in the Orkney Isles, where she and her family are restoring a Victorian Gothic mansion with no money or practical skills. This is her first short story (apart from one about pox-ridden-ghost-whores, which was confiscated by the nuns in her Catholic school).

Kevin Patrick McCann

Kevin Patrick McCann has published seven collections of poems for adults, one for children (Diary of a Shapeshifter), a book of ghost stories (It's Gone Dark) and Teach Yourself Self-Publishing (Hodder), co-written with the playwright Tom Green. Kevin is currently working on his selected poems (his previous collections are out of print) and a new edition of the ghost stories. He now publishes under the name of Kevin Patrick McCann to avoid further confusion between himself and other Kevin McCanns currently roaming cyberspace. His Facebook feed is @Diary of a Shapeshifter.

Barry McCann

Barry McCann lives in the north of England and is a writer, editor, broadcaster and speaker. He is a features writer for various magazines, newspapers and websites such as Cultbox and the Spooky Isles. This has led onto regular appearances on BBC Radio Lancashire as resident writer, Radio Cumbria as Folklore Correspondent/storyteller and Radio Merseyside as cultural historian. His short stories are regularly featured in the Lancashire Post and American anthologies such as *Dark Gothic Resurrected* and *The Horror Zine*, as well as being performed to audiences all over the UK and Ireland. He is also editor of the art and literature journal *Parnassus* for Mensa International. He is currently working on his first anthology.

Jaki McCarrick

Jaki McCarrick is an award-winning writer of plays, poetry and fiction. She won the 2010 Papatango New Writing Prize for her play 'Leopoldville', and her play 'Belfast Girls', developed at the National Theatre, London, was shortlisted for the Susan Smith Blackburn Prize and the 2014 BBC Tony Doyle Award before premiering in Chicago in May 2015 to much critical acclaim. Jaki has also recently been selected for the Irish Film Board's 2016 Talent Development Initiative to adapt 'Belfast Girls' for the screen. In 2016 she was shortlisted for St. John's College, Cambridge's Harper-Wood Studentship for her short play 'Tussy' about Eleanor Marx. Jaki also won the 2010 Wasafiri prize for short fiction and followed this with the publication of her debut story collection, *The Scattering*, (Seren Books) which was shortlisted for the 2014 Edge Hill Prize. Recenty longlisted for the inaugural Irish Fiction Laureate, Jaki is currently editing her first novel and a second collection of short stories.

Rachel Steiner

Rachel Steiner lives in Oshkosh, Wisconsin. She graduated from Saint Mary's University of Minnesota in 2017 with a degree in literature with a writing emphasis. She writes horror and fantasy fiction, often with a basis in folklore. This is her first publication.

Will Graham

Will Graham is a former professional forensic investigator specialising in computer forensics and electronic evidence. That career inspired his 'Spider's Trilogy' (Spider's Tango, Spider's Dance and Spider's Kiss). His short story Point of View is included in the anthology "Protectors 2", a collection nominated for the Anthony Award at Bouchercon. Will's musical tastes pretty much stopped with The Rat Pack, and he still reads Leslie Charteris, Sir Arthur Conan Doyle, Dame Agatha Christie, and Ellery Queen.

Petula Mitchell

Petula Mitchell lives in Billingshurst, West Sussex in South East England, close to the edge of the South Downs National Park. She has two grown-up sons and five grandchildren and has spent almost thirty years working for the NHS. She has three dogs (a lovely old springer spaniel and two big, black, handsome retired greyhounds who keep her busy but are immensely rewarding to care for). She enjoys visting London's art galleries to see new exhibitions, as well as visiting paintings that are now 'old friends', as well as handicrafts and singing in her local rock choir. Her first reading love is sci-fi but she also enjoys detective fiction, hIstory and art books.

RA Goli

RA Goli is an Australian writer of horror, fantasy, speculative and erotic horror short stories. In addition to writing, her interests include reading, gaming, the occasional walk, and annoying her dog, two cats, and husband. Her short stories have been published by Broadswords and Blasters, Deadman's Tome, Grivante Press, Horrified Press and Fantasia Divinity among others. Check out her website https://ragolifiction.wordpress.com/ or stalk her on Facebook https://www.facebook.com/ragolifiction.

DC Merryweather

DC Merryweather has contributed to online music publications such as Stylus and Drowned in Sound, where he was a contributing editor, writing scathing and needlessly wordy reviews of hapless indie bands before admitting defeat and settling for factory work. He has since written short horror stories, mainly about old things not entirely disappeared, which have featured in magazines such as Starburst and Music From the Empty Quarter, for whatever that's worth.

Lightning Source UK Ltd.
Milton Keynes UK
UKHW01f1849310818
328138UK00002B/247/P

9 781916 422704